THE ROOTS OF THE OLIVE TREE

THE ROOTS OF THE OLIVE TREE
COURTNEY MILLER SANTO

HAY HOUSE

Australia • Canada • Hong Kong • India
South Africa • United Kingdom • United States

First published and distributed in the United Kingdom by:
Hay House UK Ltd, 292B Kensal Rd, London W10 5BE.
Tel.: (44) 20 8962 1230; Fax: (44) 20 8962 1239.
www.hayhouse.co.uk

Published and distributed in the United States of America by:
HarperCollins Publishers, 10 East 53rd Street, New York, NY 10022.

Published and distributed in the Republic of South Africa by:
Hay House SA (Pty), Ltd, PO Box 990, Witkoppen 2068.
Tel./Fax: (27) 11 467 8904.
www.hayhouse.co.za

Published and distributed in India by:
Hay House Publishers India, Muskaan Complex,
Plot No.3, B-2, Vasant Kunj, New Delhi – 110 070.
Tel.: (91) 11 4176 1620; Fax: (91) 11 4176 1630.
www.hayhouse.co.in

Copyright © 2012 by Courtney Miller Santo.

The moral rights of the author have been asserted.

Designed by Jamie Lynn Kerner

This book is a work of fiction. The characters, incidents and dialogue are drawn from
the author's imagination and are not to be construed as real. Any resemblance to
actual events or persons, living or dead, is entirely coincidental.

A catalogue record for this book is available from the British Library.

ISBN 978-1-84850-976-4

Printed and bound in Great Britain by TJ International, Padstow, Cornwall.

For Winnie and Sofia,
who are the beginning and
the end of my family's five generations

In the olive grove, a wise man at the feet and a wild man at the head.
—ITALIAN PROVERB

Anna — Wealthy Davison (1888-1943) is older brother to **Anna** Davison, who was born in 1894. She married **Michael Keller** (1893-1934) in 1915 and they had four other children: Michael (1918-1963), Christopher (1919-1991), David (1921-1942), and Timothy (1924-2001).

Bets — Born in 1917, Elizabeth, or **Bets** as her family calls her, married **Frank Wallace (1916)** in 1937 and they had four other children: Matthew (1942), Mark (1944), Luke (1946), and John (1948-1972).

Callie — The owner of the Pit Stop, **Callie**, or Calliope Wallace, was born in 1941. She married Greg Rodgers (1925-1978). Their other children include Jim (1965), Nathan (1966), and Noah (1970).

Deb — **Deb**, or Deborah Rodgers, was born in 1964. She married Carl Ripplinger (1956-1986), her husband, in jail for shooting Carl in 1982.

Erin — Born April 1, 1982, **Erin** was raised by her grandmothers.

Anna in the Fall

CHAPTER ONE

Arrival

*A*nna Davison Keller wanted to be the oldest person in the world. She felt she was owed this distinction, due to the particular care she'd taken with the vessel God had given her. In her morning prayers, she made a show, in case God himself was watching, of getting out of bed and onto her knees. She spoke to God in his language—asking for a length of days to be added to the one hundred and twelve years she'd already lived and pleading for health in her navel and marrow in her bones. She didn't say outright that God ought to strike dead that jo-fired man in China who was keeping her from the title, but after all these years, surely, God knew her heart.

In 2006, summer overstayed its welcome—giving the entire Sacramento Valley the look of wildflowers sat too long in a vase. Dawn was still an hour away, and although it was early November, the air that morning was warm and stale. Anna dressed in the dark, while her terrier, Bobo, nipped at her heels—urging her to the door. Rising before the sun gave her privacy enough to be pleasant with her daughter and granddaughter, who shared the tidy house with Anna. People often mistook them for sisters. Rubbish, Anna always thought, but that was the young for you—to anyone under thirty everyone over sixty looked the same age.

She didn't want the toast and marmalade on her plate—making it was part of her routine, but she was realizing that too many minutes of her days were taken up by unexamined habits. She forced a bite, tossed the remainder to Bobo, and stepped onto the back porch. For the past several days, she'd been preoccupied with the impending arrival of a doctor, a geneticist, who was coming to study Anna and her progeny. As it had been explained to her, the man hoped to unlock the keys to longevity that hid in the genes of certain people—superagers, they were called. Anna thought of it as a holy grail search, although she sensed saying this aloud would be tomfoolery on her part.

Thank God he was finally arriving today, the anticipation had kept her from giving full attention to normally reflexive activities, like sleeping. Last night she'd been plagued by dreams filled with half-formed images of umbilical cords and the face of a woman she didn't recognize. Then, there was her appetite. Each time she tried to eat, her stomach seemed to be full of its own acids. Anna needed a distraction, and today, with the harvest finally over, the olives would be waiting for her.

In the dark, the long slope of lawn was gray and heavy with dew. She stayed at the porch railing and watched Bobo run down the steps and across the lawn to where the grass ended and the family's orchard began. There was not enough light to see the olive trees, but Anna could hear the leaves rustle as the Northers blew through the valley. She pursed her lips. A muttering, anxious voice inside her clawed its way to the surface: *There's fruit to glean. Olives plumped up so tight that the skin'll split at the slightest touch. Dozens of drupes dropping to the ground with each sway of a bough. They're out there rotting, an ample feast for pests.*

She felt this guilt after every harvest. The pickers were only ever able to collect nine-tenths of what the grove had to offer. Anna had never been able to abide waste. She blamed her frugality on her parents and their heritage. What was it people said? Shown the Eiffel Tower any good Scot-Irish would ask what fool wasted good steel. Anna pulled on the muddy galoshes they kept on the porch and emptied the basket where they kept kindling. God knew; if she didn't glean, no one else would. It was futile, but she felt certain that one year she would succeed in stripping a tree of all its fruit.

Bobo met her as she descended the hill. She bent down to rub his ears before he trotted back to the house. She was surprised to find when she raised her eyes that her mind was not on that November morning, but on a memory more than a century old. For Anna, time had a way of folding up on itself. There were certain seasons when she felt the reminiscences about her father and mother, both dead since the early 1930s, as freshly as if it were the day they'd formed. She knew that every second she'd breathed had been recorded by her brain and that occasionally, her mind surprised her by recalling a moment she'd not remembered before.

The smell of wet flannel tickled her nose, and she heard the echo of giggling. It was an old memory, she couldn't have been more than ten. She and her brother, Wealthy, were gathering fallen olives from the squares of gray wool laid on dewy ground. The perfect olives were put on one, the split and shriveled fruit on another. They were dutiful children for a spell, but before long, they were sitting cross-legged, playing slapsies. She was much slower than her older brother, and the backs of her hands were red from being hit so many times. Her hands hovered just above Wealthy's. She watched his eyes closely for the first sign of movement. She ached to win, to get a chance to slap her brother's hands. Neither of them noticed their father, standing half-hidden behind an olive tree, with a deep frown across his face.

He was a thin man. Anna imagined that if her father's skin were to be peeled back, like whittled bark, there would be green wood underneath. His blows always felt like those from a switch. There was rebound in his strikes. He boxed Wealthy's ears with open palms and roared at them both about the wasted time. Anna, seeing her opportunity, slapped the tops of her brother's hands and ran off. She remembered turning to look at her father and brother, their mouths open, their expressions changing from anger to laughter, and then she tripped.

It was a small cut, one that healed without leaving a scar. But it bled like an artery had opened up. "Scalp wounds are always bad," her father said, peering at the small cut above her left eyebrow. He dabbed at it with his handkerchief and then sent Wealthy to collect all the spiderwebs he could find. When he returned, his fist was clamped tight around sticky threads pressed into a gray oblong. Together they picked off pieces of the ball and pushed them into the cut until the bleeding slowed to a trickle.

Anna stopped near the end of the lawn and cursed. The early dawn light didn't provide enough illumination to go into the grove, which absorbed and diffused the sun's rays so that even at noonday the inside of the orchard was dim. She should have remembered about the light. *Hell.* She hated to be made to feel foolish, especially by her own actions. This lapse made her wary and with her fingers, she reached up and felt along her eyebrow. She pushed the wrinkles aside and ran her finger along the few brow hairs she had left. *Nothing.* No slight bump, or irregularity in the skin to authenticate her memory, and yet she knew it was true.

The sky turned from purple to blue. She treaded along the edge of the grove, where there was just enough light, and picked fruit, reaching for the limbs on the outer edge of the orchard and feeling for the drupes by touch. A lifetime of this touching meant that she knew—by the shape, the heft of each fruit, if it would be good for pressing. That word, *drupe,* had confused her for many years. Her mother would tell her the pansies in the window boxes were drooping and needed to be watered, and Anna would run to the window, wondering what wonderful fruit the yellow and purple flowers would produce.

That was a story she'd told before, but the miracle of spiderwebs was a newly remembered tale, one that she needed to tell her daughter, her granddaughter, and anyone else who would listen. All that the generations beneath her did not know worried Anna. She wanted to find someone who would listen to her. *Really listen.* The world hated old people. Even her own family thought they'd learned all they needed to know from Anna. She was no longer consulted, and she couldn't start a story without her daughter, or granddaughter, interrupting to finish it for her. They had no perspective, no understanding of how much still needed to be preserved. It would take a lifetime to tell them her secrets, and Anna had already lived two lifetimes.

The light touched the edges of the valley and Anna moved to step into the grove.

"Mama," her daughter called.

"Grams," echoed her granddaughter with her high, thin voice.

Then their voices took on the sharper edge of need and worry.

Anna sighed and turned back toward the house. It was good to be wanted. The dew evaporated off the leaves of the olive trees like smoke. Walking out up the hill, she gave quiet thanks that the firstborns had all stayed near—tied to the olives, the reddish soil, the adobe home, and Anna.

"You're here!" said Elizabeth, no—Bets: no one called her daughter by her full name any longer. Out of nervousness, Bets played with the chain of her necklace.

"How can you just wander off in the dark like that?" asked Calliope.

"Dog was with me for a bit," she said. It always disconcerted Anna to see her daughter and granddaughter with so much age on them.

"I still worry," Bets said. Her daughter was a solid woman, darker than the rest of the family, except for Anna. She had heavy brows and deep-set eyes. In the next year, she'd turn ninety, but she had the Keller genes, which meant she hadn't been slowed down by age. Her hair had gone gray about ten years earlier, but then in the last few years it had lightened, so that in the morning light it shimmered like silver.

"That makes two of us," Callie said through the screen door.

Anna pulled off the muddy boots and sat in one of the rockers on the back porch. *Callie should let her hair go gray,* she thought. This month, her granddaughter's hair was a brassy blond and frizzed at the ends. She'd also refused to give in to the shapeless shelf that all women's bustlines moved toward in old age. Even though Callie was in her midsixties, and it was no longer fashionable, she strapped herself into corsets and brassieres that molded her soft bosoms into sharp points. Her walk, though, was the only aspect of her appearance that Anna argued with her about. The accident had left Callie with a noticeable limp, which she'd turned into a provocative tilt. Callie claimed she walked as she'd always walked, but Anna thought the come-hither movements appeared only after her granddaughter's leg had been all torn to pieces.

"Grams? Are you listening to me?" Callie said through the screen door. "What do you think?"

"About what," Anna asked.

Bets opened the door a crack. "About feeding the doctor when he arrives."

"Tell Grams to set those boots on the grass and I'll clean the mud off later," Callie said, and then she started listing off the contents of their refrigerator and wondering aloud if there was enough time to defrost a roast.

"It's only lunch," Anna said. The geneticist had been Callie's grand idea. Her granddaughter mythologized the family; she wanted to be set apart from the world around her, even from the time she was small, she'd spent all her energy on being unique. Anna blamed the girl's father for that. He'd been the one to insist on such a fanciful name. "Calliope," she said thinking it was a fine word, but a terrible name. She usually shortened it to avoid saying it.

"Are you okay, Grams?" Callie asked through the screen door.

Anna assured her granddaughter she was fine and asked for a cup of hot water with a drop of olive oil and a wedge of lemon. Then she settled into one of the rockers and sorted through the olives, throwing the few bad ones to the fat robins who were digging for worms in the yard.

"Is this your secret?" Callie said, handing over the cup and then sitting in the other rocker. Because of her leg, she could never stand for long. "Shall we tell Amrit there's no need for a blood analysis, the secret to longevity is citric acid, olive oil, and H_2O?"

"Amrit? I thought it was pronounced Hashmi. Dr. Hashmi," Anna said. New people never quite understood that she had all her faculties. She knew that her age and the way her face resembled crumpled linen made them assume she didn't understand what was happening around her. She'd been practicing the geneticist's name for weeks now, even reading up on his research, so that it would be clear when they met that she was old, but not infirm.

Callie blushed. "No, no. You're right, we should call him Dr. Hashmi. I've just been talking to him so often that I feel like we're friends."

"Talking about what?" Anna asked.

"About us, about you. All of it." Calliope looked away from

Anna toward the orchard. She took a small white pill from her pocket and swallowed it. "It's not just your age that he's interested in. He's fascinated by the generations, the firstborns. I guess in India, daughters are considered a liability."

Unable to help herself, Anna answered with the Irish proverb she heard from her own mother's lips more times than she could count. "A son is a son till he takes him a wife, a daughter is a daughter all of her life."

Anna's sons had all died. The last one five years earlier, but the line of daughters remained unbroken—five generations of firstborn women. She rocked and whispered her own private litany—Anna begat Elizabeth, Bets begat Calliope, Callie begat Deborah, and Deb begat Erin.

"There's always a place for sons," Bets said, coming out on the porch. Anna knew her daughter was proud of her own boys, even though they'd all left California and settled into towns where their wives had grown up.

"Callie was telling me that wherever this doctor comes from that daughters are a burden," Anna said.

"Everyone always wants sons. But it isn't like it used to be. They're the ones who leave now, got to get off in the world and explore," Bets said. "I haven't seen my boys in two or three Christmases now, although Matthew tried to fly me to Boston last year."

"It's different in India," Callie said. "You have to pay money if you have daughters, for them to get married."

It occurred to Anna that perhaps Callie had a romantic interest in the geneticist. Anna, despite being widowed for decades, had never wanted another man in her life. Her granddaughter, however, was a fool for love.

"Think of all the money I could've had. Five able-bodied sons might've brought in enough money to leave Kidron and move back to Australia," Anna said.

"They might have been able-bodied, but they certainly weren't able-brained," Bets said. She had never been able to resist a dig at her brothers, even if they were dead.

"I think it's romantic," Callie said.

Anna took a good look at her granddaughter. She'd put on her Sunday makeup, even though it was a Saturday, and she was wearing hundred-dollar jeans the saleswoman in Nordstrom had insisted made her look merely fifty, instead of the sixty-five she actually was. Anna thought dungarees were ridiculous no matter who was wearing them. She smoothed the fabric of her own skirt and pulled a stray string from the seam.

"This is science, not romance," Anna said. She wanted to warn Callie, to keep her from getting her hopes up. This had happened before. One of the suppliers for her store would strike up a relationship with Callie on the phone and she would think she'd found true love.

"She knows," Bets said. Her daughter didn't like disagreements. Anna wasn't surprised when she changed the subject. "How long until the good doctor gets here?"

"Before lunchtime," Callie said. She pulled on the neckline of her shirt until it fully covered her bosom.

"Help me with these olives then," Anna said. "If we get them in the press now we'll have fresh oil for lunch."

"The pickers did a good job this year. The Lindseys said their crew pulled down a ton an acre and we got at least that," Bets said.

Anna didn't agree. "There's a lot of picking left to do."

Bets sighed and took the bait. "Didn't they strip it clean enough for you? I know Benny hired that new foreman, but he's Diego's son, and you know he'd been out with his daddy in the Lindseys' fields since he could walk."

Anna looked at the funnel that fed the small handpress they kept on the porch. She needed another basket of olives to fill it.

"Pickers didn't do any worse than any other year. Definitely no better than the year all our men were at war and the harvest was left to the women and children."

"Daddy always said women made the best pickers. What's that old proverb?" Bets asked.

Anna grinned as she spoke. " 'In the olive grove you've got to be wise in the feet and wild in the head.' " She smiled thinking about her own father and how he'd always claimed that women were the only souls wild enough in the head to pick a tree clean. He never meant it as a compliment, but Anna took it as such.

Callie shook her head. "I never did understand that. I think you ought to let the pickers use those machines. We could probably get a ton and a quarter an acre." With this statement, her granddaughter had started an old argument, and Anna understood Callie raised it mostly for the conversation.

"The noise would kill me and the pounding is likely to kill the trees." Anna smiled as she said this. She knew her granddaughter was just finding a way to argue, since Bets had cut off their conversation about the doctor. This was better. Callie liked to tell people that the day her grandmother wasn't outraged, they'd start planning the funeral. It made folks laugh, especially young people, who couldn't imagine that Anna, as old as she was, hadn't already planned her interment twice over.

They stood on the porch, hashing out old complaints until the dry November wind drove them inside. Just as Anna moved to pick up the basket and head to the orchard for a second time, she heard the crunch of a car coming down the gravel drive out front.

"He's early," Callie said, rising and moving with her awkward gait quickly through the house to the front door. The dog, who was too old to hear the car, trotted after Callie as she thumped past him.

Bets held the door open for Anna and then glanced at the ormolu clock on the piano in the corner of the front room. "I don't see how he made such good time from the airport. Oakland traffic is never easy to get through."

There was no porch off the front door. Three concrete stairs stepped down to the gravel driveway, a carved semicircle in the front yard. Anna remained standing on the top step, shading her eyes against the sun as a dark blue sedan made its way down the drive.

"Why doesn't he hurry up already?" Callie asked.

"Probably didn't get the rental insurance," Bets said. "They'll get you for the tiniest ding."

Anna squinted and saw that there was a woman behind the wheel. Bobo surprised them all by rising up on his hind legs and pawing at the sky before turning a flip. It was a trick he hadn't done in years. Anna was just realizing it was not who they expected when the car stopped and Erin, her great-great-granddaughter, stepped out of the car.

CHAPTER TWO

Erin

$\mathcal{E}$ rin left Kidron two years earlier, after graduating from college, and hadn't been home since. She talked too fast for Anna to catch most of what was said, but it was clear that her great-great-granddaughter was in trouble. Erin's voice was thin, her skin sallow, and her gestures moved in opposition to her words. Anna heard her say, "I just needed a break, the stress—" and watched her hands make a circle, as if to indicate that there was some larger problem, an issue so big it couldn't be spoken about. Callie settled next to her on the couch and the dog climbed into Erin's lap and curled into a ball.

"You need to eat," Bets said, bringing in a plate of olives and saltines. "You're too thin and your cheeks are all sunken in. What do they feed you on tour? I'd think in Italy it would be all pasta and bread."

Callie picked up where her mother left off. "Did you lay over in New York? Why didn't you call to tell us you were coming? You didn't have to rent a car, I would've picked you up."

Erin leaned her head on Callie's shoulder and closed her eyes.

"We should send her to bed." Anna wanted to talk to the others without Erin present. They needed to piece together an explanation of the child's behavior.

"I'm old enough to send myself to bed," Erin said. Her eyes were still closed, and Anna suspected she was crying. "I didn't know I was coming home until I got here and by then it was too late to tell you."

Bets stroked the girl's hair and murmured soothing words. The scene wasn't much different from the one that unfolded when Erin had been a child, one who lost her parents and had come, quite unexpectedly, to live with them at Hill House. Anna listened to Bets's hypnotic voice—there was some lilt, pattern to her speech that soothed the instinct to run and then watched as her daughter—old enough to need help herself—walked Erin down to the bedroom that had been hers when she was four. Bobo went after them.

Anna pulled open the secretary in the living room and took out all the papers she had about Erin's time in Italy. There were a handful of airmail letters written on tissue-thin paper full of vague descriptions of the other opera members, anecdotes of day trips they'd taken, and one particularly long missive when Erin thought she'd left her sheet music on a city bus. She also had the initial packet of information that Erin had received when she signed her contract to sing mezzo-soprano for the Academy of Santa Cecilia.

Callie and Bets came down the hall and settled back into the couch. The exchange with Erin seemed to have restored some of their youth. They talked quietly, and Anna didn't even try to listen. She'd never admit it, but she couldn't hear as well as she used to. Instead, she searched for the copy of the contract that Erin had given her when Anna demanded to know how she was going to pay for her living expenses. There was money that Erin didn't know about—money from an insurance policy that had paid out when her father died—but Anna was holding back, waiting for the right

time to give it to Erin. At last Anna found what she'd been searching for at the bottom of the pile of letters. When she unfolded it, she
realized every word was in Italian. It would be of no use to them.

"She's in trouble," Bets said, at last bringing Anna into the
conversation.

"I've never seen her look so much like her mother," Callie said.
"Should we look in the car for clues? There has to be some indication of why she's here."

Bets took the paperwork from Anna and scanned it. "You can
read some of this," she said to her daughter. "Spanish and Italian
aren't that much different. Both romance languages, right?"

"They're nothing alike," Callie said, not even glancing at the
papers. "I'm not sure we should pry. Chances are she'll tell us when
she's ready."

"Her mother never told us anything," Bets said, pulling at a
silver strand of hair that escaped the low bun she always wore.

Anna knew she should step between them, knew that the
blame and the guilt for what had happened with Erin's mother was
deep enough to threaten the bond between the two of them. It had
been ugly for so many years after it happened.

"A woman is entitled to her secrets," Anna said. She thought of
all that she'd kept from her own mother, her daughter—suspicions
that none of them were who they thought they were.

Bets stood, quickly gathering the papers up off the couch. She
had her father's height and his chin—pointed and heavily angled,
although he'd always worn a beard, which softened his face. Bets
didn't have that option and as a result, people often felt accused
when she spoke to them. "We could have stopped it if we'd known.
I'm not going to let this become another festering secret we keep
because it's easier to tell ourselves that privacy is important. To hell
with privacy."

Anna listened to the front door slam and the heavy crunch of

Bets's feet on the gravel. "She's not going to find anything," she said to Callie. "I got a good look when our girl jumped out of the car crying and I didn't see a bit of luggage and not so much as a burger wrapper."

"Doesn't matter. Mom thinks you took my side again." Callie glanced down the hall at the closed door to Erin's room.

"There aren't any sides," Anna said, reaching for her grand-daughter's hand. "There've never been any sides. It's all just one big endless circle."

"I don't want to be sitting here when she comes back in," Callie said.

She sounded petulant, like she had at fourteen when her hair was a tangled mess and her feet were summer-browned. As a girl and then as a teenager, she'd been a blur running from Bets, run-ning from Hill House, never wanting to be contained. Every spo-ken wish tied inextricably to leaving Kidron. Callie had thought the big wide world was holding its arms open for her. "Come down to the orchard with me. I need another basket of olives to get enough oil pressed," Anna said. The orchard had a way of calming people.

Callie rubbed her leg through the stiff denim. "In too much pain to do any serious walking. I'll start lunch, I need to figure out another vegetable, since Erin won't eat any of that ham we've got baking."

Anna rose and thanked God that her body functioned well enough for her to move around. She'd never been one to be idle. Not that her granddaughter's leg kept her idle, but it allowed her to hide in kitchens and storerooms doing only the work she wanted to. Anna pulled a sweater from the front closet, grabbed her basket, and headed out the back door to the orchard. With Erin's arrival, the day seemed cooler to Anna.

The house would be in disarray when the geneticist arrived. Anna wondered what sort of man Dr. Hashmi was and whether he'd notice the chaos around him. Men weren't blessed with the same intuition as women. At the bottom of the hill, she turned to look back at her house. It was a home built in stages, with rooms added as their family grew in size and in wealth. Like many of the homes in the Sacramento Valley, it had been patterned after the missions that the Spanish abandoned when they lost the war. It was one story with an adobe roof and stucco walls. From the back you could see the two wings that ran perpendicular to each other off the main structure. The kitchen, which for many years had served as a place to process the family's olives, took up most of the north wing. The south, comprised of three bedrooms and a bathroom, was slightly longer than its counterpart. The main building held a master bedroom, renovated most recently, a sitting room, a dining room, and a library.

This home, which had always been called Hill House, had been built by Anna's father, Percy Davison. Over the years, she'd often wondered how a man had constructed such a perfect home for the women who'd come to inhabit it. When they moved from the canvas tent where they'd lived waiting on the fledgling orchard to sprout, providing enough collateral for the bank, her father told them their temple awaited them. Hill House was not the oldest home in Kidron, but because it was one of the few plots of elevated land in this part of the valley and the orchard was still family owned, it was one of the stops on the tourism route drawn up by the town. The brochure, which Anna had hanging on her refrigerator, called it Kidron's own San Simeon. It was, of course, not even a third of the size of that mansion, but Anna privately agreed with this assessment. She never said as much, afraid that what the world perceived about her town, about her house, was not her reality.

The closer she came to the orchard, the younger she felt. She stepped into the grove of trees, which were not even a foot taller than she, and breathed in the musk of decomposition. Fall was coming fast, but there, among the olive trees, summer was still suspended in the gray-green of the leaves. The fruit had just started to turn from lime green to purple. She reached up and cupped her palm around one of the nearest branches. The noise the leaves made as she moved her hand quickly upward, the friction sending the fruit falling into the waiting basket, sounded like the voice of her father, who held as many stories as there were stars and each one always began and ended with the trees.

CHAPTER THREE

Kidron

*A*nna had loved her father, but she never liked him all that much. She suspected most people felt this way about one parent, or at the very least, a sibling. It wasn't God's way to stick you with people who were easy to like—life was all a big test. Can you love your sniveling, sickly brother? Can you love your dumb but well-intentioned mother? Can you love your hard-as-steel father? Anna used to tell her children that God never gave one commandment about liking a person and she'd learned over the years that it was possible to love without having a lot of like in your heart.

Under her father's inscrutable gaze, Anna always felt disappointed in herself. This feeling of not measuring up is what made her older brother, Wealthy, leave home, and it is what made Anna stay in Kidron. Funny how two people raised in the same home could have such opposite reactions. Of course, you are born who you are. In Anna's experience, raising children was less like molding clay and more like chipping away at granite with a butter knife. Her father had never tried to change who his children were, he just remained disappointed that they couldn't become what he expected of them. A week or so after he died, Anna found a slip of paper in his Bible that confirmed this for her. On the top of the paper in his deeply slanted writing, he'd written "The Accomplished Life of Percival Keenan Davison." Following that was a numbered list:

1. First man to cultivate olives in California
2. Two-time collar-and-elbow champion of Meath
3. Discovered the world's fifth largest alluvial gold nugget in Australia
4. Moved Kidron to present-day location
5. ~~Father to Wealthy Davison and Anna Davison Keller~~ Flew on a plane

Anna didn't know whether he'd crossed his children off the list because those weren't the type of accomplishments he'd intended to document or whether in the end who his children had grown up to be was less of an achievement than riding in a biplane at the state fair.

She did know that his list wasn't entirely accurate. The Spanish were the first to bring olives to the New World. When they conquered California, they planted groves wherever they planted their missions—using the oil for the church's anointing and consecrating. The olive tree, like most religions, required civilization to survive, and when the Spanish were conquered, left-behind trees became feral, barren bushes. Percy arrived half a century after the Spanish ceded California, meaning that Anna's father could truly only claim to have resurrected the crop.

Veda, Anna's mother, who was called Mims, claimed the gold nugget was as large as two clasped hands. Percy's mining partners cheated him, and in the end, Anna's parents left Australia with just enough money to start over in California. Because Anna was only four when they left Brisbane, she never fully understood why they needed to start over—only that the move was connected in some way to Wealthy's asthma and Mims's grief over the babies she'd lost between the births of Anna and her brother.

The people in Kidron held a dozen stories about Percy that differed in a dozen different ways from the truth that Anna knew about her father. If he'd talked more, maybe the history books would agree on a few facts, but the only story anyone had right was what happened once he arrived in the Sacramento Valley. The Davison family arrived in San Francisco in 1898. After weeks on a cramped ship, Percy couldn't take even the smallest crowds. He wrinkled his nose at the stench of the city and went in search of arid land with mild seasons.

Anna, Wealthy, and their mother stayed in a rooming house guarding the family's most precious possession—six wooden boxes filled with rootstock. As Anna understood it, there had been more trees when the family had left Brisbane, but they'd not all survived the voyage. For many years, her parents used these boxes as night-stands, and it was only when they both died that Anna tossed them into the woodpile and put in their place a matching set from the Penney's catalog. She sometimes wished she hadn't done this, but for many years, she didn't appreciate that objects could have a history.

Ultimately her father was only able to untangle half his trees. He spent the money he'd planned to use to build the family a house on buying year-old trees from Spain and then he grafted bits of his trees onto the new rootstock. The earliest written account of Percy's contribution to Kidron notes that he went in search of the feral trees at the back of abandoned missions—snipping branches from the heartier specimens. After seeing how quickly his rootstock with the feral cuttings took to the soil, Percy allowed himself to feel hopeful. In a year's time the trees were as big as those that were three years old in Brisbane. He calculated that instead of ten years, it would only take six for his trees to bear enough fruit to pay back his outlay and start putting money in his pocket.

Money remained an obstacle to easy success—her father didn't have enough cash to wait six years for a crop. He needed to find people with money who would believe in him and understand his vision of small ten- and twenty-acre lots producing just enough for a family to make a living. Two of the largest landowners in Tehama County, James Mayfield and John Woodburn, quickly signed on to make Percy's vision a reality. They waited until the location of the railroad became public knowledge and then they announced the creation of the Maywood Colony. They divided up the acreage of Mayfield and Woodburn into ten-acre plots and planted them ninety trees to an acre, then they took out advertisements in major magazines offering more than 100 percent profit on the land. It was nearly true, too. The trees provided enough income for purchasers to make their installment plan payments on the houses and land and earn enough money for a family to buy house goods. They hired Percy to manage the olive and fruit trees and paid him a small percentage of each sale.

It was a good plan. Even now, fourth grade teachers in Kidron during their sections on local history tell their students that Percy saw the future—he was a man who sensed the growth of the West would come by bringing in the people who were neither rich nor poor, but wanted more space than the congested East could give them. Then there were the children of farmers who knew enough to want more than to raise livestock or depend on the volatility of wheat prices at harvest. Olives were a steady crop with predictable payouts. Her father lived long enough to read a few of these history passages about the colonies, and it delighted him.

Before it could be a triumph—and the Maywood Colony was hugely successful—Percy had to appease George Kidron, who felt anyone's success but his own as if it were sand in his underwear. As the town's founder, George held opinions that people respected. When asked about the colony, he predicted failure and called Percy a foreign con man come to fleece California. His blustering made Percy's investment partners nervous, and they asked him to make peace. Percy could read men like he could the earth, and he knew that the failure of Kidron to find success as a railroad town had left a great, gaping pit in George's heart—so instead of offering him money, Percy told him that he knew how to move the town.

For this part of her father's story, Anna didn't need to rely on the town's history books, or what Mims and Percy had told her. Her first clear memory—one that moved beyond emotions and senses— was of this move. She thought of that fall day in 1900 as the day she was born. There existed in her mind still images from Brisbane—a woman she didn't recognize in a flour sack apron, a tortoise as big as a table, and her father lifting a basket of sun-blackened olives. She sometimes wished she could find the key to start these images rolling into a movie, felt that they would give her insight into herself, but they remained still and slightly out of focus. The day the town hauled itself a mile toward the railroad was a moving picture, but unlike the story of her father and how he brought the olives, it lived and breathed in her cells.

There was no school on moving day. All the children were released and told to stay out of the way. Some of the older boys, like Anna's brother, Wealthy, assisted their fathers by tying ropes and holding harnesses. Anna volunteered to take care of her mother, who was five months pregnant. There was optimism that Mims would be able to carry this child to term, but the midwife, after hearing her history, had confined her to bed. Anna had no talent for ministrations and her mother soon sent her to town, telling her to watch over her father and brother. "If we lose them, we're lost," Mims had said.

As it happened, Mims blossomed when all the men in her life had left her. With her petite, round figure and her small-featured face, Mims had, when she was thin, resembled a mouse. As she aged and put on weight, her face filled out and looked like a child's illustration of the sun. This was how Anna's children remembered Mims, but on that day in 1900, her skin was drawn tight over her skeleton—all the worry about the baby, the orchard, and the colony had eaten up every last reserve of fat she had.

The hot air pushed up the valley from the desert to the east of Kidron and brought with it the fine grit of sand. After two years of living in the valley, Anna still felt out of place. It was a sentiment shared by most of the other residents of Kidron. She overheard her father tell the men at the general store that most mornings he felt like he'd put on another man's pants. There was less permanence back then, when the people who lived in the valley had only called it home for one or two generations. Now, everywhere she looked, Kidron was filled with the grandchildren and great-grandchildren of those men standing around the store, agreeing that the hot wind just didn't feel like home.

The general store was an imposing rectangle with annexes stuck off the sides like stacked boxes. To Anna, the buildings hadn't seemed old, but now that she was six, she'd only recently decided that the world hadn't started at her birth. She considered the things that had been there before her as she fed the horses bits of carrots on moving day.

It had been decided that the saloon no longer fit with the character of the town and it would remain, along with what her father called the "ladies" house on old Main Street. When her daughter Bets first married Frank, she lived on old Main Street, and visiting them Anna was surprised to find that both buildings had survived. The ladies house, which she now understood had been a whorehouse, was home to an eccentric pair of brothers who rented rooms to vagrants during the winter. The saloon had become a restaurant that capitalized on the building's history. Although the owners had installed swinging doors, like those one would find in a

John Wayne picture, they had not been present when she was a girl. Anna told Bets that the saloon had never had swinging doors. "Such an impracticality. Good only for gunfights, and we never had those," she'd said.

Those two buildings had large black *X*s painted on their sides on moving day. Anna walked among the teams of horses waiting to pull the buildings, and stopped to listen to the butcher tell her father and a few of the other men who'd come into town from Maywood Colony about seeing an outpost in Iowa attempt a move. "Damn fools killed half the horses in town and had to put the other half down from injuries. I saw a man flattened when a house rolled over him," said the butcher as he spit tobacco juice into the street. "It wasn't like you'd think. No popping or bursting right when it happened. Naw, that came later."

The men went on to discuss death and how the bodies they'd seen never looked like one expected. The butcher said the flattened man's body had started to swell, and the skin on his legs split like a peach left too long on the tree. "He was dead before the sun set," the butcher finally said. Some men standing around him edged away and found a way to busy their hands with horses or uncoiling rope. Her father, though, stepped closer and put a hand on the man's shoulder. She frowned and remembered her mother telling her father that morning that the easiest solutions are often impossible. Although Anna was only six, the image of that man's skin splitting open like overripe fruit stayed in her mind as if she had actually been in that small Iowa town to watch the man suffer.

She watched her father as he threaded his way through the town taking notes on who was ready to move. Anna kept a few paces behind him, stepping into a doorway when he turned around, or reaching to stroke the neck of one of the hitched horses. The town smelled different then; there was always straw thrown down over some low spot in the road, and a man's sweat mixed with that of the animals. The horses were damp with perspiration that day and the smell of their sweet, heavy sweat overpowered Anna. She watched him write numbers on buildings to indicate the order that they would be moved. At last he came to the general store, and he drew a chalk line up one side of the store and then handed off the chalk to the men on the roof, who completed the line. He took his chalk back and marked the store's halves each with a different number.

Anna felt no compunction to watch over her brother. He'd been so sickly in Brisbane that her parents let him roam all hours of the day and night around Kidron. Anna complained about how Wealthy never had to help, and her parents said that God was likely to take his miracle back if they stopped him from exercising his good health now that he had it. It made her wish him ill. She watched him shimmy up the side of the general store to help the Lindsey boys dismantle the chimney one brick at a time and hoped that he'd fall and break his leg.

Logs had been stripped of their bark and made smooth, and they sat like the legs of giants in the middle of the road. Each of the two dozen buildings in town was surrounded by piles of furniture and goods, and Anna left her father and his chalk numbers and amused herself by wandering among the stacks to examine the insides of houses she'd never set foot in. All around her the noise of steel teeth cutting through planks and men swearing as horses pulled unevenly filled her ears. The breeze pushed back at her as she walked, and although there was no salt in the air, there was the sweetness of newly cut lumber. She felt proud of Kidron, emboldened by a town that refused to die because the Southern Pacific Railroad had plotted a route out of its reach.

The town worked together to move the butcher shop first. Two dozen men slid planks under the foundation and forty others circled the structure. On the count of three, men pushed down on the planks and those circling the building moved in to take their place along the front or sides and hold up their section until the logs could be rolled underneath. It took no more than three minutes for the butcher shop to be placed on rollers. Anna watched as it was secured with ropes and then as six teams of horses were hitched to the logs. At that point every man put a hand on the building and walked with the horses to where lines had been burned into the prairie grass to mark the place for the shops. Anna returned to where the butcher shop had sat and poked her toe at the bone and dried blood that had dropped through the cracks in the floor.

Wealthy and the Lindsey boys began scavenging for bits they could use in their cowboy games and pushed Anna aside. "This is no place for girls." Anna pocketed a palm-size bone fragment the color of weak tea and settled herself on a stack of flour sacks. It took nearly ten hours to move the remaining eighteen structures. For the last two—the pharmacy and the blacksmith—the children were given lanterns to set atop their heads and told to walk the path between old Main and new Main. After the last had been settled into its new foundation, Anna watched her father set his foot on the path toward Hill House and then scurried back with her lantern to find what had fallen through the floor cracks of each of the buildings. That night was the only one she ever remembered staying out later than Wealthy.

Anna kept that pile of treasures tied up in a blue handkerchief far into adulthood. It wasn't until one long summer day when her children were small and in need of a distraction that she dug the pile from her hope chest. She doled out the buttons, shoe buckles, nails, and even the bone to each with a made-up story of the item's owner and the special powers it held.

From the orchard, Anna heard the grind of tires on the gravel and knew that the geneticist had finally arrived. She quickly ran her hands up several more branches, trying to pull as much fruit as she could. The basket at her feet was nearly two-thirds full. It would be enough.

CHAPTER FOUR

Supercentenarian

*A*nna watched the good doctor fill his plate with olives, green beans, and potatoes. He passed on the meat but took three of Callie's dinner rolls. His muddy brown eyes flicked around the table, and he nodded each time he made eye contact with any of the women. He looked to be in his midfifties. Callie was probably too old for him. In Anna's experience, men his age wanted a wife young enough to take care of them as they aged. Still, he had kind eyes, and they glanced most often at her granddaughter.

Bets, who'd overseen the cooking of the ham, picked up the platter and tried to urge it on him. "It isn't beef, if that's what you're worried about. Fresh meat, we only got the hog butchered last week."

Dr. Hashmi's gaze dropped to his plate. "I'd not expected such a large lunch."

"Most of the Hindus I know are vegetarians," Erin said. She'd come out of the bedroom during the introductions. They'd told him right away about her unexpected return, and he'd clapped his hands, offering that he was delighted that he'd get to meet the fifth generation in person.

"Ah, yes. American food is quite complicated," he said, bringing an olive to his mouth. "But quite good."

"Well I don't eat the meat either," Erin said and turned toward the doctor. "Philosophical grounds. Humane treatment and all that."

Anna stiffened. "Your second cousin Charley Spooner raised this pig up from when it was small. Bought it at the 4H auction, and it followed him around like a sheep. How much more humanity do you want?"

Bobo growled and then Erin surprised them all by reaching for the platter and moving a slice onto her plate. She tore a bit off, tossed it to the dog, and then licked her fingers. "Oh God that's good," she said. Anna wasn't sure if she were speaking to the dog or to those seated around her.

Erin blinked rapidly. "I've been away too long. I forget that you don't see the world the way everyone else does. I forget it's still possible to get a pig that someone took on daily walks." She cut the meat into small squares and then put a bite no bigger than a pea on her fork. "I'd also forgotten that Bets can make a ham so tender it melts in your mouth."

Anna didn't know what to say. Erin's strange behavior wasn't an issue they could raise in the presence of a stranger. Bets put another slice on Erin's plate. "You're so thin, maybe a little ham will put some meat back on your bones," she said.

In the end, Erin was the only one of them to have an appetite. Anna watched Bets clear half-full plates with food pushed around the edges. In the corner, Callie and Dr. Hashmi stood, holding their plates as if on their way to the sink, but instead they talked to each other in low voices.

"Should we start?" Anna asked.

Dr. Hashmi ended up sandwiched between Erin and Callie on the low living room couch. Erin, who appeared revitalized by lunch, asked question after question, with hardly enough space between her words for the doctor to answer. "Your accent is slight," she said to him. "Where are you from?"

"Tennessee. It was my father who immigrated to America in the 1940s to be part of the nuclear experiments."

He'd shared this information as if they wouldn't know what he was speaking of, but Anna corrected that notion. "At Oak Ridge, right? One of the Lindsey boys was out there at that time working security. Of course we all thought he was a peanut farmer. Maybe your parents knew him?"

Dr. Hashmi raised his shoulders as if to answer her, but Bets cut him off. "One of the faults of being so old is that you tend to think everyone ought to know everyone else." She changed the subject, asking if he'd been born in Tennessee.

Dr. Hashmi shook his head. "I'm afraid now that you know I wasn't it gives away my age."

"Age is nothing to be ashamed about in this room," Callie said. "You don't get to be the head of a department if you're under fifty." She leaned forward, exposing a bit of her ample cleavage. "I just couldn't get over that his assistant put me right through to him."

Anna watched the doctor closely. He dipped his head slightly in Callie's direction, but she couldn't tell what he was looking at. It had become apparent to Anna that Callie had developed feelings for Dr. Hashmi. She wondered if he felt the same.

"I've been searching for a family such as yours nearly my whole career." His hand briefly touched Callie's knee.

"And here we are in the middle of nowhere California," Erin said. There was an edge to her voice that set off alarm bells in Anna's head. She brushed her concerns aside to concentrate on the doctor, who opened his briefcase and passed around a thick packet of papers.

"The questionnaires are first, but I want you to do this over the next few weeks. The oral interviews are why I'm here and of course, your DNA. I *vant* your blood." His attempt at humor was greeted with silence. Callie's laugh came a beat late.

Anna pitied him and despite herself, she felt her suspicions melting away. She'd been strongly against the idea of having a geneticist study their family. *Lab rats,* she'd said to Callie when she brought them the idea. Her granddaughter explained how well his research suited their family. He was specifically interested in studying supercentenarians, both living and dead, and the resulting longevity of their offspring. He, along with several financial backers, believed in the existence of a longevity gene.

Callie's fascination with their family's age sometimes exhausted Anna. That girl was always trying to find the why behind the Keller women's ability to age gracefully. Anna, although she would never vocalize this, felt that if there were something special about the family that it would somehow lessen the feat of living to be the oldest person in the world. Like when those baseball players got into trouble for taking drugs. Anna just wanted Callie to leave well enough alone, and yet here she was again. All it took this time was reading some of an article in *Newsweek* about Dr. Hashmi and his research.

Callie immediately contacted his office at the University of Pittsburgh earlier that year, and in the spring, he'd sent a brief questionnaire and arranged telephone interviews with all the firstborns. Getting permission to speak with Deb, who was incarcerated, had been difficult. Fortunately, there was money attached to the project, and the warden at Chowchilla, where she was housed, accepted a substantial donation from several backers of the study the week before she approved the interview request. During the phone interview, Anna had been grumpy—providing only one-word answers and muttering about the presumptions of this man who thought he could divine the secrets of longevity by asking about the diseases of long-dead family members.

Now, Anna paid close attention as Dr. Hashmi took them through the lengthy questionnaire. She didn't want to give him any opportunity to think she was addled. She did notice that Erin ignored his guided tour and leafed through the pages, stopping when she came to section six, which was headed "Dietary Considerations."

"Glad to see you're interested in what we're eating this time around," Erin said over the top of his explanation about section two, which discussed environmental toxins.

"Yes, food is an important consideration, although I've no training in—" Dr. Hashmi inclined his head and let Erin speak.

"It's the oil," she said.

"The oil?" Dr. Hashmi, who was flustered at being interrupted, didn't understand what Erin was trying to say. Anna knew, as did Bets, who was shaking her head to warn Erin not to speak.

"Olives. You had some earlier with lunch. Didn't you notice driving through the grove how beautiful the trees were? I arrived just before you, and with the slight breeze blowing in from the west I saw not only the greens of our leaves, but also the silver underbellies. They call that Athena's eye. I don't know if they've told you all their secrets, but here's one for you. That stock of trees traces its roots back to a time before Christ ever walked the earth. You ask Anna, she'll tell you how her father smuggled his special stock over from Brisbane." Erin sat back in the recliner and smiled, satisfied that she'd made her point.

"The groves." He paused before continuing and glanced at Callie, who shrugged slightly. "They are quite striking. And you process the oil yourselves?"

"Process it, sell it, cook with it, and if you listen to Erin long enough, she'll have you believe that we sleep in it," said Bets, tightening her grip on her own questionnaire until the paper started to crumple. "The good doctor is looking for answers, not hocus-pocus."

Erin frowned at her great-grandmother. Bets had never believed in the power of the groves, and every time Erin or Callie, who was the true believer, talked about it, her voice took on a dismissive tone, as if she were explaining how the magician pulls a rabbit out of a hat.

Anna closed her eyes. Bobo came to her and began to paw at her knees.

"Perhaps I've stayed too long," said Dr. Hashmi, rising from the couch. Callie had been sitting so close to him that when he stood, she fell over into the space he left behind.

"No," Erin said. "We just need a snack. That's something else you should know about the Keller women, we're all a little hypoglycemic. You don't feed us every four hours and we're likely to start a fight over a feather."

"I didn't realize you called yourselves that," he said. "It is your married name? Am I right?"

Anna failed to answer him. She had been trying to catch Bets's eye. She knew what was wrong with Erin and wanted to see if Bets knew as well. The hunger was the giveaway. Erin had just eaten. When she was small and had first come to live with them, her eating patterns had been erratic. She'd gorge on a meal and then, like a snake, not eat for two or three days afterward.

"It's of no consequence," he said when no one answered him. He moved into Erin's seat across from Anna and squeezed her hand. "You're amazing. Most of the supercentenarians I interview fall asleep before we've even turned the first page."

His praise made Anna less stoic, and she admitted that she was tired. "I don't nap. I know that's what everyone thinks, but I close my eyes to conserve my energy. I'm still aware of what's happening around me. There's too little life left for me to miss out."

"Like bears. Hibernation is a myth. It isn't a long sleep, it is a long rest." He continued to hold her hand. "I'll let you hibernate for the rest of the day if you schedule a time for our interview. I've actually got to meet with everyone here and then, of course, Deb."

Erin came back into the room, cradling Mims's yellow cookie jar. Anna's gaze settled on the girl's midriff. Seeing Erin in the hallway with the fading afternoon light turning her black hair purple, Anna was reminded how much the girl looked like Violet, or what Anna's sister would have looked like had she ever become a woman. Her great-great-granddaughter finished chewing the half of peanut butter cookie she'd crammed into her mouth and then smiled at Dr. Hashmi. "You can come down to Chowchilla with me. Mama is up for parole again, and I thought I'd try to see if I can help her get out."

CHAPTER FIVE

Violet

*A*nna's little sister Violet was born in October 1900. After her father had overseen the town's move, his investors had given him enough money to build a house for his family. The stucco had not yet dried and the floors had not been laid, but Mims was moved indoors when her contractions started, and Violet Philomena Davison was the first child born at Hill House.

Her presence marked the beginning of good fortunes for the Davisons, and in those early years the trees prospered and the plots of land for the acreage sold quickly. By Violet's third birthday, Maywood Colony had bought out three more ranchers and two alfalfa farms, bringing the total acreage of the colony to forty thousand. The Lindseys, who were one of the first families to buy into the colony, purchased land near Kidron's old Main Street and built a processing plant that was run as a cooperative.

Until Anna was thirteen, the only sour note in her childhood was when her brother, Wealthy, rejected their father's offer to buy him his own plot in the colony. Instead, he bought a train ticket to Texas to search out his fortune. Her father refused to see him off and then he forbade any of them from so much as waving good-bye to the train. Anna, who liked that she and Wealthy called the mailman postie and asked for snags instead of sausages with their eggs, skipped school and walked the four blocks to the station on the day that he left. She found him quickly; he was the only man besides her father in town who had red hair. His head was leaning against the window, and Anna threw pebbles at the train car until he turned and saw her. He nodded, and it was the first time her brother looked like a man to her. She hummed to herself as she left the station, planning to make good use of her day out of school by heading to the swimming hole. She heard a low whistle and turned to see her father in the shadows of the station. He winked at her. It was one of the only times she liked her father.

Two months later in early May, the schoolhouse on West Street in the oldest section of Kidron caught fire. It was unusually hot and windy that Spring, and before the fire all that the town talked about was the weather and how it would affect the fruit set of the olives. Anna's father was especially concerned about fruit set because his trees would be six years old that season. His reputation had been built on the promise that in 1907 all the trees that had been planted the first year they sold plots would bear a full harvest—they would be as mature with as much fruit as trees that were a decade old elsewhere.

Anna and Violet had little supervision. The wind made Anna itchy and she often ducked out of school after lunch to go to the swimming hole she and the Lindsey boys had discovered their second year in Kidron. The creek forked at the edge of Anna's land and cut through the property that the Lindseys had purchased. Just after it forked, there was a sinkhole that in the Spring, as the snow from Shasta melted, filled with water.

When her father found out about playing hooky he sent her to bed without her supper, but that year, her parents barely registered the notes the teacher, Miss Dupont, sent home. Violet liked to be praised and enjoyed having her sister punished. Anna knew it bothered her little sister when she was told to mind her own business when she complained about Anna not being where she should be.

They attended Kidron Public No. 1, a wood clapboard structure with an old-fashioned bell tower at the top of its three stories. In the West, where no one family had more than a generation's claim on the land, the social pecking order was determined by proximity to downtown. Those who got in early were seen as forward thinkers and admired, while those who went to school No. 5 were deemed to have unimaginative parents who'd followed the pack. Those with real money boarded their children in schools in the East.

By May it became apparent that the crop yield for 1907 would be far lower than expected. The wind had been too strong to pollinate the trees. Instead of gently blowing the bits of yellow dust from one blossom to another, it swept all the pollen north and into the foothills of Mount Lassen. Families who'd taken out large loans based on the previous year's yield prepared for bankruptcy. The town itself was still flush with revenue under the direction of George Kidron, who was the mayor. He moved to bring the town into the twentieth century. The week before the fire they began replacing the Kidron's electric arc lamps with incandescent ones, and they purchased thirty gallons of a new red paint that the distributor promised would last for thirty years because of the addition of thermite to the mix.

The schoolhouse was half-painted when it caught fire. Twenty-six of the forty-two children died, including Violet. Years later, when Anna was in her eighties, a researcher interviewed her about the fire; although she'd not seen it herself, she related the accounts of those survivors, yet long dead, of a strange quality the fire had, almost chemical in the way it popped and flamed, with geysers of fire igniting. He sent her a copy of his paper, which blamed the fire on the paint and the thermite, which had later been used in World War II to help bombs ignite.

The schoolteacher, Miss Dupont, who had been brought in from the teachers' college in Illinois, survived the fire, although her left arm and neck were badly burned. She left Kidron after the funerals but remained a presence in the lives of those whose children died. Every year on the anniversary of the fire, she wrote letters to those who'd lost children. These letters were hopeful and imagined what each child would have accomplished that year had he or she lived.

On the second anniversary she wrote to tell Louisa Farris's parents that their daughter had won the school-wide spelling bee and Miss Dupont expected her to place at the state level. On the tenth anniversary, she wrote to George Lee's parents to tell them she was quite sorry to find out that his eyesight had not allowed him to join the army but was proud to know that he had raised so much money for war bonds. On the fourteenth anniversary, she wrote to Emily Rose Burnam's parents to tell them how proud she was that their daughter was so skilled as a nurse that she'd saved fourteen others from the influenza epidemic. On the thirty-fifth anniversary, John Pickerling's sisters discovered that their brother had narrowly lost the election for governor. On and on went her letters, every anniversary these children who'd perished in the fire escaped wars and epidemics and had lives of prosperity and notoriety. When parents died, siblings began receiving these letters, and in the case of George Lee, who'd been an only child, the letters went to a distant cousin in Arkansas who'd never met the family. This continued until Miss Dupont's death in 1972. The month after she died, each family received an obituary of their child that Miss Dupont had written out. Some relatives refused to open them— this would have been the case with Anna's parents, but by the time that Violet's obituary arrived in the mailbox, she'd been opening Miss Dupont's letters for decades.

Ten years before the woman's death, Anna had the occasion to visit Miss Dupont in Illinois. That year Callie was selected to attend the United Airlines' stewardess school at O'Hare in Chicago. Bets and her husband, Frank, were overloaded with the orchard, which had grown to three hundred acres, and asked Anna to accompany their only daughter on the train. It was an uncomfortable trip, not only because the train was stalled in Nebraska for two extra days, but also because Callie had wanted to travel unchaperoned. They didn't speak much during the trip, although when she dropped Callie off at the dormitories the girl held her tight and whispered, "Thank you."

She took a cab to the southern suburbs of Chicago and met Miss Dupont for coffee in her brownstone. The scar tissue had not softened over time, and it reached from Miss Dupont's neck, like tendrils, and wrapped around her jaw, stretching toward her left eye. Once she stopped looking at the deformity, Anna, who was in her sixties at the time, was surprised to find that time had compressed the difference in age between them. All around the scar tissue, Miss Dupont's skin was as wrinkled as Anna's, and her eyes had a similar red-rimmed wateriness to them. They ate the pimento-stuffed olives that Anna had brought and talked about how small the world seemed now that man had been in space.

They talked about their lives, the good years, the lean years, and complained that age had sneaked up on them. They circled around their families, each unsure how to talk about children and grandchildren without thinking about Violet. When Anna relaxed into the camelback sofa, Miss Dupont finally brought up her children. Miss Dupont had outlived three husbands and birthed nine children; she counted off her grandchildren, occasionally pointing at a photo set on her brick mantel. "That's thirty-seven altogether.

It's more than I lost, but I know it's a big debt to pay and I'm not sure God'll take mine in exchange for them." They sat quietly, two gray-haired women gazing at photos of children. Then she patted Anna's hand. "Your sister was beautiful. Like a Botticelli angel."

"Violet looked like Mom. I used to watch them play mirror—they'd sit face-to-face and mimic each other's every move. I'd watch, hoping to see a trace of myself in either of them, but there was never a gesture, a freckle that I could lay claim to. After she died I realized that the one thing she never had was Mom's accent."

"I kept wondering when you'd start to sound like you were from Kidron. Wealthy dropped his accent and picked up the Lindseys' Italian."

"My brother was a chameleon. You thought he was related to whoever he was standing by. Had a way of parroting folks. When he was sick, before we came here, Mom said he used to lie in bed and practice bird calls. It got so he could summon any bird in Brisbane to the tree outside his window."

"He was in my class the first year I taught at Kidron. Him and Michael Keller tormented me—"

"You know I married Michael? He's been dead more than twenty years now."

They traded stories for a while and then in a lull Anna reached up and smoothed her iron gray hair, which as far as she could tell didn't belong to anyone in her family.

"You must look like your people," said the teacher.

"My mother said one of her grandmothers married an Italian, which is where—"

"Your father told me about you being a half-caste. So you don't have to—"

Anna looked away from Miss Dupont and then at her watch. She'd not known that her father ever spoke those words aloud. Wealthy used to whisper it to her at night when she'd showed him up at spelling or tree climbing, but she refused to give weight to his taunts.

Miss Dupont rubbed her scars, which took on a purple-red hue when she blushed. "It was in the hospital when we couldn't find you and thought you dead along with Violet." She went on to talk about that day, and as she got closer to the climax of the story, when Anna appeared with the Lindsey boys, wet and muddy from spending the afternoon in the creek, her voice dropped to a whisper.

Anna surprised herself by giving away the ending. "My mother slapped me and then told whoever would listen that I was to play hooky whenever I wanted."

Miss Dupont was crying. "But you never came back to school. None of us did."

Half-caste. She'd forgotten the sound of those words until Miss Dupont said them. They stayed with her, pulling up memories she thought she'd forgotten. She remembered being eight or nine and beating Wealthy in a foot race on the playground. He'd said it then, spit on the ground and told her she was just a *half-caste* anyway. Anna was not a woman who liked change. Violet would have grown up to become the type of woman who would have confronted Wealthy—demanded to know the truth. Anna waited nearly thirty-five more years to ask.

In 1941, two years before Wealthy died in a mining accident, he came home to Kidron for Christmas. His red hair had turned white and his mustache yellow. The skin around his eyes was deeply wrinkled from spending so much time hatless out in the sun. He was lucid, but there were moments when he confused Bets with Anna or asked when Michael, Anna's husband, was expected home. A night in between Christmas and the new year when the wind was still, but the air chilled, they walked through the orchard, each of them reaching out to brush their fingertips against the gray-green leaves of the olive trees.

She'd not wanted to ask him about her past because she was afraid that what she believed about herself would be changed. But that night as they swapped stories about Kidron, their father, their mother, and even Violet, Anna felt time collapse on itself and she sensed that whatever her brother said it only confirmed what she'd always known—the story of her life was not the same as the truth of her life. She didn't have her mother's Irish complexion nor did she ever get sick. She was four inches taller than her father, stronger than her brother, had curly black hair, and skin the color of polished olive wood. She thought maybe she was nobody's child, but what Wealthy told her was that she was their father's child and that although Mims loved her as if she were her own, she'd not given birth to Anna.

"I wish I remembered more," Wealthy had said. They were sitting in the two rocking chairs on the front porch, huddled under heavy wool blankets. "It seemed important when I was younger, when I knew there was a difference between us. But once I was grown and you were grown, it all seemed quite unimportant."

Anna pressed him for any details, and he told her that before she came with them on the boat that he remembered seeing her riding a tortoise and hanging around the fire where the women boiled the wash.

"I used to know more," he said, again lamenting his age and the loss of memories. He looked so pained that Anna shushed him. They were quiet for a long while and then he asked her where Michael was.

"He's dead. Been that way a few years now," Anna said.

Wealthy laughed and then asked her what her secret was. "You're aging so well. The rest of us move slower, can't see as well, and have enough aches and pains to keep a doctor in Cadillacs. But you, you are just a little more wrinkly and only slightly slower than you used to be."

"I wish I knew," she'd said.

Anna told no one about her conversation with Wealthy. She was afraid to believe him, and so over the years, she pushed that memory deep into her mind until she'd convinced herself that she'd forgotten it. She blinked at the paper in front of her—filled with questions about her family, what she ate, how much time she'd spent in the sun as a child, and a chill ran through her. None of her children suspected there was any complication to their genealogy. It was as straight as it could be—a line from Erin back to Mims. Anna shook her head. There was nothing special about her family. No matter what Callie was looking for, the Kellers were ordinary women with ordinary stories. Over the years, she'd found little to lend weight to Wealthy's claims—a yellowed ticket that the immigration officers had pinned to her coat and her parents' sworn statement that although they could produce no birth certificate she was born January 18, 1894, in Brisbane. And that was enough for Anna.

CHAPTER SIX

One in Seven Million

*A*nna's interview with Dr. Hashmi began the next morning. They had the house to themselves. Bets had taken Bobo with her to the assisted living facility for her weekly visit with her husband, Frank, and Callie had dragged Erin to the Pit Stop to help with inventory. The last time Anna had been alone with a man was when the cable guy had to come over to string new lines after a late-March thunderstorm. The boy caught her watching him climb up his ladder, and when he brought the bill in for her to sign, she had trouble meeting his eyes and felt the urge to giggle.

Men had stopped appraising Anna around the time her youngest child, Timothy, had gotten married. His wedding had been a lavish affair held in the ballroom of the Fairmont in San Francisco. Her husband, Michael, had been dead nearly two years then, and when people asked her why she never remarried, she liked to tell them that by the time she was ready to get over her husband, the country didn't have enough men to go around. The war had taken so many. Girls no older than eighteen were throwing themselves at the feet of widowers, and youth with its dewy edges triumphed over age.

Anna finished putting together a tray of olives and crackers. It worried her that Callie had a crush on the doctor. He was the sort of man young women went after, and she didn't see how her grand-daughter could compete. The doorbell rang. Anna knocked over the jar of olives. She cursed her clumsiness, threw a kitchen towel over the mess, and hurried to the door.

Dr. Hashmi looked much as he had the day before. He extended his hand to her with the palm down and she grasped it in more of a grip than a shake. It was small and soft like a woman's.

"Have I come at the right time?"

"Yes, of course. I just spilled a jar in the kitchen and it took me a moment to make it—"

He held up his hand. "You have near perfect mobility. I am just making sure that the others have gone."

As Anna told him about the inventory at the store and Bets's weekly visit with Frank, he unpacked his briefcase onto the coffee table. He laid out a syringe and other tools for drawing blood. Then he ate several olives and asked her about the orchard.

"We used to have several hundred acres, but with all the offspring it's been divided and quartered and sliced up so much that all we're left with is fifty acres," Anna said. She gestured toward the windows that lined the back of the house. The curtains were open, giving them a clear view of the trees at the bottom of the hill.

"Everything's still so green," Dr. Hashmi said.

"Those there," she said, pointing to the center of the grove, "are the original acres, the trees Daddy planted." Anna took an olive and began to suck on it. The brine coated her tongue. There was a lull in the small talk. They sat in silence for several moments, watching the branches rustle in the wind, their green leaves turning over to reveal their soft, silver undersides.

Dr. Hashmi picked up a length of rubber cord. "You must be

used to this. I had to learn it a few years back after the university cut my travel budget. Used to bring a nurse along with me."

Anna shook her head and rolled up her sleeve. She'd worn the purple caftan she bought for Erin's graduation and all her best jewelry. The bracelets clanked as she slid the bell sleeves of the dress up onto her shoulder. "No. I haven't been to see the doctor in about a decade. The last time I went was for a hearing aid, but I don't use it anymore. Can't get the batteries in."

"But you can still strip a tree of its olives in less than twenty minutes. Remarkable." He found the vein and slid the angled point of the needle into her arm.

It took nearly half an hour to fill the six vials he'd brought with him. When they were finally finished, he held her hand and apologized, telling her she had thick blood. The doctor insisted Anna remain seated while he brought her a glass of lemonade to drink.

"What are you going to do with all that blood?" she asked after emptying her cup.

"See what it is made of." Dr. Hashmi smiled. "Before we're through we'll know all your secrets, and if we look hard enough I might be able to find that gene I've been looking for."

"Secrets. What makes you think I've got any secrets?" Anna had never considered that the doctor would be looking for more than a reason why she'd lived so long and how she'd maintained her good health.

"Everybody has secrets. There are so many clues hidden in DNA and we're just beginning to understand what they mean." He packed up the vials and the equipment and took a small silver device from his coat pocket. "That's why the interview is so important. It helps us figure out those secrets."

Inexplicably, Anna felt the need to protect her family from Dr. Hashmi. He'd done nothing threatening and his manner the entire time had been jovial and kind, but seeing him lock her blood up in his cooler made her wary. "We try not to keep secrets anymore," she said.

He fiddled with the device and then stated the day and time and Anna's full name. "Is that because of what happened with Callie's daughter?"

"That's part of it," Anna said.

"I'm not after those sorts of secrets. I just want your blood to tell me about your family. Can you tell me about your parents? What do you know about their backgrounds—where they came from and how old they were when they died?"

She didn't tell him about her vague memories of another mother, or about Wealthy's confession. He was a scientist, and she knew he'd want facts. Anna also knew that she wasn't ready to face the possibility that she was anyone other than the daughter of Percy and Mims. They talked about her childhood and then about her husband and his family. She speculated on why her brother, Wealthy, had never married. To keep the genealogy straight, they drew it out on a paper together, and seeing all the branches made Anna dizzy. They ate their way through a second platter of olives and crackers. As the doctor finished his prepared questions, they began to talk about his work.

"Do you know how rare you are?" he asked.

Anna shrugged. "There aren't too many of us, but I'm telling you I'm not only going to outlive that man from China, I'm going to outlive that French woman who died at a hundred twenty-two. I got at least a decade left in me."

Dr. Hashmi turned over the paper with her family tree on it. He drew a bell curve and then circled the far right corner of the graph, where the line nearly touched the bottom of the paper. "You're here. One in seven million people live to be older than a hundred ten. So right now on Earth there are probably only eight hundred and fifty people alive right now as old as you, and none of them, at least the ones I've met, can remember their name, let alone have enough teeth to eat crackers. So I'm giving you at least fifteen more years to live."

At this assurance, Anna forgot all her reservations about Dr. Hashmi and his tests. She grabbed his hand and held it tight. "I knew I liked you," she said.

CHAPTER SEVEN

Ovuli

Anna's obsession with staying alive longer than any other human being didn't begin until she celebrated her hundredth birthday. Prior to that milestone, she'd had no real interest in age and felt little of the nostalgia that infected her peers. She'd focused on what was right in front of her; however, that year the local newspaper sent a young man to Hill House during her birthday celebration to interview her about her legacy. The reporter was a small, plump adolescent with a smattering of large freckles across his cheeks. He sucked on the inside of his cheeks when he wasn't talking. "Just pretend I'm another party guest," he'd told them, following Anna around like Bobo did if he wanted to be fed. He was silent for long periods and then would corner someone from the family and let loose with two dozen questions. He didn't take notes, a fact that Anna returned to time and again when the article was published.

Near the end of the afternoon, he sat down and ate a piece of cake with Anna. "You don't look that old," he'd said. "I thought you'd be half blind and deaf and there'd be someone here, a nurse or an orderly, wheeling you about."

She did not start to lose her eyesight until ten years later, just before her hundred and tenth birthday. That day she had two pieces of cake and ignored all the boy's questions about longevity. Instead, she told the story of when they moved the town and took a few of the treasures she'd found underneath the stores—a bit of bone from the butcher's shop, three pearl buttons from the seamstress's shop, and a watch fob from underneath the bank—and laid them on the table. They were trinkets her children and grandchildren had loved playing with. Erin, who was twelve years old at the time and beginning to be interested in adult stories, was more entranced than the reporter. Still, that boy had the nerve to hug her as he left (the younger generations had no proper sense of formality any longer) and told her he felt blessed to have been able to get her stories from her before—. She cut him off.

"Before what? I die?" Anna was four inches taller than the reporter, and she'd glared down at him.

He stammered and blushed and then apologized before turning and rushing out the front door. Her confrontation had made little impact on him. He wrote about none of that but penned an article that painted Anna as he'd expected her to be—a senile, wrinkled woman who was the town's last remaining link to its past. "Reading this," Anna said to Bets, "you'd think I'll be dead before the year is out." The article had a tone of near tragedy, and although the reporter acknowledged that Anna was in good health, he quoted a nurse as saying that the elderly often deteriorate rapidly.

The nurse worked at Golden Sunsets, where Frank lived, and Anna made a point of ignoring the woman when she visited the home with Bets. The reporter left to work at a larger paper in Fresno, and every Christmas, Anna sent him a card that she signed, "still here." As awful as the story had been, it awakened her to the realization that everyone expected her to die, and soon.

Those around Anna had died because of illness or war. She didn't know of anyone who'd died of old age—just diseases and infections related to aging. What a load of crap that phrase was—"related to." She read the obituaries and kept a tally of the causes of death. By her hundred and first birthday, she had categorized nearly one hundred and fifty deaths from heart attacks, cancer, strokes, falls, drowning, suicide, and snake bites. Not one mention of old age. That year she went skydiving and was given a ten-year renewal on her driver's license. Neither event merited another story in the *Kidron Observer*.

She asked Louise Bells, who had gone to school with Bets and now volunteered at the library three days a week, to find the person who'd lived the longest. "You mean besides Methuselah?" Louise asked. The woman Louise found was French and was one hundred and twenty. Jeanne Louise Calment lived on her own until she was one hundred and sixteen and claimed her longevity could be traced to chocolate, Bordeaux, and olive oil, which she poured over all her food and rubbed into her face every night. Anna felt that this was a quip designed to put off reporters and other intrusives, but Callie took it as gospel truth and photocopied the news accounts of Mme. Calment to hang in the Pit Stop. She wrote to the French woman to request an autographed photo, which was framed and hung next to the tin cartons of imported olive oil. Callie liked to have visitors guess the woman's age—they always picked a number between eighty-five and ninety-eight.

Callie took this as proof that olive oil was a cure for old age, but Anna thought the more likely story was that people couldn't conceive of anyone living longer than a century. She kept this thought to herself and let her granddaughter believe in the miracle of the oil, although she couldn't help but point out that she herself had far fewer wrinkles than Mme. Calment and had never once put olive oil on her face.

"You should start," Callie had said one night at dinner. "Then in twenty years we can put your picture up and claim it works wonders."

They'd laughed, and Erin, who'd grown up around wrinkled

women, took to stealing olives from the refrigerator and rubbing them across her cheeks. There'd been an argument about the child's behavior. Anna and Bets thought the act was frivolous and wasteful. Callie, who'd been overruled about the tooth fairy and Santa Claus, threatened to move out and take the child with her. The courts had made her the legal guardian of Erin, and although they'd all agreed to raise her together, if she decided to leave, Anna and Bets couldn't stop her.

"The child has nothing to believe in," Callie had said. "What's wrong with letting her believe in the olives? Neither of you can say that the olives had nothing to do with your remarkable health. You don't believe that they've kept you younger than your years, but that's not to say that they haven't."

It disappointed Anna when Bets took Callie's side. "Let her believe in this," she said.

Anna understood how Callie might see the orchard, the olives, as having magical properties, but Bets knew better. There had been so much work when Anna was a child helping her father and even more during the years Anna raised Bets. Children were let out of school during harvest, and they worked as hard as the adults picking olives from the trees. The cheap labor came not from Mexico, but from the households of Kidron. When Anna thought of the orchard, she recalled blisters, splinters, arms that ached during harvest. Her memories of the trees were of sweat. Bets had the same childhood, and then they'd had to work together to keep the business alive during the years when the men had been gone for war. She wanted to shake Callie and Erin and explain that the olives were nothing more than the fruits of their labor. But Callie and Erin had never worked in the orchard, and that allowed them to find mysticism in the fruit.

By the time Callie was born, the orchard was picked by immigrants who moved up the valley with the ripening of crops every fall. They still owned the land, but they paid a neighbor to manage the orchard and split the profits with him every year. The groves became a playground for Callie—row upon row of places to hide or climb or sit in the shade and watch the leaves rustle with the wind. Frank had indulged his daughter; he'd indulged all of Bets's children but especially Callie, because she was the first and there had been such a long time between her and the others. Deb, Callie's daughter and Erin's mother, had never spent much time in the orchards. Callie and her first husband had bought the Pit Stop when Deb was first born, and her experience had been one of canned olives and fluorescent lights.

Deb would have brought up Erin in the store, too, giving her a sterile view of the olives, if she'd gotten the chance, but she'd screwed everything up. When the three of them finally got Erin, Callie had just lost her husband and was working eighty hours a week trying to keep the store afloat. In the end, Erin was raised by Bets and Anna, who were overwhelmed by the preschooler. For the first time in their lives, they felt truly old. To keep the house tidy, Anna kept Erin out of it as much as possible. Before she was old enough for school, they spent most afternoons walking through the orchard, showing Erin how to climb trees and during harvest the best way to pick olives.

Bets surprised Anna by telling stories. This respite from the constant motion of the small child was a blessing, and Anna found she enjoyed hearing her daughter talk about how the goddess Athena showed up her brother by creating the olive tree, which was of much more use than a spring of salt water. Erin had gray eyes like the goddess, and the legend held that the leaves of the olive tree were patterned after Athena's eyes because although they were green, the undersides were a soft gray. It would be these stories that gave Anna the courage to tell her own, disguising them as being about about the Tortoise and the Girl.

The day after Anna caught eight-year-old Erin rubbing olives across her face, she took the girl into the orchard and began to teach her about the trees. This was what Anna knew. She couldn't give her Greek myth, but she could give her truth disguised as myth, which held more mysteries than a thousand fairy tales. It was February and the weather had finally turned cold enough to ensure budbreak in the spring. They were buttoned up against the cold, and Erin's green scarf kept getting caught on branches as they walked among the trees. Anna wanted to show her great-great-granddaughter the first trees, the ones that her father had planted when the family first moved to Kidron.

The older trees were easy to find; they had much thicker branches, and the leaves held the same shape as a hawk's flight feathers—oblong and tapered at the ends. The high wood-to-foliage ratio meant the trees produced fewer olives than their offspring, but in Anna's experience the older trees produced larger fruit heavy with oil. Her father had started with a hundred trees, but over the years, they'd lost several to frost, disease, and pests. There were two dozen that remained, and they'd become Anna's trees. The foreman knew that she would take care of the trees and they were not touched except to harvest. If a younger tree was struggling, Anna often took cuttings from these old trees and grafted them to the immature trees.

As spring came, she would show Erin how to slice off a stem the size of a pencil and grow a tree of her own, but on that winter's day, Anna just wanted to sit her great-great-granddaughter in the tree and tell her how the trees were brought from Australia and before that from Spain. She helped the girl climb up into the crown of the tree and then leaned in so that the branches surrounded them. It was warmer inside the tree's canopy and their breath no longer came out in white puffs.

In the tree Erin showed Anna the underside of a leaf. "See," she said. "The same color as my eyes, but nobody else's. I guess I get that from my dad."

"You've got his fingers, too," Anna said. "I always thought his hands were too feminine, with such long fingers that had the look of a refined man. Those fingers are what made us start you on the piano." They didn't often talk about Carl, her father.

The child was quiet for a long bit, and then she reached up and ran her fingers across Anna's high, wide cheekbones. "You and I match here," she said. "Maybe I'll be like you and live forever."

Anna laughed. "How old do you think I am?"

Erin shrugged. "As old as the trees?"

"Smart girl. You know what's amazing about olive trees? They have a real sense of survival." Anna wasn't sure if at eight, Erin knew what *survival* meant, but the little girl nodded. "If we cut down this tree today, in the spring, it would have about a hundred shoots growing up out of the side and top of the stump."

Erin looked skeptical. "You just told me the tree was older than you. How do you know it'll be all right if you cut it down?"

"These shoots, they're sometimes called suckers." Anna made a noise like she was sucking on a straw. "They suck up all the energy they need to grow from the roots that the original tree left behind. It's the roots that are important."

"Where do the suckers come from?" Erin asked.

Anna was surprised at the question. She'd thought the girl would want to talk about the miracle of a dead tree coming to life. She held out her hand and helped Erin out of the tree. Then she took off her gloves and dug around in the soil around the trunk. The ground rarely froze in Kidron, although the red dirt had just enough clay in it that it clumped together. She dug down about two knuckles deep and exposed the gnarled bumps on the bark. "Burr knots. They're sacks of nutrients and energy, and that's where the suckers come from."

Erin ran her fingers over several of the ovuli and smiled. "It's like someone put olives underneath the bark."

CHAPTER EIGHT

Sixth Generation

*A*fter the geneticist left, Anna took a rest. She awoke to the sound of dinner and found the others in the kitchen eating ham sandwiches on olive loaf. Although she rarely had an appetite, Anna's nose was as sharp as ever. The smell of the facility where Frank lived was all over Bets. To Anna, the rankness reminded her of rotting fruit, but the rest of the family insisted the odor was nothing more unusual than the combination of antiseptic and sweat. Anna gagged and turned her face away from her daughter.

"Stop it," Bets said, swatting at Anna. "I could always put you in there."

"I'm not decrepit enough. Still have my brains and my beauty." Anna smiled, showing off that she still had most of her teeth.

"It only takes losing one of those two." Bets turned away from Anna.

"You know what stinks?" Anna asked, taking a seat next to her daughter. "It's the perspiration. That's what smells like rot. I've attended enough deathbeds to know the smell of death, and that home you've got Frank in reeks of it."

Callie put her hands on both women's arms. "Stop it."

"What do you expect?" Bets asked. "I bet two or three people a week die in that place."

Erin giggled. "I've missed you all so much. I haven't had a nonphilosophical argument about death since I've left."

Death was not an abstraction to Anna. When she was a girl, the world was a more dangerous place—men died in farming accidents, mothers died in birth, and children died when schoolhouses caught fire. Erin had never been to a funeral. They'd not allowed her to attend her father's service, and since then no one she was close to had died.

"Death is all part of the cycle. It's neither here nor there, it just is," Callie said, turning to Bets to ask about Frank. "How's Dad? Any sign he's getting better? Or worse?"

"He's got a new friend," Bets said. She continued to talk, describing the man, in his late fifties, who rolled around in a specialized sport wheelchair. Anna noticed that Erin was again eating meat and that as she listened to her great-grandmother's story, she pulled strands of hair out of her head. Anna got Callie's attention and nodded in Erin's direction.

"Later," Callie mouthed and then got up to clear the table.

"So. Who's coming to visit Mom with me?" Erin asked. Her voice was high and she spoke quickly. Anna knew she'd waited until Callie left the room to ask. In the twenty years Deb had been at Chowchilla, Callie hadn't visited her daughter once.

"We'll both go," Bets said.

"Just not right away," Anna said. "You've only just gotten here, and we have so much to catch up with. Can we go next week?"

Erin looked at the floor. "I'm tired. I think the time change is finally catching up with me."

They ushered her off to her room, with Callie pulling down the shades and drawing the thick brocade curtains.

"She should sleep a good bit," Bets said outside the girl's door. Anna wanted to talk about Erin, to discuss her sudden appearance and her strange behavior, but they all went to their own rooms, coming out a few hours later when Anna warmed milk on the stove.

Anna knew they were digesting the news about Deb. None of them had known that she was up for parole again. As they learned last time, the California State Parole Board was only required to inform the victims of the prisoner's crimes about parole hearings. Erin was both a victim and family.

"She's dead asleep. That jet lag of hers should buy us a few more hours," Bets said. She'd opened the can of instant cocoa and spooned it into her cup of warm milk.

Callie scooped an additional teaspoon of chocolate powder into her cup every time she took a sip. "She wasn't much help at the store. I had to go back and redo all her counts and I finally just put her at a cash register."

"She didn't say anything?" Bets asked. She turned to Anna. "Did you find out when the hearing was?"

Anna had called after the geneticist left. "We've got about two months. It'll be in January. The warden was surprised we knew anything about it. He seemed to think the family didn't find out until the hearing was about a month away. I guess they don't like getting anyone's hopes up."

"The last hearing was all formality," said Bets.

Anna watched Callie add two more scoops of cocoa to her milk. "There's got to be more to this than a parole hearing," Callie said. "Have we had any luck trying to get in touch with the opera? I'm fairly sure she's broken some sort of contract with them. It was a three-year deal."

Bets shook her head. "I can't get the times right and I'm not sure if they'll return a call to the U.S. or even understood what I was trying to say."

"None of you know anything about her life? How she spent her time over there? Who her friends were? Wasn't there a girl from Boston who signed on the same time as her?" Anna's frustration came out in these rapid-fire questions. The guilt about not knowing these details turned into accusations of Bets and Callie. All that Erin had given her in letters were platitudes, and it was what Anna accepted. She wanted to believe that they'd been successful, that they'd made up for Deb by raising Erin the right way.

Callie broke under all the veiled accusations and guilt. She had the deepest regrets about Deb, and they carried over into all aspects of her life. The need to be forgiven for failing her own daughter made her fragile. Anna disliked tears. She thought they were wasteful, and the sight of her granddaughter blubbering jolted her out of the pleasantries.

"Have you considered the obvious?" she asked.

Bets sighed. "I don't want to think about it. She's too young."

"Her mother was only seventeen," Callie said. She'd pushed her milk aside and dabbed at her eyes with a dinner napkin. Anna saw a mound of cocoa had piled up at the bottom of her cup.

"We need to know what we're dealing with," Anna said. "I'll wake her up and we can just ask her."

"What if we're wrong?" Callie asked.

Anna stood up, but Bets put her hand on her elbow. "Let me."

Despite Bets's hard facade, she had always been the closest to Erin. Callie felt too much guilt to be anyone's mother figure.

"What if it's true?" asked Callie.

"She's made a hard choice," Anna said.

Bets grimaced. "I don't want it to be true. We've worked so hard to give her the kind of life where the choices aren't hard. Damn it to hell and back."

Anna didn't want to listen to their supposing. She knew it was true. She'd felt it the moment that Erin had stepped out of her rental car. There was going to be a sixth generation. Anna had dreamed of the child the night before and felt a pull between them, as if the umbilical cord were attached not only to Erin, but also to Anna.

EXCERPT FROM "THE END OF AGING," A TALK PRESENTED TO
THE AMERICAN COUNCIL ON AGING IN DECEMBER 2006

BY DR. AMRIT HASHMI

Many of mankind's myths are inextricably tied to the quest for immortality. The driving force behind most religions—whether one believes in reincarnation or resurrection—is the promise to extend the span of time for which our consciousness exists. The idea of starting over in a new body or restoring an existing body to its prime might seem laughable to us, until you consider that most of us in this room are attempting to accomplish these feats on a much smaller scale in our lab animals and Petri dishes. We are at the cusp of a new age—one in which mankind turns not to his gods for an answer on eternal life, but to his scientists.

My particular interest lies not with immortality, but with agelessness. Most of us are surely aware of the tragedy of Eros and her lover Tithonus. This goddess of the dawn, one of the immortal Titans, had the misfortune to fall in love with a mortal. When he began to age, Eros begged Zeus to give Tithonus the gift of everlasting life. In her haste and in her passion, Eros forgot to also ask for eternal youth. This mistake cost Eros her heart, but it cost Tithonus the world. Long after his body had withered, his mind remained. Eros could not bear to be near him in this babbling and immobile state. She entombed him in a room with no windows and a red door. There he remains, wanting only death and wondering how it was that as Tennyson said, "The Gods themselves cannot recall their gifts."

We should be mindful of this fate. I've sat among this very group and heard the hypothesis that the first person who will live to be a hundred and fifty years old has already been born. While that is extraordinary, I pity that woman (and our research shows it is most likely to be a woman, firstborn in her family, who was raised on the West Coast in a large family). If we cannot unlock the mysteries of the process of senescence, we will continue to prolong life without any measurable benefit to mankind. We will produce an entire generation of elderly who, like Tithonus, will end up locked inside the prison of their own decaying bodies. We must commit together to work toward discovering the key to stopping the aging process. This is what I've devoted my life to. At the University of Pittsburgh, I've spent the last decade searching out and cataloging people who I, and my staff, have come to call *superagers*. That is to say those individuals for whom the natural markers of old age appear to have little effect, or I should say a lessened effect.

These are people who scale Mount Everest in their seventies, swim the English Channel the same year they turn ninety, or run a marathon at age a hundred and one. I believe that is the kind of old age we all want. I don't have to tell the people in this audience about the raging debate over what causes senescence. There are a dozen theories about the process—aging is a disease, aging is a by-product of evolution, aging is psychological, aging is the accumulation of damage from radiation, etc. The list is endless, and this room is filled with researchers probing every possible avenue for an answer because the simple truth is we don't know what causes aging.

We also don't know the exact mechanism by which aspirin works, or how placebos can be more effective than treatment. It has been said that age is merely the accumulation of defects, but why is it that some people have so many fewer defects? The only way to discover this is to gather as much information as possible about superagers. We've been cataloging what they ate, where they lived, how much time they spent in the sun, how much time they spent exercising, how long their parents lived, and searching for some commonality among them. I've long suspected that dietary and environmental influences were microscopic in their influence on this process, and through surveys and observation, this conception has been borne out. Many of my superagers are active nonsmokers, nondrinkers, but just as many of them still gleefully embrace the habits they've been warned against all their lives. Every time I interview a smoker, they inevitably point the end of their cigarette at me and say, "You were wrong you know, smoking doesn't kill all of us."

What these superagers have in common is the large disparity between their chronological age and their biological age, as determined by the Zyberg scale. In most cases, superagers have the physical, psychological, and social lives of people half their age. They have sex, they sleep through the night, they remember phone numbers and acquaintances' names. Because Zyberg does not take into account physical appearance, which is primarily influenced by genetics and environment, some of these superagers may look as old as they are, but across the board, their physical health and mental health is usually on par with someone half their age.

What all of our research points toward is that the ability to stop or at least slow senescence exists within the body—inside the very cells themselves. To prove this, I need evidence of a genetic mutation, and to find such a mutation, I need a family of superagers. The problem with that is not only the rarity of superagers—there are fewer than a thousand in the entire world, but also the unavoidable fact that an accident is just as likely to cause a human's death as complications from aging. You know how difficult the search is—a twin brother will have died in war, a daughter in childbirth. No matter what we do about aging, the world is still a dangerous place for human beings.

I was quite discouraged until earlier this year when I came across a remarkable family in California. There exist five generations of women—beginning with the matriarch, who is a hundred and twelve years old, and continuing down through the generations to the youngest, who is in her midtwenties and pregnant. I can't be sure that all of these women are superagers, but after preliminary questionnaires and extensive interviews, I believe I have found a family who carries the genetic mutation that holds the key to slowing aging.

Researchers at the University of Pittsburgh have already begun to sequence the entire genomes of these women. Our hope is that within a decade we will be able to identify the genes that slow senescence and then develop drug therapies to activate them in those who age at a normal rate. I also suspect that we will find that in these women several harmful genes have been essentially turned off. But I'm getting ahead of myself. Let me take you through the research that has gotten me to this point. I will just say that if that child has indeed been born who will live to be a hundred and fifty, that by the time she is middle-aged this research should have produced therapies that will allow her agelessness along with longevity.

Erin in the Winter

CHAPTER NINE

Haircut

By January, the uproar of Erin's arrival and pregnancy had settled. With long hours to fill, Erin often thought about her first pregnancy scare. Unlike some girls, she hadn't had hers until college. She and a boy from her music theory class had been playing at dating. She brought him small tokens of her affection—greeting cards, superhero stickers, his favorite soda, and in return he helped her into her winter coat and paid for dinner. She liked how his deep brown eyes always seemed to be wet, as if at any moment he could be moved by the world around them. They slept together. And once that happened, it was all that ever happened between them. Sex became recreational.

One of them would call the other and make up an excuse to come over. "I left my glove at your place," she would say. Or he would claim to have lost his notes from their shared class. After one of these terse exchanges, Erin's roommate, a thin girl from Vermont, offered her appraisal.

"So, you've finally figured it out."

"What," Erin had said, pulling her hair from its ponytail.

"That all that boyfriend, girlfriend stuff is for high school."

Erin blushed. "We're together. I mean—"

"It's not serious though. And you're not in a relationship, right? I mean he could sleep with someone else if he wanted to."

There was no point in protesting. Erin couldn't imagine a future with the boy. She nodded.

"You're still so naive," the roommate said. "Most of us figured this stuff out before we got here. But I'll tell you what you need to do. Especially with this guy. Try just enjoying the sex. Make sure you get off, that he goes down on you. They all claim not to do it, but every boy I know does."

Once Erin got over the shock of what she'd said, she realized it was the only useful information she'd learned that semester. From then on when Erin slept with boys, she held on to her heart— offering them nothing more than smiles and an offhand attitude that hid her natural earnestness.

This new approach served her well when weeks later, Erin missed her period. Ben walked with her to the student health center, talking the whole way about how much he enjoyed Frisbee golf. When Erin came out of the examination room grasping a negative pregnancy test, he was gone. She didn't see him again until just before graduation when he showed up at her doorstep with a bouquet of carnations and tried to tell her that he was in love with her, that he'd always been in love with her. She slept with him, and the night was a disaster. He cried and then as she held him, patting his back, she got the worst case of the giggles. One that left her gasping for breath and Ben shooting her angry looks, his wet eyes finally blinking back actual tears as he grabbed his wilted bouquet and left.

She thought that she'd cured herself of the sincerity that her grandmothers had instilled in her. And then, five months earlier, in Rome, all of her earnestness came back to her when the pregnancy test turned up positive. She was the one who cried during sex, and although her lover wiped away the tears and promised that he'd make everything between them right when the baby came, all she saw in him was a reflection of her despair. That look and the letter that came two days later from the parole board gave her a reason to leave.

She should have told him she was going back to California, but she couldn't bring herself to cry in front of him in the daytime. Plus, she was still angry that after she'd told him she was late he'd still wanted to go to dinner.

"But I think I'm pregnant," she'd said to him as a shopkeeper swept around their feet.

He took her elbow and steered her away from the pregnancy tests. "Of course, of course."

"I'm not even hungry," she said, trying to get him to slow his pace.

"We all need to eat, and The Swan has such lovely food."

She'd eaten dinner with him that night and they didn't speak once about the pregnancy. She put the unopened test on the table, and he never once asked about it—instead speaking the entire night about his problems with the orchestra and asking her opinion about an alto who was also an American. They discussed plans for an upcoming performance, and despite her frustration, she found herself agreeing to a weekend in Milan.

The next morning, on the way to the airport, she considered that part of his callousness was that he and his wife had never had children. The cabdriver had a picture of an elderly woman and a young girl taped to his dashboard. "She's lovely," Erin commented as she paid him. He took her money and held her hand for an extra few seconds while he described his wife and daughter. He referred to them as the "women of my heart." Erin lifted the handle on her suitcase and considered what he'd said. In the anonymity of the crowded airport, she let her hand rest on her stomach and for the first time in her life stopped wishing for her mother and started to consider what type of mother she would be.

In the months since returning to Hill House, Erin found herself still trying to answer that question. The day before the parole hearing, she filched her grandmother's sewing scissors and cut heavy bangs. "Just wanted a change," she'd said when Callie witnessed her slipping the shears back into the older woman's mending basket. In trying to explain, Erin's voice took on the same thin quality it had when, as a child, she'd been caught getting into any one of her grandmothers' belongings. Callie took Erin's chin in her hand and turned her head toward her. Erin shut her eyes against the late winter sun that filtered in the front room.

"I never did like you with bangs. Reminds me of when Bets took you down to Supercuts for a six-dollar haircut and you came back crying, saying you didn't realize it would stay short."

Erin pulled away and sat in Anna's chair. "I was eight. I thought bangs would make me look like a princess."

"You look all of eight now," said Callie, taking her knitting from the basket. "Next time use the kitchen shears, you'll dull the blade on these."

Erin's forehead itched. "Fine."

"Did you clean up the mess in the bathroom? Hair has a way of getting everywhere. Especially with the furnace going all the time, blowing dust onto every surface of this house."

"I'll get to it. Thought I'd have some time to myself." Erin listened to the click of her grandmother's needles for a bit. She knew Callie expected her to get up immediately and clean the bathroom, but Erin didn't move. Now that she was having her own child, she felt less compelled to respond to commands. Instead, she tried to get

Callie to talk with her about the hearing. "You're home early. Bets took Anna with her to see Frank. Wanted to get a second visit in, since she can't go tomorrow."

Callie didn't look up from her knitting. "It was a slow day. No one feels like going out after lunch—it gets dark too early. I'm surprised Bets went, she doesn't drive as well when it is dusk."

In all the years Deb had been in jail, Callie had never visited, written, or so much as sent a word of greeting, not even when Bets or Anna made their monthly trek to Chowchilla. Erin considered asking again if Callie would come to the hearing. She thought of all the ways she'd asked before, of overhearing Bets tell her that *God doesn't give do-overs—even to mothers.* The baby turned somersaults in her uterus, and Erin moved to the edge of the chair and stretched her spine. She'd never understood Callie's decision to excise Deb, her own daughter, from her life.

"Baby's moving," she said and reached for her grandmother's hand. Callie counted out the last row of stitches and set the beginning of a delicate pink bootie aside. They sat quietly with Erin's hand on Callie's—moving it when the baby changed places—for several minutes.

"How far along are you now?"

"Doctor said about five months."

"Have you talked to the father?"

Erin felt herself blush. "A bit. I'm just not ready."

"They would never say it, but it does bother them. You know this, right? That Anna and Bets just can't understand how you got yourself into this situation."

"I guess you understand, though, how people get themselves into this type of situation?" Erin had learned, living with her grandmothers, to meet an attack with an attack

Callie looked much smaller. "We all understand that. Each one of us, and you've gone and grown up on us."

Erin wasn't sure whether Callie felt deflated by Erin being an adult or by the reminder that her daughter had also gotten herself knocked up. She considered that there might be sadness in her grandmother that she might never know the cause of. "Had the ultrasound last week," she said, offering a truce.

"And you still won't find out whether it's a girl or not? It would be good to know, for the publicity. I mean, it's a girl. But to know for sure might help."

Erin wasn't frustrated with this push to find out the sex of the baby. The grandmothers had all been anxious to let modern medicine prove their suspicions correct. None of them could understand Erin's reluctance. The absurdity of lying on the table while the technician slid the sonogram wand around her belly made her laugh. "What's the use of knowing? You, Anna, and Bets have told me to expect a little girl. It's in our genes—besides, everything you've made the baby is pink. Who would dare mess with all that work? Not even God."

Callie reached into her pocket for the vial of pills she kept with her and swallowed one. Then she stretched her bad leg out and after leaning back into her chair spoke. "I'm sorry I can't go. It's our busiest season, with the casino buses coming in nearly every hour, and I've just hired some men to work in the orchard. They'll need supervising and I—"

"You just said it was slow."

"Slow today. It gets busier."

"It'll always be there. The store isn't going anyplace, but—" The look of panic that crossed Callie's face made Erin swallow what she was going to say next. "—It'll be fine. Just fine." It wouldn't be, but she knew when to quit.

Callie rubbed at her leg. "Did you hear about that Lindsey grandchild?"

Erin shook her head and looked out the window as the sun

made its slow, steady descent toward the coastal mountains. They gossiped and traded stories about babies and knitting. It was nice to sit and talk as equals, and for a moment she felt a glimmer of hope about becoming a mother. She realized that the light in the room had all but disappeared and pulled the cord to the reading lamp. As she did, her hair came loose from the twist she'd spun it into while they'd been talking.

Callie came at the hearing sideways. "You'll look even younger if you braid your hair."

"Gotta pee," said Erin and left the living room. She hadn't understood that Callie knew her so well.

She stood in front of the bathroom mirror, plaiting her hair into a single braid and then into two low, loose twists. She worked on different expressions, moving her eyes and mouth around and trying to settle on a look she could wear in the hearing room. One that made her appear vulnerable, like a girl who needed taking care of. The bangs did make her look much younger than twenty-four. It helped that the pregnancy had plumped up her face—gotten rid of her sharp angles. With the darkness of her hair so close to her brow, her own normally light gray eyes appeared darker and, Erin thought, needier.

She started to recite her statement as she brushed bits of black hair that had fallen on the lip of the sink into the bowl. It was important that it not be too rehearsed, but she knew that the appearance of effortlessness took work. She could not trust herself to speak from the heart, which was the only advice Deb's lawyer had given her. She'd sat in his leatherette chair, staring at his liver-spotted face, and thought that despite the fifty years between them, she knew what he didn't. The heart was as likely to be full of treachery as of love.

CHAPTER TEN

Chowchilla

The pregnant and the old have weak bladders. Erin confirmed this during the four-hour drive to Chowchilla. She remembered from her teenage years the constant torture of stopping, but this time around, because the baby seemed to be using her bladder as a punching bag, she was grateful for each of the five gas stations they pulled into. Neither Bets nor Anna responded to Erin's one-sided chatter, and so after the third stop in Yuba City, Erin kept her mouth busy snapping chewing gum and kept her mind off the monotony of the drive by chasing one pop music station after another down the whole of state route 99.

Erin still wasn't used to the special treatment often afforded her because of the pregnancy. As she approached the guard gate at the Central California Women's Facility, she steeled herself for the hostile appraisal of the guard. The gaze they always gave her, with hard eyes that seemed to be assessing the worst acts Erin was capable of, had made her itch when she was a teenager. This morning though, when she'd handed the sentry the papers indicating their intent to attend the parole hearing, he'd looked into her eyes as he raised the gates and given her a nod, which to Erin seemed to say "you're right to do this." The unexpected welcome made the cool January day seem a bit warmer.

At check-in, the women were assigned a corrections officer, who was overweight in the way that sometimes happens to college athletes as they age. They followed the heavyset man into the nearly empty hearing room and settled themselves in the row of chairs reserved for civilians. The air in the small room had a stale, sour odor that reminded Erin of the smell of the alleyways of Rome. A blue weave that was more burlap than fabric and felt scratchy to bare skin covered the chairs. Anna adjusted herself several times and then took off the yellow scarf she'd tied carefully around her neck that morning, and draped it over the back of her chair. She moved as easily as a person half her age and her voice was still strong. "I expected it to be more Perry Mason and less—" Anna paused, searching for the right comparison.

"DMV," said Erin.

"It's all scripted anyway," said Bets, grimacing. "You should have been here for the last one. The district attorney, the commissioners, Deb—they all will play their parts, the parts they've always played, enforcer, judge, petitioner. It's all a farce."

Anna patted Erin's knee. "Except for our lovely granddaughter. Erin is most certainly not part of their script."

There was no script, Erin thought. For a moment, she wished she were back in Rome, or that she'd even once considered not having the baby. Her face burned with shame when she thought of how rash her decisions had been since peeing on that plastic stick. She wanted to blame some other force for her actions. Her mouth trembled, and not wanting to draw any attention to how truly vulnerable she felt, Erin turned her eyes to the paperwork that had made her presence at the hearing possible. Normally parolees weren't allowed to have anyone testify on their behalf and instead their supporters were encouraged to write letters. It took Erin weeks to craft her letter. She believed that she fully supported her mother's release, but no matter what she wrote, her pleas to have her mother with her for the birth of her first child felt empty when put on paper. Then, in December, as the hearing neared, she discovered a loophole that would allow her to have the last word at the parole hearing.

Erin's thoughts were interrupted by the appearance of two male members of the Board of Parole Hearing. They strode to the front of the room, took their places on the far side of the folding table, and were then joined by a tiny woman of indeterminate age who set up a portable stenography machine. Erin looked at the two commissioners and worried about what Bets had said earlier. Sitting there, she felt as if she were involved in a first-class hoax—a pseudotrial to determine whether after nearly twenty years in prison Deb was suitable to reenter society. Too much time in an institution made it impossible to be suited for life outside. Erin studied the men who would decide Deb's fate. They each had a stack of papers more than a foot thick in front of them along with a tabletop microphone. The larger of the two commissioners wore a short-sleeve dress shirt without a tie. He had a substantial white mustache that was yellow at the ends and a scar that zigzagged up his left forearm. His eyebrows were as thick as his mustache and they nearly covered his small brown eyes. He was not looking through his file but scanning the handful of observers, relatives, and staff who were installed in the hearing room. Erin blushed when his gaze landed on her, and she looked quickly away toward the other man, who had not yet lifted his head from the papers.

The second commissioner was thin, like a long-distance runner, and wore a yellow polo shirt with khaki trousers. His blond hair was cut unevenly and his fingernails were bitten to the quick. He paged through the file with speed and randomness. Anna, when she saw Erin watching the man, leaned over and whispered, "He's a good-looking one, no ring."

"I'm not looking," said Erin louder than she'd intended and the guard left his post near the door to stand behind them.

Erin felt that pregnancy had not heightened her beauty but obscured it. The swelling overwhelmed her delicate bone structure and gave her skin a mottled appearance. Overall the effect was one of a ripe tomato on the verge of splitting its skin. This change altered how men now reacted to her—before, they'd let their eyes linger on her breasts or the curve of her waist and now they could find nowhere to rest their gaze. She knew her best strategy would be to appear to the commissioners like a motherless girl. She'd taken Callie's advice and tied her black hair into braids, put on a touch of mascara and a glancing sweep of lip gloss. She kept her eyes on her shoes while they settled themselves into the first row of seats behind a folding table set up at the front of the room. She thought of the mannerisms of schoolgirls—their hesitations, their habits. And now, as the commissioners watched, she crossed one arm over her stomach and brought the other to her mouth and began to tear at her thumbnail with her teeth.

"Stop that," said Bets and grabbed her hand, bringing it to her lap.

"Don't be nervous," said Anna.

Erin willed the men to keep their eyes on her—she needed them to look up and see a young girl comforted by women too old to take care of her.

Bets waved an embroidered handkerchief in front of her face and sighed. "It's too hot in here." She directed this at their corrections officer, who had visible sweat rings under the arms of his short-sleeved uniform shirt. Then she turned to Anna. "Mother. This heat can't be good for you. You look peaked."

Anna dismissed her daughter's worry with a slight shake of

her head and pulled her cardigan tighter around her shoulders. "I'm fine."

"Erin?"

She shrugged. And then seeing the concern that settled into the mustached-commissioner's eyes, she said, "It is stuffy. Maybe if there were a fan or—"

"A fan!" Bets clapped her hands together, and the two commissioners looked up. The guard nodded at Bets but didn't make eye contact. Before Bets could push the issue further, the door opened and Deb and her lawyer entered the room.

Instead of her prison blues, Deb wore a yellow cotton jumper covered in delicate pink roses over a long-sleeve pink shirt that was badly stained at the cuffs. This was the first time Erin had seen her mother outside of visiting hours at Chowchilla, and she had never considered that her mother's plainness had not been by choice, but by regulation. She studied her as she crossed the length of the small room to sit in a folding chair placed on the opposite side of the same table the commissioners occupied. With her black hair carefully curled into ringlets, blush that was too orange and applied too low on the left cheek and too high on the right, and eyes obliterated by blue shadow and clumpy mascara, Deb looked like she belonged in a mental institution.

"Didn't someone give her a mirror?" asked Bets. "Maybe she can rub some of it off before they get started." She leaned forward and tried to get Deb's attention by waving her handkerchief and clearing her throat.

"No communication with the prisoner," said the guard who had escorted Deb into the room.

Deb turned her head and shook it quickly, but forcefully, at the three of them. Then she glanced at Erin, who looked away and then brought her hands to her belly. She'd written her mother about the pregnancy, but they'd not spoken about it.

"I forget that she's got her mother's eyes. They're so blue today," said Anna.

"Frank's eyes. Deb got them from him." It was not uncommon for Bets to clarify Anna's statements, and this normalcy in the hot, windowless room made Erin feel slightly less strange.

"Why didn't they let anyone help her? We could have brought her something more tasteful to wear. She looks old enough to be Grandma Callie's mother, not mine," Erin said. The lawyer should have prepared them for this. He didn't even suggest clothing or help with her makeup. She should have hired someone with actual parole experience, but none of the grandmothers volunteered any money to help. She clenched her fists.

Anna patted her back softly. "It's not important. Stay calm. Make eye contact with the commissioners. Let them see the sort of family she has behind her. Let them see her as a person, not as a murderer."

It was strange to hear Anna speak so plainly. In the years that she'd lived with her grandmothers, Erin had felt that the three of them felt safest with Deb in prison. Callie, Deb's own mother, had never visited her daughter and she refused to allow Erin to visit until she was in high school. Only Bets, who Erin often thought of as the hardest-hearted of the grandmothers, had visited Deb with regularity. It had been Bets who fought Anna and Callie on the issue of bringing Erin to the prison. It wasn't until Erin got her learner's permit that they relented and let Erin go with Bets. She wasn't sure what really made them change their mind, only that Anna claimed she was worried about Bets driving the four hours to Chowchilla by herself every month.

Erin watched as Bets passed the lawyer her handkerchief and motioned for him to get Deb to wipe away some of the makeup. She wondered why Bets felt such responsibility for her granddaughter, especially because she and her daughter, Callie, rarely spoke. They'd tried to hide it from Erin, but she knew that they kept to their separate wings of Hill House. She was in her teens when she first felt the silence between her grandmother and great-grandmother. Erin had never asked about the distance between them, but sometimes she heard Anna rebuke them about unrealistic expectations.

And yet, when she was finally allowed to visit Deb, Erin was astonished at the tenderness between her mother and Bets. They were rusty with each other and the small talk never came easily, but when Bets visited Deb, they were like mother and daughter. Erin often found herself full of envy and wishing she were grown up enough to talk with her mother as an adult.

CHAPTER ELEVEN

The Prison Song

*E*rin was fourteen the first time she was allowed to visit her mother in prison. More than a decade had passed since the trial and she was more afraid than she would admit to anyone about seeing her mother again. That summer it was unusually hot. The women had all been cranky with one another, especially Bets and Callie, so Erin had been surprised to find Callie in the kitchen packing biscuits and dried fruit for the drive. Her grandmother had hugged her tightly, and although she'd not said it, Erin came away from the embrace feeling as if she'd been told not to go. It was the year that the Olympics in Atlanta were bombed, and when Erin watched the chaos unfold later that summer, people kept repeating that the scale of the tragedy was smaller than it could have been. She felt similarly about her first trip to the prison to visit her mother.

Chowchilla was nestled in the dead center of Central California surrounded by pistachio and almond orchards. The trees were small, about as tall as the average man, with umbrella-like canopies covered in waxy green leaves. The order of the orchards reminded Erin of the olive grove in Anna's backyard. Her eyes followed the parallel lines of trees as their car left the interstate and made a series of turns. The car slowed to a stop, and looking around her, Erin realized that there was a line of cars along what appeared to be a service road for farm vehicles. Straining her eyes, she saw in the distance a glint of wire and several blocky, sand-colored buildings that appeared to move with the heat. Bets turned off the car.

"We're early. They start letting visitors in around eight A.M." She reached across the seat and took the visitation papers from the glove box.

"Lots of cars," said Erin.

"Lots of prisoners," said Bets.

"Does she know I'm coming?"

"I wrote her a letter last week."

"What should I call her?"

"I can't answer that."

Erin had spent much of her life referring to her mother as Deb. It was how her grandmothers spoke of her and it gave her the distance she required to make sense of the situation. But she wasn't sure she would be able to call her by her first name when she saw her. Bets opened one of her *Reader's Digest Classic Readers* and Erin slid the only photo she had of her mother, her father, and herself out of the notebook she'd brought. She thought her mother looked like Elizabeth Taylor, but plumper. Her father was the same height as her mother, but he was thin with a long neck and a prominent Adam's apple. His nose had the same sharp angles of his elbows. In the photograph, he gazed at an object outside the left frame of the picture. Erin's chubby toddler hand was on her father's cheek, as if she were trying to get him to turn toward her. She didn't remember having the picture taken, but her grandmother had told her it was snapped the summer before "everything happened."

It was nearly nine thirty by the time Bets and Erin were allowed in the waiting room. She'd had to leave her belongings behind, and

Bets carried her car keys and a small amount of cash, all in dollar bills, in a clear change purse. Her great-grandmother had ushered them through the checkpoint and security with the exactitude of one who tolerated the rules but didn't respect them. "It gets worse every time," she'd said to herself as a female corrections officer gently patted up and down her legs and checked around the underwire of her bra.

They waited with the other prisoners' families in a rectangular room with small oblong windows near the ceiling. There were dozens of children—all running and jumping around the room, their exuberant shouts made all the louder by the bare concrete floor and walls. Bets stiffened each time one of these children came near them. Erin understood that her great-grandmother didn't think of Erin as a child any longer. And then she felt a surge of rage that she'd never had the chance to be one of these unruly children waiting to visit their mothers. These children, as lawless as they were, knew what she didn't, and that knowledge gave them power far beyond their years. She was more a child than they were.

When the guard called their name, Bets stood and nudged Erin toward the heavily guarded door that led outside to the courtyard. A female guard who looked to be about Callie's age held the door open with her baton and reminded them that embraces were only allowed at the beginning and end of the visits. The midmorning sun had reached the valley floor and Erin was momentarily blinded by the light, which reflected off every inch of the metal fence and the rolls of razor wire that snaked around the tops of the fences, like ribbon curls on a birthday package. She blinked to clear the tears from her eyes and when she focused again, she found that Deb was standing in front of them. She looked nothing like her picture. She was thin and her skin had a waxy, sallow texture. She wore an oversize denim jumpsuit and her hair had been tightly bound into hundreds of small braids. It was still the color of a ripe olive, but it held none of the sheen that was present in the photographs.

"Your mother sends her love," said Bets, leaning in for the briefest of hugs. Erin wondered why Bets lied.

"How is she?" asked Deb.

"She's fine, she's working."

Erin wanted to say "She's not working. She just didn't want to come," but instead, she extended her hand toward Deb. "I'm finally here."

Instead of shaking her outstretched hand, her mother clasped it with both her palms and squeezed gently. "I should have insisted that they let you come earlier, when you were smaller." Her voice was low and the words had a vibration to them, as if they'd been hummed instead of spoken. All around them children climbed on their mothers and babies were being cradled. Erin sat next to Deb, but far enough away that their legs didn't touch.

In the weeks leading up to this trip, Erin had carefully planned her reaction to seeing her mother. She would be restrained, distant, even a little brisk if necessary. All of these intentions left her when Deb spoke. The vibration in her mother's voice felt familiar, and almost instantly an energy sprung up between them that obliterated Erin's hesitation. Deb fired question after question at Erin: *Favorites? Turquoise, pearls,* Anne of Green Gables, *Backstreet Boys, math, linguini, chocolate,* Sound of Music. *Boys? Tommy Kilpatrick. Skateboards.* When the questions stopped, Erin was almost dizzy—it was not often she'd ever been the center of attention.

Bets coughed, and although Erin couldn't be sure, she felt that her great-grandmother was clearing a sob from her throat. After that, Bets began to brag about Erin's accomplishments. She said that Erin's algebra teacher was convinced that she could be an engineer and that she'd been the only freshman with a speaking role in the musical. They talked about her singing and that her voice coach was sure she'd be able to get a scholarship to Berklee or Juilliard or anyplace she wanted to go. This chitchat continued and then it slid into what her grandmothers always talked about when they ran out of words—the olives, the weather. It was always the same, sound for the sake of not sitting in silence. Erin couldn't stand it. She couldn't bear for a moment to be wasted talking about the number of buds per branch.

"Why did you shoot my father?"

Deb squinted hard at Erin and then turned her back to her and studied her fingernails.

"Mom!" Erin raised her voice, and several families turned to look at them. Bets, who sat across the table, shook her head quickly and tried to fill the silence with stories about Frank. Erin looked around the cement slab where the prisoners sat with their families. She saw that most of the women there were young, and her eyes settled on a middle-aged black woman disciplining her son for climbing on the table. Her prison blues were wrinkled and her hair had been flattened, but not styled. She was the sort of woman who would wear a wig if she weren't in prison. Probably had a different one for every day of the week and three different ones for Sundays. Erin expected the woman to grab the boy and yell, but was surprised to see the woman wordlessly put her hand on the boy's shoulder and then gently lean in and whisper to him. Erin had been yelled at as a child. Callie, especially, shouted and swatted. Her grandmothers were of a different generation.

Bets looked at her watch and began to set out the food purchased earlier from the prison store. It was the stuff of convenience—chips, soda, and soggy sandwiches. Erin realized that they were going to move past her question, to ignore her need to understand. Later, when she was older and had read the newspaper accounts, the trial transcript, and talked with her therapist, she realized that even if her mother understood why she'd killed Carl, it was not something she could put into words. But that day, Erin felt like it was deliberate action, a conspiracy to keep her from entering their grown-up world.

The sandwich Erin ate was tuna fish and the bread was so soggy it fell to pieces. The prison photographer made her way to their table, and the women slid around to one side and put their arms around each other as she gave them a thumbs-up and told them to say "parole." In the following years, Erin would put together a collection of these photographs tucked into the frame of her mirror at home. None of her smiles went past her cheeks. Bets circled back to Erin's singing.

"Have you heard her sing?" she asked Deb.

Erin's mother shook her head. "When she was little, but it was nothing but the alphabet and that song about the wheels on the bus."

"She placed third as a mezzo-soprano this year at the state competition."

"I keep up on things," said Deb, nodding.

Erin had sent her mother the ribbon she won. She didn't know if it was the sort of item they let prisoners keep, but when she sang *Com'è bello* she thought of her mother and father. She made sense of their story by thinking of it as an opera. In Lucrezia Borgia's renaissance world, rife with treason, murder, and illegitimate children, the story of a woman killing her husband felt like a minor subplot. She wondered if her mother knew much about opera.

"Do you know the aria?" she asked Deb.

She shook her head. The movement of the tight braids gave the gesture more force.

Bets rushed to speak over Deb, who was fumbling around an excuse. "We never listened to opera until you started singing it.

Heck, even Mom never liked the classical stuff, she sang folk songs and then it was all jazz growing up."

"Sing it for me?" Deb spoke quietly.

Erin knew she could pretend not to hear her mother, but she didn't want to let this opportunity slip by. She needed to show her mother how different they were. How different she was from all the Keller women. She stood.

She thought of what her coach had told her about Lucrezia. She considered the emotions of a woman singing to a child she had not seen and then she opened her mouth and with a raw intensity and earthy richness, she sang, *Com'è bello quale incanto.*

She finished, and there was sporadic clapping and some laughter, as if this audience wasn't sure what to make of the thin child with hair the color of asphalt singing in a voice that belonged to an older woman, a larger woman.

Deb wiped away her tears and asked, "What does it mean?"

Bets translated the first bit before Erin could answer. "Holy Beauty. Child of Nature."

"It was lovely. I wish I could have been there." Her mother reached for her hand and then stopped, deciding instead to tuck a strand of Erin's hair behind her ear. "Just lovely."

A bell rang and all around them visitors gathered their possessions and made a stab at last embraces. Guards were supposed to allow only a quick hug and a kiss, but they turned their eyes from the children clinging to their mothers' legs and let the women with infants walk with them cradled in their arms right up to the door. Deb's good-byes were quick and followed the guidelines exactly. She tried to hold on to Erin a bit longer, but she pulled away from her mother after just seconds into her embrace. It was Bets who turned for one last wave as she walked through the door.

In the car, more than an hour into the drive, Erin asked Bets why she'd changed the subject when she'd finally found the courage to ask Deb about the murder.

"Why did you take her side, Bets? I have a right to know why she did it."

"It isn't the sort of question you can surprise a woman with."

"It wasn't a surprise. It's what I've wanted to ask her my whole life."

"But you know what happened. There's no hidden complication, no other suspect. Your mother shot your father during an argument. What you need most is to get to know each other again."

"I've never known her. I don't even know what Deb does all day in that place."

"You mean your mother?" Bets narrowed her eyes. "It's all quite routine. Get up. Wait. Get dressed. Wait. Eat breakfast. Wait."

"She must do something," Erin insisted.

"There's television and the other inmates."

"So she has friends?"

"No. Not exactly. They're more like—"

"Frenemies?" She'd learned the word this summer reading *Seventeen*.

"Is that what you call it these days?" Bets smiled. "Then yes."

Erin was silent for a while. She pushed the car to go faster and was thrilled when Bets didn't seem to notice they were flying by the other cars. She had been angry the whole day at her mother, about her mother, and now that she was behind the wheel—only the second or third time since she got her permit—she felt the anger slip away, and a sadness that she'd always had overcame her. "I should have asked her about that instead. Asked her about her friends, about what she does with all her time."

Bets sounded tired. "She wouldn't have told you. Deb waited nearly ten years to see you. She wanted nothing more than to hear your voice and let you tell her about your life."

"Then you can tell me what it's been like for her."

"I can't. That's why I brought you today. You need to see it, to hear it in her voice." Bets leaned her head against the window. "Slow down."

Erin eased up on the accelerator but stayed in the carpool lane. "Why won't Grandma Callie come?"

"God only knows," said Bets, closing her eyes. "My daughter has a stone heart."

Erin had never thought of Callie as cold. It was Bets who distanced herself from the other women, and this trip had begun to change Erin's perception of Bets. There was a tiredness about her—because of the strained relationship with her daughter Callie, and the dementia that had taken her husband away from her. Erin wanted to erase some of the distance between Bets and all those she loved. With an open face, she turned to ask Bets about Callie, what she'd been like as a girl, but as she did, she heard her great-grandmother's snoring. Erin pushed down on the accelerator, turned on the radio, and instead began to wonder what her grandmothers' lives would have been like if she'd not come to live with them.

CHAPTER TWELVE

The Other Side

The hearing started late. The heat of the room made every second seem like a minute.

"Why are we waiting?" asked Anna.

"It's ten after," said Bets loud enough for everyone in the room to hear.

Deb's lawyer spoke quietly with her and then turned to the grandmothers. "Carl's mother had an episode of some sort in the waiting area."

"Episode?" Erin looked at Deb, who had folded her arms on the table and laid her head down. The few times she'd asked her mother about her father's family, or even about Carl himself, she'd shut down—turned away from Erin or ended visits abruptly. It was also a difficult subject with the grandmothers. Erin put her hand on her stomach and wondered if her father's family knew about her pregnancy. At five months she was showing, and today, to draw attention to herself, she wore a tight T-shirt that emphasized the swell of her abdomen.

"Panic attack, I think. The attorney from the DA's office is with them," said the lawyer and then turned back to his note cards and the massive file Deb had amassed during her twenty years in prison.

At Deb's first parole hearing, Carl's mother, Lucille, and his sister had testified under California's victim's rights law. That winter, after coming home from Rome, Erin had read the transcript of the hearing in preparation for Deb's second chance at parole, and that was when she'd realized that she too qualified as a victim under the parameters of the law. She was the child of the murder victim, which gave her the right to speak at any parole proceedings. The law was intended for testimonies like those of Carl's mother: impassioned demands and tear-filled pleadings that the murderer of a loved one not be allowed to serve anything less than the life portion of their sentence. A life for a life.

In 1986, when a judge had sentenced Deb to fifteen years to life for the second-degree murder of her husband, no one expected her to serve more than seven years. Erin remembered Anna telling her that her mother would be home before she was a teenager. However, in the years since, sentiments turned against convicted criminals—especially in California. At Deb's first hearing, the board had denied parole and given her another thirteen years before she could seek parole a second time. This devastated Erin. She was eleven, and her dreams of her mother coming home were the puff and hue of a child's imagination. But two months ago, reading the transcript, she was surprised to discover that she empathized with Carl's mother. She didn't sleep well for days and was on the verge of abandoning the whole idea of getting her mother out of jail, when she realized she alone had a way of overcoming the bias intrinsic to the parole process. As victim of the crime, she was expected to speak on behalf of her dead father, but there was no provision to keep her from instead speaking on her mother's behalf. She had the right to speak, and they could not censor her words.

There was a small commotion when Carl's family entered the courtroom. Ms. Rivera, the attorney for the DA, had her arm around the waist of Carl's mother. The older woman clutched a white handkerchief embroidered with pansies that she dabbed at her nose and eyes. Every few steps, she let out a ragged sigh and leaned heavily on Ms. Rivera. It was strange to think that if Carl hadn't been killed, Erin would have called this nervous wreck of a woman grandmother.

"That woman never could hold herself together," said Anna.

"Didn't she collapse at the trial?" asked Bets, who leaned over Erin to speak directly to her mother. "At least her daughter isn't crying."

Carl's sister, Loraine, took her mother's elbow and guided her to a seat across the aisle from Erin and her grandmothers. She was the same age as Deb, but with her bleached hair teased into a chignon and her charcoal suit, which was immaculately tailored, she looked ten years younger. There was a hard edge to her, though, and as she gently helped her mother into the chair, she let out an exasperated sigh as the old woman scooted forward and complained that the chair itched.

Ms. Rivera, the attorney who represented the state, sat on her side of the table in front of Carl's family and smiled warmly at the commissioners and then at Erin and her grandmothers. She was young—maybe only a few years older than Erin. Her coffee-colored skin had a golden sheen to it and her overall roundness gave off an appearance of warmth instead of gluttony. There was a hint of foreignness to her speech, but it was more of a purr than an accent.

"We're ready," she said to the commissioners.

The men relaxed in her presence, and the tension that Erin had felt build up in the room evaporated as the wait dragged on. Erin took up Anna's hand and stroked the cool paperlike skin on the back of it. The feel of Anna's hands had calmed her since she was a child. From the moment they'd learned of her father's death, Carl's family had wanted nothing to do with Erin. The closest they'd come to an explanation was a card she received on her thirteenth birthday with a long note from her paternal grandfather who had prostate cancer and wanted to clear his conscience before he died. The only line Erin recalled from the card had stuck in her memory like an overplayed pop song. *We didn't have it in us to take a chance on you. You are your mother's daughter.*

"I've been waiting twenty years to tell that woman what I think of her," said Bets as the commissioners made procedural statements. "Abandoning a four-year-old child. And what she said at the trial—"

"—hush. This isn't the place; besides we wanted Erin all to ourselves," said Anna. "It would've been awful to have to share her."

Deb looked back at them anxiously, and Erin tried to catch her eye and smile.

"Are you okay?" Deb mouthed. She was not allowed to speak directly to anyone but her lawyer and the commissioners.

"Fine," said Erin, standing and then stretching with her hands on her lower back and pushing her abdomen out in front of her.

At that moment, the daughter leaned over to Carl's mother and spoke loudly, "I should think they'd force those women to stop breeding. Nothing good comes of their blood."

Carl's mother looked over at Erin, and a furrow appeared over her artificially tight skin and sculpted nose. "It seems a little too timely. Probably a ploy to get sympathy from the board. Poor me. I'm pregnant and my mother's in jail."

Erin and Bets both started to stand, but Anna, who sat in between them, put her hands on their knees and whispered, "Not now." Deb's lawyer looked back at the audience and shook his head quickly back and forth. The blond commissioner, with the ravaged fingernails, looked up and spoke sharply into his microphone, which wasn't plugged in.

"They'll be no discussion from those present until statements are taken at the end of the proceedings. Failure to comply will result in removal." He then looked at the stenographer and nodded.

As the district attorney's representative, Ms. Rivera waded through several formalities, cleared her throat, and drank nearly all the water from her cup before opening what looked, to Erin, like a prepared statement. "I'd like to remind the commissioners of the violent and horrific nature of Deborah Keller Ripplinger's crime and I think that is best done by reading a description of the crime scene, which the responding officer called 'a bloodbath.'"

At the original trial, the responding officer testified that he had found the body of Carl Ripplinger on the floor of the rented room he shared with his wife. He had been shot multiple times, mostly in his chest and groin area. Erin lowered her head and placed her hands on her stomach. It had started so quickly, hardly enough time to realize that the agenda of Ms. Rivera was not to let anyone forget what Deb had done. Erin didn't want the baby to hear this. She didn't want to hear this. She began to sing that lullaby from *Dumbo* in her mind. *Baby mine, don't you cry / Baby mine, dry your eyes.* Erin willed the baby to hear her voice, to listen to her thoughts and not to the vulgar description of its grandparents' legacy.

CHAPTER THIRTEEN

Constructing the Story

As far back as she could remember, Erin had collected slivers of the story of her mother and father. She eavesdropped on her grandmothers, studied family photographs, dug through the attic boxes with KEEP FOR DEB scrawled on the side in careless cursive. She'd spent hours puzzling over that handwriting and the bits and pieces of her mother's childhood stored in those boxes. The contents told her that at one time, Deb had fallen in love with porcelain cats, at another, based on the contents of two different paper sacks, rainbow erasers and rabbit feet. The real find came when Erin was sixteen and opened her mother's copy of *The Call of the Wild*. Tucked inside in a hollowed space created by cutting pages out of the book was her mother's diary.

The powder blue, imitation leather volume had thick ivory gilded pages. Her mother held no regard for margins—every available inch of space was filled up with scrawling purple handwriting. The looping cursive letters were the same width and height, making the words difficult to separate from one another. Erin felt a vague uneasiness when she read the journal—thinking that such intimate confessions should only be read when the writer was dead. She wasn't sure that Chowchilla counted as a cemetery.

Still, she came to view the diary as the truth. She realized as she grew into adulthood that the grandmothers were holding on to a crucial piece of information about Deb. There were silences to some of the questions she asked, and occasionally, Erin would catch the tail end of a conversation between Anna and Bets expressing concern at the time that she spent with her mother at Chowchilla. The year she found the diary, she got her unrestricted license and drove herself there nearly every Sunday. Erin almost always left Kidron with the intention of asking about the diary and about her father, but by the time she saw the glimmer of the razor wire atop the fence, she'd lost her nerve.

Despite her desperate faith that being able to see her mother, to touch her, would create a bond between them, it had not. She pinned her hopes on the diary, only to find that nothing she read reminded her of the woman she'd come to know during her visits to the prison. Deb seemed like an echo of the person on the pages of the blue journal. It carried over into her actions, into the letters sent from prison. The handwriting was even altered. Deb's script was compressed, subdued, as if she knew that what she wrote was for everyone's eyes and it needed to be small and compact to avoid letting these secrets out. The secrets in her journal, however, were almost gleefully revealed—in large loopy script.

Erin read the diary four times before she went in search of other stories about her mother. The first page was dated January 1, 1978: *What's crackin? I can't believe I have to go back to school next week! I know that Heidi and little Miss perfect, Natalie, are going to be laughing at me and trying to get all the other kids to pick on me. I figured it out, though, I'm going to be really nice to Natalie and then sneakily let her know that Heidi only likes her because of her horses.*

Natalie even looks like a horse with her long nose and big fat nostrils!!!!
I should draw a picture of her and pass it around. Mom better keep her
nose out of my diary. Daddy promised he wouldn't let her read it. And I
know what she'll say. Just because she's got that stupid limp and people
make fun of her for it, she'll tell me I'm being mean. But they were
mean first. Heidi was my best friend not Natalie's.

The subsequent entries were full of scheming, plotting, and vows to find a best-friend necklace that splits three ways. *I will make them like me again and then I will make them hate each other.* The first time she read it, the anger surprised Erin. She'd never seen such rage from Deb during their visits at Chowchilla, and Erin had never experienced that level of passion during any of her friendships. When the natural ebb and flow of high school pulled one girlfriend away, she always found another. The entries, taken together, revealed Deb to be impulsive, intolerant, fearful of betrayal and most of all of being alone. Erin searched for signs that she would have liked her mother as a teenager, but the picture she kept coming up with was one of a slightly overweight tyrant.

The entries became sporadic and Deb only seemed to write when she was having trouble with her friends. But then Deb met Carl and the entries became part of Deb's daily ritual. Reading those pages, Erin learned that her parents fell in love at the annual Redding Round-up. Deb was supposed to be in algebra class, but at sixteen, she was often places she shouldn't be. Kidron was too small a place for teenagers to find trouble, and so on a warm day in May, Deb and her girlfriends ditched—driving an hour north to Redding to sit on dusty bleachers that were downwind of the stock pens, but within shouting distance of the men. *Cowboys.* That was the word Erin's mother used in her diary. The girls covered their noses with scented hankies when the breeze rushed through the arena and then waved them at the cowboys as they straddled pens, waiting for a turn to ride. It was late afternoon when the steer wrestling competition started, and Carl was first out of the gate. She'd never seen bulldogging before and was stunned when Carl leapt from the saddle of his galloping horse and wrapped his forearms around the horns of a 750-pound steer named Monkey Lip. It took him less than four seconds to turn the tar-colored beast on its side—fast enough to win a little prize money and Deb's interest. She wrote that it was *love at first sight,* but she'd written that often in the pages of her journal. There had been other boys, but as far as Erin could tell, no other men.

Carl was a short man, built like a fire hydrant, with eyes the color of an empty bottle of pop—translucent green. He was twenty-seven, but his round cheeks and soft mouth made him look ten years younger. Deb watched him closely as he dusted off the seat of his Wranglers, took off his hat, and bowed to the crowd. She saw that his reddish blond hair was damp with sweat and before she realized what she was saying, she screamed *mine, mine, mine.* The other girls laughed and teased, but she didn't care. Looking at him made her think of necking with Bobby, the neighbor boy, in the olive grove that summer and how she'd pushed his boy's hand away every time he slid it up her skirt. She knew that if she ever got the chance to neck with this cowboy that she'd let his hand travel all the way up.

Erin kept her virginity until the summer before college. She knew the feelings her mother wrote about in her diary, but she'd only imagined them, her kisses with boys had been chaste and few. The grandmothers monitored all her social activities closely, but more than that, they filled up her days and left her no time for foolishness. There were dance lessons, cello lessons, performances with the community theater group, the three-hour drive on Saturdays to San Francisco where she worked with an ex-principal from the Royal Opera, and afternoons working for Callie at the Pit Stop. It wasn't until she returned home from college for winter break and for the first time faced unfilled days that she realized the busyness had been a deliberate strategy on her grandmothers' part.

Those early sections about Carl had given Erin a bit of hope that her mother was growing out of being a bratty teenager, but the entries ended two months after they met in 1981 when she wrote: *knocked up, getting hitched* in the same blocky script that Erin would later recognize in her mother's letters from jail.

The rest of her mother's story came the summer before Erin left for college, when she spent several hours hunched in front of the microfiche machine at the county library. Hundreds of stories had been written about the murder. They were all versions of the same story—scorned woman shoots husband in fit of rage. They differed only in the smallest details. Some reporters focused on the gun, others on her family's history in Kidron, and one or two near the end of the stories in paragraphs that could be cut off if their editors needed more space for furniture or car ads, pointed out that all of this—the shooting, the fighting, the drinking—had taken place with their four-year-old daughter on the floor of a closet in the bedroom.

Erin knew soon, very soon, Ms. Rivera would get to that detail, and when she started to talk about the way the pillows had been arranged and the Rainbow Brite doll, Erin would have trouble breathing. She'd spent most of her life making herself forget, but when she had to remember, a terror like the hard, dry Santa Ana winds would sweep through Erin as if she were nothing more than the scrub grass in Kidron. She wanted to rush from the small room and into the car and leave the women in her life, leave the trouble. She curled her fingers tightly around the arms of the scratchy blue chair and held on. The baby rolled and twisted and then began hiccupping, as if to tell Erin that it felt what she felt. This fear wasn't about the shooting, it wasn't about not knowing her mother, it was about not understanding her own part in Carl and Deb's story. She'd felt it before—remembered bending over the screen of the microfiche machine, feeling the relief of being able to in the year 2000 still hide behind its beige partitions and read about the murder in the *Chronicle*. She had been hungry for the details, desperate to find an answer to the question no one would answer, and then three-quarters of the way into the sparse account, she found herself. *A four-year-old child in the next room.* There she was, in a place she didn't remember with people she no longer knew, and that was where the fear came from.

CHAPTER FOURTEEN

What Erin Believes Happened

*I*n the small, hot room, Ms. Rivera spoke to the commissioners about finding Deb in the bedroom with the gun. Erin closed her eyes and started to tell herself, tell the baby, what she believed happened the night her mother shot her father. It was what she did to get control of the terror. Part of her understood that what she imagined couldn't be true, and yet what she imagined had to also be true. She closed her ears to the legal story of the shooting, to the black-and-white, letter-by-letter, word-for-word account of the shooting and remembered it the way she had come to view it. She was, after all, there.

It was not the marriage Deb had imagined. She was too young and Carl was gone too often. He didn't settle down and take the job at the processing plant that was offered to him by Bets's husband. He continued to ride rodeo, which meant that nine months of the year he was gone for long stretches of time—sometimes ten days would pass before Deb would get a collect call where over the operator's voice Carl yelled the time his bus would arrive.

Deb would wait for Carl's call, and if it took more than a week, she'd be consumed with the fear that he'd left her. She'd take the schedule of small town and no town rodeos off the beige fridge and stare at it for clues, pull the atlas out and use a bit of shoelace to figure exact miles between Malta and Roundup, Montana. She'd eat nothing but cantaloupe and celery, hoping to lose enough weight so that he wouldn't think of leaving her. And sometimes if the wait for the calls stretched past ten days, she'd leave Erin sleeping under her mother's watchful eye and take up a stool at the Green Doors Tavern. Erin learned this about her mother from the interviews with Tavern regulars, like Bobby. Deb liked to flirt with him and pretend that even though he had two kids with Natalie and was barely supporting himself, that he was a place she could go if Carl decided not to come home. When Carl was home, they stayed at Mrs. Castello's boardinghouse, where Carl worked as a handyman in exchange for their room. The boardinghouse was a place out of time, filled with old men who'd never thought to get married (youngest sons without an inheritance or the gumption to go someplace else to make their fortune) and depended on Mrs. Castello to cook and clean for them. Carl liked it because it got him out from under the watchful eye of Callie.

It was near the end of rodeo season in 1986 and Carl had been gone twelve days. He'd spent more money on travel than he'd earned in prizes and had cracked two ribs and his ankle after a bad fall in Pocatello. The night before Carl was to return to Kidron Deb had been at the Green Door Tavern, telling one of the regulars there, Bobby, that her marriage was over, that she was sure he was never coming back. It was nearly 3:00 A.M. when Carl called collect, shouting over the operator that his bus from Pocatello would arrive at 10:55. Deb was drunk when she answered the phone in her mother's house and started crying, telling the operator long after Carl had hung up how much she loved him and what it felt like to know he was on his way home.

The next morning her mother, Callie, found her asleep with the phone still cradled next to her ear. Callie nudged her daughter with her foot until she woke up enough to stumble to bed and then, knowing that she wouldn't see her granddaughter for a few days, dressed Erin and took her to the Pit Stop with her. No matter what was true, at the trial, Callie testified that Deb expressed happiness at Carl's impending return. Erin imagined her mother took a long time to prepare for Carl's homecoming, that she packed her clothing into the matching set of luggage she'd been given on her wedding day by Uncle Lester, took a steamy bath, and painted her toenails bubble gum pink.

Near dinnertime, she picked up Erin from the Pit Stop and drove to the boardinghouse, where Deb and Carl had moved after they were married. Mrs. Castello, who had inherited the place from her own mother and still ran it as if it were the 1930s—including meals in the common dining room for an extra fee. Because Deb had never learned how to cook, they took dinner at the boarding-house. Mrs. Castello presided over dinner and offered a blessing before passing around the warmed-over dishes. It was said that night that Erin had her first bite of shepherd's pie, and then asked for seconds.

Mrs. Castello treated Carl like a son. She told the prosecutor that she didn't think Deb was planning to kill him—how could any woman plan the death of a fun-loving, high-spirited man like Carl? As much as she thought Deb took Carl for granted, she still believed that shooting him had been an accident. Like kicking a dog, she'd said. You know the old cuss don't understand, but at the same time you got to stop him from pissin' on your geraniums.

The night of the murder, as it neared time for Carl's bus to arrive, Mrs. Castello volunteered to watch four-year-old Erin, who was asleep on the floor of the closet, which her mother made into a room when they stayed at the boardinghouse. This had been their routine the last four years. When she read the trial transcript, Erin had been surprised about how much Mrs. Castello knew about her parents. *No. She'd never seen Deb with any bruises, no she didn't seem particularly afraid of her husband. The child? They adored the child.* It made her wish the house hadn't been torn down and replaced by a pharmacy, that the old woman's mind wasn't as addled as her great-grandfather's, and that she wasn't sitting in Golden Sunsets talking gibberish. Mrs. Castello could have given her real truths about her parents.

In the police report, Deb said she'd gotten the time wrong, or the bus was late. Erin imagined that her mother sat on an aluminum bench next to the Greyhound sign on Antelope Drive and waited. The heat from the day dissipated quickly and left her shivering in her lightweight cotton dress. As she waited, the adrenaline that had pushed her through the day evaporated, leaving her drowsy, with aching muscles. She began to dream about the type of life she could have had, away from Kidron, away from Carl. The squeal of the brakes from the large silver bus woke her, and she leaped up from the bench. She couldn't be caught like this, unaware, inattentive. Carl was the only passenger to disembark.

He was limping. One of the steers that Carl had wrestled to the ground at one of the small towns in eastern Idaho stomped on his foot, and although he'd not had it checked out by a physician, he was sure at least three of his toes were broken and maybe a rib.

Seeing him wince, she pressed herself against him and whispered in his ear. He pushed her away and grabbed his duffel bag from the driver who'd found it among the jumbled luggage in the outside compartments of the bus. The driver waited for a tip. Carl brushed him off and headed for the truck, which was parked across the street. Deb pressed a dollar into the man's hand.

It was not the reunion either of them had imagined.

In the *Chronicle*'s account of the murder, Carl's sister said that her brother was a willful man. "Frankly, I was surprised he married her. Mama told him he didn't have to. She knew Carl best, and that boy didn't want to have anything to do with a family. He was running away from us when he started bulldogging."

The night he was shot, Carl was preparing to return to Idaho for another stretch of rodeos that crisscrossed that frying pan of a state. He would have made small talk with Deb. Told her how ugly he thought Idaho was, said that looking out the bus window all he saw was brown grass, dirt, hills, and buildings the color of mud. They would have been whispering, trying not to wake Erin, who was always asleep by 7:00 P.M.

Deb saw that he was packing more than the usual road items. That in addition to spare jeans and underwear, he put in his lucky belt buckle and the flask his father had given him. She knew his secret before he was ready to tell her, and it made her consider her own secrets. At some point in the preceding weeks, she'd taken her grandfather's gun from Hill House. Erin, when piecing together this part of the story, tried to consider all the reasons her mother could have had for taking the gun. Maybe she was afraid her grandfather with his increasing dementia would use it, or maybe she took it for protection when she stayed at the boardinghouse. She wondered if her mother was depressed and had considered suicide. What she never allowed herself to think was that the taking of the gun was premeditated.

Erin imagined the airlessness of the room at Mrs. Castello's house. It wouldn't smell like lemons and Murphy's oil soap, like Anna's house on the hill in Kidron. It would smell of other people, of misery, of liver and onions taken in rooms, and of industrial soap purchased by mail order from a generic supplies company.

When he finally admitted the truth, that he was leaving her, Deb would have felt like she was being bulldogged. A steer set loose to run and then out of nowhere grabbed by the horns and pulled down. How long would it have taken him to say those words? A second? Deb would have thought of Monkey Lip. Of the three and a half seconds it took for Carl to leap from the back of his horse and lean with all his weight on the horns of that half-ton steer. And just when the bovine thought it had a fighting chance, reared its head up and sideways, Carl's hand would have come around and clamped tight on its nose. Maybe dug a finger up in the nostril to give the steer a little pain as they stumbled to a stop and rolled over each other.

She wouldn't have had enough life, not with having that baby right away and not with growing up with the grandmothers, to know that a steer could get up and shake off the weight of a two-hundred-pound man, bringing it down. Trot off like it'd just tripped on its own feet.

But there was the trouble with the gun. She'd taken it. Taken it long before he told her he was leaving. Told her that for a long time he'd been sleeping with women like her, who saw him wrestle that beast to the ground and wanted nothing more than to be wrestled to the ground themselves.

"She took it for protection." That was Bets telling the reporter that she'd given it to Deb. Pressed it into her hands as she left for the boardinghouse that week. Because Carl had become unpredictable, she said. His drinking had increased and his anger was like a thunderstorm—just as likely to fill up the sky on a clear blue day as not. She also mentioned the quality of characters at

Mrs. Castello's and that there were rumors of drugs and whores and that she wanted her granddaughter and great-granddaughter to be safe, to feel safe.

Loraine, Carl's sister, saw it differently. As the lawyer reminded the probation officer of the trial testimony, Erin heard clearly Loraine's sour voice whisper, "That's just a story they come up with. And I'm surprised the jury believed her. You know the judge didn't or he wouldn't have given her fifteen to life. Would have let her just sit for seven or so years. That's what they give the accidental murderers. She wasn't part of any accident."

Erin tried to tell herself that the whole situation was an accident, but it only made her feel worse, because her conception was the accident that triggered all the other missteps, mistakes, miscues. Her presence in her mother's womb was the first change from girlish scrawl to tightly compressed scripted lines.

Six shots.

"I need you to stay," Deb would have said. Maybe she grabbed his collar or emptied his bag as he packed it.

Each time Erin thought about it, the details were different. There was information in the trial that she never envisioned. Her father never hit her mother. No one ever hit her. There were no bad guys, just accidents and anger. She shook her head, brought her hands to her ears, and tried to obliterate Ms. Rivera's talk about the quarts of blood that were found at the scene, the six shell casings. She closed her eyes and again remembered that day in her mind, even though she'd been asleep holding fast to Rainbow Brite.

She thought of another scenario, one with more detail, one where both her parents shared the blame. They'd run out of beer. Carl left to walk to the 7-Eleven at the end of the street, and while he was gone, Deb had unpacked his duffel bag and found a pair of women's panties, or lipstick on one of the buttons of his Wranglers, and that was when Carl walked in, keys jangling, whistling. Erin remembered that her father always whistled. Usually "Buffalo Girl" or the theme to one of the old westerns. *Shane.* She hadn't known then that the tune she associated with her father was from a movie until she watched it with the first boy she'd ever kissed. When she realized, she cried so hard she couldn't talk and had to wipe her face with her shirt. After that, she could never bring herself to return the boy's phone calls.

"Why do you have to sleep with them? Why can't you just take their kisses and their winks and come home to us?" Deb would have yelled this. Erin knew her mother well enough, knew that the women she'd lived with didn't have rational logical discussions, but were full of anger and accusation.

"Leave it alone. We've got enough going on without you bringing what I do when I'm away from you into it." Erin had started to think of Carl as one of the interchangeable leading men from the westerns, and so in her mind he spoke in the clipped way that all men from those movies talked, as if syllables were rationed.

"I'm not sleeping with you. Not going to have you stick me with something that's been up and down the bars of Idaho."

"You know there aren't many bars in Idaho. To get good whiskey a man's got to duck into the barn of a fellow he just met. It isn't my fault those barns sometimes have women."

"I think it's time you stayed. Gave up steer wrestling."

"You make me stay and I'm going to leave for good. Not much holding me here now." Erin liked to think that her father spoke of her during this fight, but no matter how she tried, she couldn't make it fit the narrative. Couldn't make it seem natural that her father would speak of his daughter, their daughter, and that her mother would respond by shooting him. Sometimes she pretended her father deserved to be shot.

"I'm not sure that little bastard is even mine."

Sometimes he spoke like Shane did to Joey. "You make sure

she grows up strong and straight, even if I'm not around. You can explain things to her."

The fight would have escalated. Mrs. Castello's pictures had been knocked off the walls, and the photos the police took of Deb when they put her in jail showed a woman with a busted lip and a slightly swollen cheek.

The first shot had hit Carl in the back of the left shoulder, passed clean through, and lodged itself in the solid wood door. He would have turned around and tried to wrestle the gun away from her.

The second shot passed through his right hand and into his upper thigh. He fell to the floor and screamed like the sound a calf makes the first time it's hog-tied. He pleaded with Deb, who stood above him, but she fired again. The third, fourth, and fifth shots hit him in the groin. He would have been unconscious. One shot to his thigh hit his femoral artery. The police were already on their way. They'd been called when the downstairs neighbor heard the first shot.

The sixth shot was through Carl's heart. Deb lay on top of him to deliver this final bullet. There were powder burns on his shirt and her blouse as if she had laid her head one last time on her husband's chest and pulled the trigger.

The police didn't find her on top of Carl. She stood when she heard the sirens, tucked the gun into a pocket in her skirt. She then went to the closet where Erin slept and curled around her daughter. Sometimes Erin knew that she was wide awake after the first shot and that her mother came into the small closet and lulled her back to sleep, but she didn't always remember it that way. In any event, this was how they slept at Grammy Callie's house—mother curled tightly around daughter, and now whenever her mother was close, Erin smelled gunpowder.

CHAPTER FIFTEEN

Erin's Performance

I'm so sorry. So very sorry," murmured Deb as Ms. Rivera finished her account of Carl's murder. At first it was a low mumble, more of a catch in her throat than words, but as the bullet count increased so did Deb's sniffles and apologies. She looked at Carl's mother and his sister as she groveled. Her lawyer put a hand on her arm and pushed Bets's handkerchief toward her. This was not a good scene. Erin felt the commissioners begin to turn against her mother, and she willed Deb to pull it together before Ms. Rivera introduced the psychiatrist's report. The younger commissioner appeared annoyed by the tears and shook his head slightly from side to side. He set his pencil down and stopped following Ms. Rivera through the report. The older man with the scarred forearm leaned over and whispered to him, and they both glanced at Carl's mother. She'd set her mouth in a deep frown and turned her body away from the proceedings. Erin hoped that the older woman didn't remind either of the men of their own mothers, she held on to the faith that they were born to kind-hearted women who didn't look as if they sucked on lemons. Carl's mother felt their gaze, and instead of softening her face, which would have made her seem frail, she leaned across the space that separated her from Deb. "Nobody cares about your apologies, my dear. Nobody cares."

Their assigned guard moved from the back of the door to stand in the aisle between the two families. Deb pulled herself together and used the handkerchief to wipe her face—taking with it much of the makeup she'd been wearing. Erin felt the mood in the room shift, and knowing that the commissioners were still on her side relaxed her, allowed her to leave the horrors of her memories behind and start to prepare for her performance. Ms. Rivera asked the commissioners to turn to the psychiatrist's report, and Erin focused her energy on her upcoming speech. She trusted that the lawyer had already painted a picture of Deb as a near-perfect prisoner, and in the rebuttals he would counter the report, which claimed that Deb suffered from borderline personality disorder. He had two evaluations by private psychiatrists that showed while Deb had poor impulse control, she wasn't crazy. Crazy might be a good television defense, but it was the kiss of death in a parole board hearing. The objections and clarifications portion of the proceeding passed quickly.

"You ready?" Bets picked at her pale peach nail polish. Her great-grandmother had asked Erin countless times if the speech she was about to give in defense of Deb was legal and wouldn't agree to come to the hearing until the lawyer sent her a copy of the rules, which specifically stated that next of kin were allowed to speak with no restraints placed on content.

"I just wish they'd let me get in the last word. Giving it to Carl's mother doesn't seem right," Erin said.

"I'm sure they're saying the same thing about you speaking," said Anna, who spoke louder than a whisper and drew a shush from the guard. A few moments later the older commissioner asked for the next-of-kin statements.

Erin struggled to rise from her chair. She arched her back, pushing her stomach as far out as it would go, and then placed her hands

on the arms of the chair to steady herself. At that moment she knew
she looked like she was twice as far along as she actually was.

"You can sit if you'd like," said the blond man, and Erin felt a
quiver of attraction toward him.

She shook her head. "What I need to say needs to be said standing up. It's not a casual request, asking a couple of men to give my
mother the chance to come home. Just doesn't feel like something I
can say unless I can stand eye to eye with you." She spoke clearly but
softened the vowels so that her words floated over the room and sort
of settled into the commissioners' ears. She'd been trained to do this,
to speak, to sing, in a way that changed how a person felt. Her voice
coach said that before television and movies, folks were used to feeling moved by a person's voice. Creating shared consciousness was a
gift that especially great preachers had, or dictators and all actors of
Shakespeare. But now no one understood live performance, and when
those transformative performers took the stage in a Puccini opera or a
Beckett play, audiences couldn't put the experience into words.

So many years of working on her singing had taught Erin about
voice modulation—how to control a crowd with the speed and tone
of her voice. It was easier to achieve with music, because certain com-
binations of notes, dissonant chords, were as good as a hypnotist's
watch. It could be done with just words. It was harder, but possible.
Pastors, mostly men, did it by increasing the pacing and speed of their
voices until if one said *jump,* the crowd would jump. Erin had studied the women who knew how to use their voices, and they were
always softer, gentler, but still with a firmness that didn't allow anyone to escape. The women were better at extracting money, the men
at extracting obedience. She needed the latter.

"I'm a girl without a father. I'm a girl without a mother. I'm
an orphan, but like Annie, I carry with me the hope that one day
I'll have a mother again, that one day she will come home and I
can put my head in her lap and feel her hand brush over my hair,

as if to tell me it's going to be okay. I don't have a locket or a letter promising my parents' return, what I do have is the promise of the State of California that once it fixed my mother, rehabilitated her, that she could come home. I trusted that California would keep its promise—" She put her hands on the table and leaned across the space that separated her from the commissioners.

"That you would keep your promise."

Erin let silence fill the room. She allowed the fan's gentle whir to enter everyone's ears to fill up the space in their minds, and then in the moment before their attention drifted, she raised her voice an octave, to make her sound younger, to make the commissioners fully weigh their authority. "I'm not going to ask you to let my mother go, but I want to tell you how much I need her"—she brought both hands to her belly and looked at the floor—"a girl's bound to make mistakes without a mother around. I messed up and I need someone to tell me that my mistakes can be fixed, that there's a light at the end of all this darkness. I need my mother to tell me so that I can tell my baby that falling down is part of learning how to get up. But right now I don't believe that. I hear other people say it, but I've been waiting and waiting for my mother to get back up again, and she's not been able to. I know she's tried."

Erin wished she could touch one of the commissioners, lay a hand on a shoulder or an arm to make the connection, but she couldn't cross the table, so she did as her teachers had taught her, she reached with her voice. "Amends. Isn't that what you call it? She's been here my whole life and she's never been reprimanded, never written up for talking back or fighting. She started the young mothers program for women like herself who came here and left children behind. But you know all this, you know everything. Except how it feels to not have a mother. To have the idea of a mother, to have my mother's mother."

She shook her head, as if this tangent wasn't where she wanted to go. The last part of the speech was tricky, she had to make the commissioners believe that what Carl's mother would say would be false, that her emotion, however theatrical, wouldn't be genuine, couldn't be real. She turned away from the commissioners and addressed Carl's mother. Her head was lowered. "I know you lost your son, but I lost my father. You got to see him grow up, become a man, and you saw him as a father. I got none of that. Please don't keep punishing me, your only grandchild, because your son is gone. I know there are no words to make up for that loss. I *know* this. But please. God please. She's served her time."

Erin nearly sank into her seat, surprised by the exhaustion and how unlike a performance her plea for her mother's life had become. She looked at Anna and saw that she was crying.

She'd never seen Anna cry and felt an oppressive culpability. She wondered again if she was doing the right thing, this gambit to get her mother released. This idea, this desire to have her mother with her had come to her just after she found out she was pregnant, and the plan to achieve this had consumed her nearly the entire winter. Now that it was almost over, now that the hearing was almost over, she was no longer sure. She decided that God would give her a sign. If her mother wasn't meant to be released, then Carl's mother would give the speech of her lifetime, would find all the flaws in Erin's argument, would make them see that to give Erin a mother who had killed her father was worse than to have no mother. She bowed her head and made the deal with God.

Carl's mother didn't make it through her speech. She began crying uncontrollably after the first sentence and could only choke out "my son, my only son" before her daughter took the paper out of her mother's hands and read the statement. Loraine, the daughter, read badly. She stumbled over the words and kept forgetting to replace the "I" with "my mother." Erin watched as Ms. Rivera's shoulders slumped, and then she looked closely at the commissioners and saw they'd stopped listening.

GUEST COLUMN PUBLISHED IN THE *Washington Post* IN MARCH 2007
"THE SILVER TSUNAMI: GLOBAL AGING"

BY AMRIT HASHMI

We're all getting older. Your knees aren't what they used to be, and names that once came easily to mind are forever lost in the jumble of memories. This isn't just a problem for the baby boomers in the United States. In every country, the population continues to age. The United Nations predicts that by 2050 the proportion of the world's population age sixty-five and older will have doubled from 7.6 percent to 16.2 percent. That will account for nearly one billion people.

So what, you might ask? Maybe you are young and can't fathom what the problem is with getting old. Or maybe you're old and have just come to accept aging as part of the natural life cycle. Although scientists can't yet stop you from getting older, we do understand one important fact about the process—it isn't natural. For most of the last century, people believed after a person became incapable of reproduction that their body essentially started the process of dying. That theory, born of evolutionary science, has turned out to be wrong. What we believe about aging today is that in many ways it mimics many other diseases we are currently in a war against, like cancer.

Many conditions that were once considered part of the natural aging process have turned out to be a result of one's lifestyle. Cataracts? They're directly related to how much exposure your pupils had to direct sunlight. Experiencing heart disease? Look back and count up how many pounds of red meat you ate over your lifetime. You'll find the correlation.

I know what you're thinking: I can prevent cataracts, but can I prevent my knees from hurting, or my hearing from going? And what about my brain? Can I prevent Alzheimer's? The answer is yes. But more than that, we are close to uncovering the secret behind slowing the entire processes of aging. And if we can identify the specific environmental causes of aging, there is a strong possibility we can eradicate aging altogether. I predict that by the end of this century, we will be a world full of Methuselahs.

Just this past year, I started working with an extraordinary group of women who seemed to have naturally, as part of their genetic makeup, slowed down the aging process. There are five generations—each more healthy than the next, and the youngest is expecting a child. A child who hasn't been exposed to the environmental toxins we've all come to accept as part of our lives. This family and their genes hold the key to not only eternal life, but also life without aging.

Yet recently, the federal government in a fit of austerity decided to cut funding to the National Institution on Aging, which administrates grants to research organizations across the United States to fund studies just like mine. These are the studies that have the potential to use the work I'm doing or others' work to uncover the fountain of youth—to give you all a chance to drink from the holy grail.

I understand there are more pressing concerns—we are fighting two wars and the economy is struggling. But consider this: The gains in life expectancy over the last thirty years alone added about $3.2 trillion dollars to national wealth, according to a study published this last month in the *Journal of Political Economy*. Want more proof? Consider that the cure for aging will in all likelihood also lead to a cure for virtually all cancers, and that would be considered a $50 trillion boon to our economy.

Without funding, we can't reverse the tide of this so-called silver tsunami. Join me in supporting an increase in funding for the National Institution on Aging. If this trend is not reversed, it has the potential to cripple established researchers in the midst of crucial projects and will have the effect of keeping younger scientists out of the field. Our populations are aging—this is an epidemic that you don't have to wait for your grandchildren to see. It is affecting your grandparents today, and soon it will affect you.

Amrit Hashmi is on the board for the American Council on Aging. He serves as director of the Center for Aging Research at the University of Pittsburgh, where he holds the Lillian G. Moss Chair of Excellence in Biology. Dr. Hashmi, an endocrinologist, was the first researcher to link longevity to genetics and is currently working with the Human Genome Project to identify the specific genes linked to prolonged life in humans.

Deborah in Spring

CHAPTER SIXTEEN

Release

She looked back. The girls who were in on short stays stood in their doorways—offering nods as she passed by. Anyone with a chance at parole ignored Deborah as the guard escorted her from her cell to Receiving and Release. It was how it had to be. There was never enough to go around in Chowchilla. If someone else had it, there wasn't a prayer of you getting your hands on it. Deborah's impending freedom very likely meant that some other woman on a fifteen-to-life with twenty years down was never leaving.

It was now late March, having taken more than two months for the bureaucracy to cycle through its hoops and red tape. And nobody but her lawyer, who billed by the hour, seemed to be measuring the time. None of her family had been down to see her since the day of the hearing. It felt to Deborah like they had checked her off on their to-do lists and started looking ahead—to the baby's birth, to Anna being the oldest, to that scientist making them famous. This realization that she was being left behind, or at the least left out, pissed her off.

Careful. She felt the rage she kept coiled up in the pit of her stomach stir. It could be dangerous to get angry in Chowchilla— she'd seen girls sent to solitary, privileges revoked, and warnings put into files for as little as pounding on a wall, or shoving another inmate. The last time she let her anger overcome her, she'd lost her husband, her daughter, the whole of life, and now she had almost as much to lose. She wasn't free yet. The guard had cuffed her too tightly. Her shoulders ached from being pulled back at an awkward angle. He'd dropped her off at the desk and then gone to retrieve the handful of other women who were also being paroled. Listening to his footsteps reverberating, she wondered at the leisure of his pace.

By 9:15 A.M., there were three other women waiting to be loaded onto the parole van. Judging by their youth, none of them had been in Chowchilla for any length of time. Two of them were black, slightly heavyset, and they stood close to each other— Deborah figured it made them less nervous to stand by their own kind. That's how it was in here. The only way to feel safe was to find a group of people who were like you. Kids that weren't going to be in for that long segregated by race, but the old-timers, like Deborah, knew better.

She watched the girls for a moment, approving of the way they kept their eyes locked on the ground and their bodies soft. They had a chance of making it in the real world. The other woman was young, too, but defiant. She stared at anyone who met her gaze and held her thin body taut. She was quite short, and because being in prison had taught Deborah to classify people, she decided this woman was Hispanic—probably from Guatemala based on the broad flatness of her cheekbones and her paper-straight black hair.

A guard came around to the front of the desk and looked each of them up and down, as if they were naked. He poked each of the two young black women in the shoulder and called them by their last names. "Ferris and Sutton, you got people waiting on you in the visitors' lot." He turned toward Deborah and the other woman. "Ripplinger and Serna, you're getting dropped off at the Greyhound in Fresno. Make sure you take a bus that gets you to your paroled county in the next twenty-four hours."

Deborah froze. Her mind raced with possible scenarios to explain Erin's absence from that parking lot.

He uncuffed Deborah second to last. She tried in her least confrontational way to tell him that he'd been mistaken. "I'm sure my daughter is waiting for me in the visitors' lot. I just spoke with her yesterday and she knows I'm getting out today. She may just be running late—Kidron's a long way from here and she's pregnant—"

"She's not there."

"No. I'm sure she's there. If you could just call—"

"Rules say she has to check into the gatehouse by nine. She didn't. You'll be going with Serna to Fresno."

He grabbed Serna roughly by the shoulders and turned her around to unfasten the cuffs. "Don't even think about it," he said as Serna's lips pursed, as if she were going to spit in his face.

He tossed the women their parole boxes, which contained a change of clothing sent by the parolee's family or friends. The Guatemalan woman didn't have a box. Next, the guard shoved a manila folder containing the $200 in release money provided by the state, a simple photo ID, and any pertinent papers about the terms and conditions of their parole into each of their outstretched hands. Deborah clutched at hers, calming her outrage by crumpling the envelope satisfactorily in her hands. The Guatemalan woman put a hand on Deborah's shoulder and squeezed gently. Her eyes seemed to say, "Don't let the bastards get to you."

The two black women entered and then emerged from the bathroom in their street clothing and were escorted to the waiting van. The guard nodded his approval for Deborah to change. Alone in the bathroom, she let some of the frustration she felt finally show. How could Erin let her down like this? How could she be so irresponsible? Deborah had told her a dozen times over the last two weeks that she had to be at the gatehouse before 9:00 A.M. She pulled on the baggy linen pants she was sure Bets had picked out, and tried to work up worry over her daughter's absence. She supposed there could have been a situation with the pregnancy, or an emergency with Anna or Frank, but it didn't feel that way to her.

They were ashamed of her. They'd always been ashamed of her. Embarrassed that she got knocked up at seventeen, horrified about the situation with Carl, and now uncomfortable with the reality of how her freedom would alter their own little, precious lives. She stuffed her prison jumpsuit into her mouth and screamed.

A softly accented voice echoed around the nearly empty bathroom. "At least you don't have to wear this." Serna stood by the sinks, holding up a shapeless flower-printed muumuu. "They made me give them forty dollars for it and then asked for five more to cover the cost of the underwear. I said I didn't wear panties, but they insisted."

"That sucks," Deborah said, and then splashed water on her face from the sink before putting on the yellow T-shirt that had been in her parole box.

"It all sucks," said Serna. "What were you in for?"

"Shot my husband."

Serna raised her thin eyebrows. "Did you now. I would have thought it was something less ugly, like kiting."

"You?"

"Got me nailed as a predator." Serna shrugged off the last of her prison clothing and pulled the voluminous dress over her head.

Deborah backed up against the wall.

Serna laughed bitterly. "It wasn't nothing like you're thinking. I got high with a bunch of boys and they all thought it would be funny if I popped his little brother's cherry. Kid was thirteen, but

I'll tell you he knew what he was doing. Got charged with all sorts of nasty, but pleaded down to felony child endangerment. Still had to do six years."

Deborah flinched. The last twenty years she'd spent in Chowchilla had taught her to be wary of certain women. To protect herself, she needed to offer Serna a reason for respect. "I took my chances with a jury. Turns out they don't like it when you empty a gun into a man."

"Cuidado con lo que dices," Serna said as she walked out of the bathroom.

Deborah understood just enough Spanish to know that she'd have no trouble from the girl during the hour-long drive to the bus station.

Fresno was south of where she wanted to go. She occupied herself during the drive by making more excuses for Erin. There could have been traffic, or a power outage that stopped her alarm from going off. Of course, everyone's life existed on their phones now. That was something Deborah would have to get used to. When she'd gone into jail, cordless house phones were rare. So, even if the power had gone out, Erin would have been relying on her phone to wake her. As they neared the downtown area of Fresno, Deborah gave up on the excuses. She banged her head rhythmically against the window of the van.

The guard escorted them off the bus and into the station. They were in a shitty part of town—it looked like it had boomed in the 1960s and then been summarily abandoned. There was a light smattering of clouds in the sky, and the wind had a chill that made Deborah think of the winter in the yard at Chowchilla. Two bearded, smelly men were asleep in Day-Glo orange sleeping bags outside the terminal. The blue *h* in *Greyhound* was missing from the sign above the institutional Plexiglas doors of the station. The handful of passengers waiting in the blue and gray plastic chairs looked poor. For a moment she thought about the last time she'd been at such a bus station.

"I'll need to see each of you purchase a ticket to the county of your release," said the guard, checking their paperwork. "After that I am absolved of any and all responsibility for you."

Faced with the wide open of the terminal, Serna hesitated before picking one of the two ticket lines. Deborah knew how she felt. She watched her traveling companion buy a ticket for Los Angeles and then fidget in front of the vending machines—folding and refolding her remaining dollars. Just as Deborah was about to purchase her ticket to Redding—the nearest station to Kidron— she heard someone calling her name.

"Deb! Wait! I'm here."

Deborah hesitated before turning around. She'd immediately recognized the rich musical tone of Erin's voice.

Her daughter stood in the doorway of the bus station, holding half a dozen Mylar balloons with welcome slogans scrawled across them in various neon shades.

"It's about time," Deborah said, taking her money back from the grinning clerk. In the rush to embrace and the awkwardness of maneuvering around Erin's large belly, the balloons slipped from her daughter's grasp and floated to the ceiling.

CHAPTER SEVENTEEN

Choices

*I*n the car Erin explained her tardiness with an airy wave of her hand. "I got a late start."

"Any later and I would have been on that bus," Deborah said.

"But you're here. I'm here. We're finally headed home together." Erin's voice cracked as she tried to continue the sentiment.

Deborah should have put her hand on her daughter's shoulder and told her it was fine. Instead she asked when they were going to stop for lunch. "Nothing cafeteria-like, I want real food."

"I know a sandwich place near Modesto," Erin mumbled. She wiped at her tears with a loose cotton scarf she had draped around her neck. After a while, she gestured outside. "Does it look different to you? Bigger? Older?"

"I don't remember enough to know." Deborah studied her daughter's profile. She must be seven months pregnant now—far enough along that she looked uncomfortable, but not so far along to look swollen. She chewed on the inside of her cheek, something her daughter had done in childhood in moments of unease.

Deborah rolled down her window and let her hand ride the

currents of wind outside the car. In the median, the normally upright oleander bushes drooped with the weight of their blossoms. They were quiet until the first exit for Modesto.

"You know where you're going?" Deborah asked.

Erin turned off the radio, which had been softly playing some opera Deborah couldn't understand and didn't particularly enjoy. "Next turnoff. Grandma Bets and I liked to stop here after—" She didn't finish her thought. "I guess she met the owner's son once."

The restaurant was in a yellow building across the street from a bank Deborah had never heard of. The place had a slightly worn look, but the parking lot was so crammed, they'd had to park on the curb. A dull hum came from the shop as they stepped inside, and immediately Deborah wanted to leave. The restaurant had the feel of a place that needed an owner's manual. She'd wanted a hostess, a plastic menu, and time to sip her soda before deciding what to order.

Erin motioned for Deborah to follow her into the disorderly line in front of the counter. "The specials are there," she said, pointing to the wood paneling above the cashier, where someone with terrible handwriting had scrawled a variety of sandwiches and salads in colored chalk.

Before she could process the list, Erin leaned into the counter and ordered a Noah's boy on whiskey with a white cow. The cheerful teenager taking her order repeated it back into a microphone and then asked her how she wanted her Murphys. Erin asked for them cold and then turned to Deborah.

"I'll have whatever's good," she said to the smiling boy. "And an iced tea, if you have that."

"Everything's great," the boy replied. "Sweet or unsweetened?"

Under the boy's expectant gaze, Deborah felt itchy. "What?"

"Your tea. With sugar or without sugar?"

For more than two decades, Deborah had never had a choice

about whether she wanted sugar in her tea. At Chowchilla it came sweetened. "However you serve it is fine," she said, scratching at her neck.

"We serve it both ways."

Deborah looked again at the chalk scrawled list above the boy and then at Erin. From behind them, she thought she heard grumbling about the wait. She had no idea of what she wanted.

"Just get it unsweetened," Erin said. "We can pour sugar in it until you like it."

Deborah nodded her head. The boy looked at the people stacking up behind them. "Do you want food, too?" he asked.

"What's that smell," Deborah asked, looking at her shoes.

"Stew," the boy said, his forehead creasing.

"I'll have that," Deborah said.

"Bossy in a bowl," he called into his microphone. He looked toward Erin and said, "It comes with B and B. Does she want that?"

Erin nodded and brought out her wallet.

"Finally," said the man behind them.

Deborah sighted a table in the darkest corner of the room and walked unsteadily toward it. Erin followed with their drinks and a large number 14 that she slipped into a holder on the table. "This wasn't a good idea," Deborah said.

Erin slid the selection of sweeteners toward her. "I thought you'd enjoy it. Plus the food is good—really way better than all that Sysco stuff they feed you at Chowchilla."

"There's no sugar here," Deborah said. Her fingers furiously flipped through the small colored packets. "Sweet'n Low, Nutra-Sweet, Equal, Sugar in the Raw, Splenda."

"What do you want? Plain sugar?" Erin reached across the table and plucked out two of the small packets. "This is what you want. It's sugar, just in a fancy package."

Deborah's hand was shaking so violently she couldn't tear open the brown envelope of natural sugar. "I should have stayed at the Greyhound. Taken the bus back."

"Definitely wouldn't have had all these choices to make then," Erin said, with a half-smile. "Sandwich or soup, tea or coffee, eat in or take away—"

"Can't you take me seriously? I'm saying none of this is right— and it can't be, because we've started this whole trip off on the wrong foot."

"You're just being petty now," Erin said, taking a long sip of her vanilla milk shake.

"Why weren't you there?"

"I told you I got a late start."

"But why? This is a big day for us."

Erin pushed her chair back from the table and reached for the number placard. "I don't want to talk about this."

"Sit down," Deborah's shrill voice pierced the dull hum of conversation in the restaurant.

From behind, you couldn't tell her daughter was pregnant. She took several more steps toward the counter. Deborah looked at all of the eyes on her and tried again to get her daughter back. "Erin Elizabeth Ripplinger. Come here."

Erin didn't even turn her head. The rejection felt as if she'd been knocked to the ground. To keep herself from literally falling over, Deborah took small deliberate sips of her iced tea. She watched her daughter wait for their food at the counter and then carry it all outside, pausing against the harsh sunlight as she opened the exit.

Next to Deborah an elderly man leaned across his table and in a conspiratorial whisper told her that in his experience it was better to give in than get left behind. Deborah nodded in agreement, and after finishing her tea and then the soupy milk shake abandoned by Erin, she left the restaurant.

The car wasn't at the curb, where they'd originally parked. Deborah looked wildly around the busy commercial street and then heard two quick taps of a horn coming from behind her, in the parking lot. She turned and saw Erin behind the wheel of the car, eating her ham sandwich. She wondered if her daughter had actually driven away, or just moved the car to be in the shade.

The inside of the car smelled like meat. "I thought you were a vegetarian," Deborah said to Erin.

"You don't know all that much about me," Erin said, handing her the paper sack with the remains of lunch.

She looked in the bag. "I guess a cold Murphy is potato salad."

Erin shrugged. "Coming here always made me think Grandma Bets knew a secret language."

"The two of you are close," Deborah said. "When you were a baby and got colicky, she was the only person who could soothe you, but she'd never admit that, she thinks she's terrible with infants."

Deborah picked at her buttered bread and searched for a plastic spoon to eat her stew with. Erin slid her seat back as far as it would go and then half-turned, so she faced Deborah. The car felt smaller. "She made me come get you. I got cold feet or close to it. Bets told me it was time I learned to want something after I got it."

"You weren't going to come?" The inexorable itching sensation crept back into Deborah's skin.

Erin looked down at her pregnant belly.

Deborah repeated herself, getting louder each time.

"Let me explain," Erin said. "Just hold on a minute and let me try to fix this."

The tender skin on her neck, which she'd been scratching at since the restaurant, started to bleed. Erin unwound the cotton scarf from her own neck and dabbed at the blood. "You have to stop this," she said. "You have to listen."

She tried, but Deborah realized that she didn't know her

daughter well enough to make sense of all that was said. Instead, she thought about the last time she'd been a mother to her daughter. A couple of days before Carl had come home for the last time, she'd taken Erin down to the park on the bank of the Sacramento River just outside of Kidron. A cushion of sawdust surrounded the small playground there. It had recently rained, and Deborah remembered that the normally sweet piney odor of the wood chips had been tinged with the smell of decomposition. She pushed Erin on the swings until her arms were exhausted and then the two of them tried to skip rocks across the water.

The spring snowmelt made the river wild and full of whorls and eddies. It was nearly impossible to make a rock skim its surface, but long after Deborah had given up and resorted to seeing how far she could launch a rock, Erin kept trying. She inched closer and closer to the river's edge in search of flat stones. Before every throw, Erin turned her gray eyes toward Deborah and with great seriousness requested that she watch. Each time, Deborah offered her daughter some advice, or positioned her hand and wrist just so. Just as Deborah was going to insist that they leave, the water in front of them stilled and Erin let a half-dollar-size rock fly from her hand. It skipped half a dozen times across the river before it sank out of view. They both jumped up and down, hugging in excitement and success.

That was how Deborah had expected them to greet each other in the parking lot at Chowchilla. She finished the last of her stew and nodded solemnly at Erin, who was still talking about how the pregnancy had magnified the hollowness Erin had felt her whole life about not truly having a mother of her own. No matter how deeply the grandmothers loved Erin, none of them successfully had taken Deborah's place. That brought up emotions that Erin had never dealt with previously—mostly how she felt about not truly having a mother.

Deborah reached out and patted her daughter's knee. "You have to remember that I really am your mother. No matter what else has happened or will happen. I am your mother."

"Do you get it then?" Erin asked.

Deborah nodded, because she couldn't think of any other option.

"Oomph," Erin said. "Baby's kicking my ribs."

"Let me see," Deborah said. Erin's T-shirt was tight across her belly, and each time the baby kicked, she could see the fabric of the shirt move. Erin rolled up the shirt and they waited. Her daughter's stomach veins stood out like lines on a map. The line that ran from her pubic bone to her belly button had darkened to the color of India ink. It bisected her stomach into two perfect hemispheres. As quick as the flash of a lightning bug, part of Erin's stomach bulged and Deborah saw the outline of a foot.

"Oh!" Tears sprang to her eyes. Deborah blinked quickly and acted as if she were about to sneeze. The air in the car stilled as Deborah focused on her daughter's heartbeat, the baby's heartbeat. She wished that the umbilical cord between them had never been cut.

CHAPTER EIGHTEEN

A Model Citizen

According to her parole officer, Deborah needed a job and a place to live. Ms. Holt kept her dark hair in a small, neat bun at the nape of her neck. She had full lips and spoke with a slight southern accent—more of a lilt that a drawl—that immediately put Deborah at ease. "I've been doing this thirty years," said Ms. Holt during their initial meeting. "Got the lowest recidivism numbers in the state. Of course, some of the other officers will tell you that's because I'm a woman or that Tehama County doesn't have its fair share of drug offenders, but I'll tell you what. You get a job, you get a place to live. You're going to be just fine."

The place to live had been easy. Deborah settled into a room at Hill House that had belonged at one time to Anna's brother, Wealthy. She thought the room, with its south- and east-facing windows, had the best light in the house, but because of its narrow shape it had been rarely occupied over the years. The furnishings were spare: an iron bed frame with its own built-in springs and a squat olive wood armoire, which served as dresser and closet. Bets offered to sew some new curtains, but Deborah liked the cowboys and Indians print on the faded ones already in the sill. To make it a place she could retreat to, she'd moved in one of the rocking chairs from the back porch and appropriated a rose-colored bath mat for a rug.

The job proved more difficult. Her mother had agreed to hire her to work at the Pit Stop, but their relationship remained strained. Most days they didn't exchange more than polite greetings. At their second meeting, Ms. Holt silenced Deborah's objections about working for Callie with a sweeping hand motion that stopped Deborah midsentence. "Do you want to know why I'm so good at my job? I'm good at the therapy part of this—only unlike those namby-pamby shrinks in their offices with couches I don't sugarcoat my advice." Ms. Holt leaned across the table and narrowed her eyes. "That's what you're looking for here, right? You've got to own up to the fact that shooting Carl wasn't an accident. It's easy to rehabilitate an accidental criminal. I don't have to mess with childhood traumas or abandonment issues. But, like I said, you aren't here because of a slipup, which means to keep you out of jail, we're going to need to fix what's going on in that family of yours." Deborah wanted to dispute Ms. Holt's assessment, but prison had taught her the value of keeping her mouth shut and her disagreements to herself.

Her mother and father opened the Pit Stop sometime during the late 1960s just as Interstate 5 neared completion. In the beginning it had been a restaurant—trading on its slogan of "we'll put olives on anything." There were stories from Deborah's childhood of teenagers ordering olive malts or peanut butter and olive sandwiches. She remembered her mother complaining about the waste (none of it was ever eaten), and her father laughing it off, saying that life should allow people to try stuff they may not like. But after Deborah's father died in 1978, her mother brought in kitschy gift items—olive platters, olive spoons made of olive wood, OLIVE YOU posters, LIFE'S THE PITS bumper stickers—until every inch of the three-thousand-square-foot store was stuffed with olives and olive-related products. The billboard, which rose from the parking lot of the store and could be seen for five miles on both sides of I-5, explained it best: *"Olive the Pit Stop!" Free Tasting Bar • Locally Grown • Unique Gifts.*

She'd asked to work in the stockroom, but her mother put her at the tasting bar, which was where Deborah had worked during high school. Back then it had been a plum assignment. The tasting bar stood in the center of the store on an elevated platform underneath a sign her father had purchased when they first opened the Pit Stop. In large green script, the words EAT HERE NOW sat above a downward-pointing arrow made up of flashing lightbulbs. When she was younger, she'd liked that every person who came through the doors looked at her, but after so many years of being watched by guards and other prisoners, having eyes on her no longer brought any pleasure.

"Stop scratching," her mother said, coming up behind Deborah.

"I'm not."

"No one's going to taste the olives if they see you up here raking flakes of dead skin all over the place."

Deborah rubbed her knuckles against her forearm. "We're out of bleu-cheese-stuffed olives."

"See right there. That was a scratch."

"There aren't even any customers right now," Deborah said, gesturing to the nearly empty store. Nancy, who'd worked checkout since about the time Deborah went to jail, looked up and peered at them through her glasses.

Her mother leaned against the counter, taking the weight off her bad leg. "The casino bus will be here any minute."

"Then I should finish restocking. Can I just grab a couple of jars off the shelf?"

"No. We've got inventory control systems now. Nothing's like it used to be."

Deborah nodded her head in agreement, watching as her mother shook two pills into her hand from the bottle she always carried in her pocket. Without being asked, she handed over a cup of water in a disposable triangular cup.

"They're here," Nancy called. "Moving as slow as ever, but they've left the bus."

Deborah was about to repeat her question about replenishing her supply of olives at the tasting bar, when her mother reached out for her hand. "I'm sorry I jumped all over you. This is going to take some getting used to. Seeing you behind the counter after all these years is just—"

Her mother's words were interrupted by the loud crash of glass. One of the senior citizens had lost his balance coming into the store and bumped a five-pound jar of garlic-stuffed olives. "Call Roberto and Pedro," Deborah yelled across the aisles to Nancy. In a moment the empty store was filled with activity. The brothers cordoned the spill and swept broken glass, brine, and olives into a metal dustpan. Although no one had spoken to him, the man who'd broken the jar loudly protested having to pay for the jar of olives.

Two dozen of the more mobile seniors crowded around the tasting bar, stabbing olives with toothpicks and asking repeatedly about the threat of a left behind pit. They were all from various retirement facilities across the central valley. The Indian casino up north sent buses down to pick them up a couple of times a week. Her mother offered the drivers vouchers for swinging by the Pit Stop on their way back south.

"It would ruin my dentures," said one particularly tall woman with liver-spotted hands.

Her companion, a rounder woman, leaning on a cane, pulled

out her partial and stuffed it into her purse. "Better not to take the chance," she said.

"Never once hit a pit," said a trim man behind the women. He looked up at the counter toward Deborah. "You're new here."

Deborah refilled the tray of pimento-stuffed olives and set out a new box of toothpicks. "Sort of."

"You're prettier than the other girl who worked here," he said.

The tall woman rolled her eyes. "Watch out for this one, he thinks he's a Lothario."

"Doesn't mean it isn't true," he said, reaching for a parmesan-stuffed olive.

Against her instincts, Deborah smiled. "Thank you."

"Where'd you come from?"

"This is my mom's place," she said.

His eyes widened. "Callie can't be old enough to have a daughter your age. I mean the two of you could be sisters."

It didn't surprise Deborah to learn that her mother didn't speak about her. "I've been away awhile."

"Well, that's what children do," he said, moving to the end of the tasting bar.

In thirty minutes, the store had emptied. Deborah sanitized the surfaces around the bar, helping herself to a few of the almond-stuffed olives, relishing the slight crunch they had. Nancy came over to help her tidy up. Deborah felt more at ease with the cashier than she did with her mother. "It's nice to have you here," Deborah said. "You've been good for Mom, I can tell."

"Your mom doesn't like things that are good for her." Nancy let out a long sigh and glanced around the empty store. "After all that, I only sold a handful of postcards, a couple jars of olives, and a bottle of oil," Nancy said.

"Is that why Mom's so tense? Is it always this bad?" asked Deborah.

Nancy shrugged her shoulders and leaned against the counter. "My guess is that most of them didn't do so well at the casino. If they've gotten lucky, they like to buy gift baskets for all the relatives who never visit. Then I get to spend the afternoon applying shipping labels."

"Who used to work the tasting bar? You know, before I came back."

"Nobody. I'd just set the olives out and let people at 'em. You realize how greedy some folks are. I don't know if it is from growing up without or just not ever really growing up. But from the register I'd see women dump an entire tray of olives in their purses."

"I get that," Deborah said, thinking of the first few years she spent in Chowchilla.

From the look on Nancy's face, Deborah guessed her mother was headed their way. The older woman gave a slight nod, took a dust cloth from her apron pocket, and dusted her way back to the register.

"Get what," her mother asked, her voice slurry at the edges.

"People who eat all our olives but don't buy anything."

"It goes against human nature. Basic goodness. They ought to feel obligated to us, not entitled. This seminar I went to with your father, back when we first started the store. That's what the expert said. That free was never free. It's evolution, you know. The need not to have an obligation to another person. Look it up. Monkeys or apes in the Congo or some other dark place do this. They give trinkets—bits of grass and twigs or a rock, and they always get food in return."

From the way her mother jumped from one topic to another and the glassiness to her eyes, Deborah guessed that she'd taken more pain pills than she ought to have. She remembered this look from her childhood. When her father had been alive, he'd regulated how much she took and when. On days when she got like this, he'd send her home—blaming the weather for making her leg act up. Deborah had seen her share of drug addicts at Chowchilla. Her mother had more in common with them than she ever would have thought.

"Didn't you ever feel like the world owed you something? After the plane crash? After Daddy's stroke? Even after what I did?"

The edge to Deborah's voice seemed to help her mother focus. "I don't care how bad your life is, you're not going to think taking a few more than your share of olives is going to fix having the world owe you something."

"It all adds up," Deborah said.

Callie pulled Deborah into an embrace. "Oh, you are still that little girl. You are still my little girl, and I know you think the world should be fair, should be balanced, but it can't be. It simply can't."

Deborah struggled to pull out of her mother's hug. The tone of her voice was an echo of her childhood. The sound of being given less than her brothers and being told it was impossible to measure all the good and bad that happened to one person in one lifetime. "It also can't be that I'm always the one to get shortchanged," she said.

Looking down at her leg, her mother frowned. "We all get shortchanged. That's the lesson, sweetie."

CHAPTER NINETEEN

Family

After being home for about two weeks, Deborah confessed to Ms. Holt that she missed her prison family. "I've seen this before," Ms. Holt said, rummaging through a messy stack of glossy papers. "They even printed up a pamphlet on it. Or maybe it was part of that larger booklet on reintegrating yourself into society."

"It's not that I don't love being around my daughter," she said, accepting the booklet Ms. Holt thrust into her hands. "There's just no way she understands—or really any of them—about what it's like being in prison."

"Being understood? That's what you're after?"

"Not exactly."

"How much do you understand about how your daughter felt when you shot her daddy?"

Ms. Holt truly doesn't pull her punches, thought Deborah. She flipped through the booklet and her eyes landed on a picture of a smiling woman wearing a blue work apron. "I just want them not to push me so hard. LaJavia got that, you know?"

"Who's this LaJavia?" Ms. Holt asked.

Deborah ignored her. "Don't they have sponsors or some sort of trained professional to talk to?"

"This isn't the Bay Area. We're small time here, and nobody in Tehama County is going to pay for warm fuzzies. If you're churched, I'm sure your pastor would lend an ear."

"Maybe I could talk to one of the girls who's been out. Somebody I knew in Chowchilla."

Ms. Holt shook her head. "Nu-uh. Most every girl in there is a felon, and that's one of the few ways I lose people. Catch them consorting with known felons. That and drugs."

"There's nobody then," Deborah said.

After their appointment, she waited outside the small building adjacent to the sheriff's office in Redding where Ms. Holt had her office. Erin and Anna had dropped her off while they went to Walmart to shop for baby items. She thought about what Ms. Holt had said and considered trying to find a church. Her mother had given up on church after her accident—insisting that she nearly died without ever seeing a white light. Bets and Anna attended services at Mount Olive Lutheran. The deaf pastor there was a compassionate listener but rarely gave advice beyond telling the troubled to trust in God. Anna's entire theology revolved around that central tenet.

Deborah wasn't entirely sure how she felt about God. Before prison, she'd never given much thought to the existence of a deity. Being in prison, at least being with the girls who had served as her surrogate family, meant that she'd paid a lot of lip service to God. The wardens liked it, paid a little less attention to the believers—figuring they still had a reason to act right. The parole board liked it, too, all that stuff about finding God meant remorse for crimes.

When she'd first arrived in prison, all the inmates had been expected to attend Sunday services. They'd worn dresses, put on hose and costume jewelry. That was when they still had access to hair spray and makeup—and you would have thought sitting on those metal folding chairs that they were in an actual sanctuary and not the rec room for Cell Block B. Those were the last good times at Chowchilla. That was how the old-timers talked about the years when there weren't enough inmates to fill the beds and the wardens treated them more like coeds than criminals. It hadn't lasted more than a few years, but while it did, Deborah held herself apart from the other prisoners, clinging to the hope that she'd be paroled before her thirtieth birthday and that whatever damage she'd done to her family could be repaired.

By 1996, nearly a decade after she'd started her fifteen-to-life sentence, she'd been denied parole, orange jumpsuits replaced the dresses, and the farm-style chain-link fence was topped with razor wire. Each week, dozens of new prisoners filled Chowchilla, and each new body took away some of the space Deborah needed to keep pretending she was on the verge of freedom. The overcrowding began the year Erin finally started visiting. Seeing her daughter lifted her spirits, but the few hours of interaction never left her emotionally satisfied. In the days after the visits, she found herself looking around for someone she could mother, someone who would accept all that she couldn't give Erin.

For most of the years she spent in Chowchilla, Deborah lived in Cell Block B. There were eight rooms down each of the four wings of her building. They tried to mix the races up—but the numbers never worked out. The year LaJavia arrived in Deborah's cell, she was bunking with two Hispanic girls, who spoke little English, and four black girls. By that point, she'd been in prison long enough she didn't care about race. She was just glad it wasn't a white girl, because the women who hadn't grown up in urban neighborhoods cared too much who was what color.

As it all turned out, it might have been better to have race problems. She and LaJavia became close. The relationships between many of the women at Chowchilla mimicked the familial relationships outside of prison. Deb and LaJavia filled the void in their lives by calling each other mother and daughter. It seemed simple until the outside, real families intruded.

She didn't like to think about the time she spent just before being paroled. It made her feel guilty, like when she averted her eyes from the mentally handicapped woman on the bus so she wouldn't have to give up her seat. The day after the parole hearing, everyone had wanted to celebrate. The guard walked Deborah into her room, counted heads, and then left to do the rest of the hall. Her bunkies gathered around, hugging her and asking question after question about the parole hearing. There was something about the shape of LaJavia's eyes that reminded her of Erin. LaJavia shushed them all and pulled out a bottle of sparkling apple cider she'd saved from New Year's.

"To the best mom I had," LaJavia said, raising her plastic cup. "It'll be lonely here without you."

They finished their cider and everyone else except LaJavia went to the mess hall for dinner.

"You okay?" LaJavia asked and then after a pause, "We okay?"

Deborah lay on her bottom bunk with her arm across her eyes. She knew that her bunkmate was asking about their own mother-daughter relationship. "Fine. It was hard seeing them. I feel older."

"Yeah," LaJavia said, sitting down on the bunk opposite her. "I get that way when I get to see my own baby girl. She's almost a teenager now. Time is sorta wonky in here. I dunno."

Those last weeks in prison, Deborah felt older than her mother, than her mother's mother—older than Anna, who stood at the head of their family with a foot in either century. No one would believe her if she said this. She couldn't begin to explain how spending twenty years confined to Chowchilla made her older than them all, but it did. She'd tried to explain it to LaJavia. "Scientists don't know shit about time," she said. She looked over at LaJavia. The girl was frowning, her eyes were wide. "They think a day is always twenty-four hours, an hour, always sixty minutes, you know. But they forget, I mean they don't even try to explain how time works in the mind, for a living breathing human being."

"Yeah," LaJavia said. "It's messed up. Like my sister says, days is long, but years is short."

"I got it figured out," Deborah said. "There's something else at work with time, and sometimes if a human being's life gets all packed up with experiences, time speeds up so that years felt like days and hours like minutes."

LaJavia nodded, but she didn't understand. Not because she didn't graduate high school, but because she hadn't been in Chowchilla long enough. Deborah didn't tell her that the last twenty years had been so empty, so devoid of the new, that an hour spent folding clothing in the prison was equivalent to a year. She'd read someplace about a guy who theorized that time was more like temperature. Degrees didn't measure how hot the air was, but how fast it was moving. Deborah thought that for the last two decades, her life had been cold—with the molecules moving around only enough to stay alive. She wanted to explain this to LaJavia, but she was afraid that she had it all wrong. That she didn't understand enough to teach someone else her theory. When LaJavia had more years in prison, and Deborah knew the girl would figure it out on her own as LaJavia's own daughter grew up outside.

If you had money and were on the right side of the wall—not stuck in solitary or processing—prison was as good as living in a Walmart. Deborah had been on the right side of the wall for two decades and there wasn't anything she couldn't get in Chowchilla.

Except out. That had been her overriding thought those last weeks in prison. The morning after the sparkling apple cider, LaJavia woke full of conversation. "There's so much to do before you go," the girl said, putting her feet squarely down on the concrete floor of the cell. She scratched her scalp, and flakes of dead skin floated down to the wool blanket that had slipped off the bed. "I need my braids redone."

Her hair was a mess. Deborah could see all the broken strands that had slipped from the tight rows, and her scalp needed oiling. The girl had been in Chowchilla almost ten years. She got arrested on attempted murder charges after trying to run down the father of her daughter with her mother's Grand Am. She made a plea bargain and would only need to serve twelve years. The boyfriend, Calvin, was in a wheelchair now.

"Maybe Louisa will help," Deborah said. It pained her to say this, but she knew LaJavia would need a new prison mother.

"Naw. She's mad at us for being nice to Nella. You didn't notice she been giving our whole family the silent treatment the last few weeks?"

Deborah didn't answer. This conversation bored her.

"Guess you wouldn't have. About the only thing you notice these days is the mail. Can't even get you to eat. Your mama isn't even going to recognize you when she comes to pick you up."

"Won't be my mama. I haven't talked to my mother since I shot Carl," Deborah said. "Get to meet my grandbaby, though."

"I sure was glad that my mama was there when I had my first one. Even with the medicine, you still want someone there to hold your hand. And not the baby's father neither. He don't belong nowhere near the hospital."

Deborah stopped listening to LaJavia's yammering. She felt a vague tug of regret that she couldn't listen to the girl, but she'd not felt the same about her since seeing her flesh-and-blood daughter again. These prison families were just placeholders for the real thing. The women knew that; they realized that on visiting day the hugs they gave their blood mamas and grandmas would be deeper and more emotional than the affection they showed one another.

Still, she'd never had an inmate that she got as close to as LaJavia. The girl understood what it was like to want the pain to stop so bad you were willing to kill to make it stop. They'd spent hours talking about how good it was that Calvin only ended up paralyzed after being dragged three hundred feet by LaJavia's car. Deborah couldn't look at the girl and not remember the night LaJavia had confessed her deepest secret—that she didn't know she wanted Calvin alive until the paramedics got him breathing again with CPR. Deborah had cried that night. Great gasping sobs that left her achy and with a headache the next day. How different her life would have been if she'd stopped at one shot, or even two. But it took all six to kill the screaming in her head, the rage that had built up over the years—from the times he ignored her, or cheated on her, or just treated her less than what she felt she deserved. And with six bullets, she needed more than paramedics to save him.

It was only six fifteen. The guards wouldn't be around for another hour to let them out for breakfast and work release. God. How had she done this for so many days? Put one foot in front of the other and acted out a routine that never altered. Hoped to God that one of the guards would get her hair done so they'd have something new to talk about. Engineered drama between the families to have some distraction.

"You 'kay?" LaJavia asked. She was standing, peering into the top bunk. "You not even out a bed yet."

"We got time," Deborah said, and for a moment the old tenderness between them returned. She stretched out her hand and fingered the box braids that she and Nella had spent hours laying into LaJavia's thick, curly hair. She closed her eyes and for a moment imagined that she was touching Erin's head, running her thumb over her daughter's straight, coarse hair.

"You ready to tell me about the hearing? All you wanted to do last night was sleep."

Deborah wasn't ready to talk to LaJavia about her freedom. "I got to get out of here."

The pain in her voice silenced the girl, and they both sat on their bunks, waiting for the morning guard to come and let them out for breakfast. She needed to be social, got to talk with Nella Santos about getting a present made for LaJavia. The women in Chowchilla had learned to improvise. Nella, an artist, made her own supplies.

A few days later, Nella undid the padlock on her locker and pulled out an eight-by-ten piece of homemade paper. She made her own paper by shredding the cheap greeting card envelopes and soaking them in the sink. Then she spread the pulp over the vent to dry. She was meticulous about it, and her paper was indistinguishable from the fancy sort that real artists used.

"I had to improvise a little—not knowing what LaJavia's kid actually looked like."

"Were you here when she lost him?" Deborah asked.

"In a different block, but we all heard about it. Some of us said she'd have a reason to sue if she wanted, but I guess it never came to that."

"I still can't believe that boyfriend of hers wanted conjugal visits. He's in a chair," Deborah said.

Less than a year ago, LaJavia had gotten knocked up by Calvin, that boyfriend that she'd tried to kill. His family had petitioned to get custody when she gave birth, and LaJavia used to say she felt like an incubator. "She took it real hard when he died, said that God was punishing her."

"I know that. When you're in here, it's hard to think you don't deserve every shitty gift the fates give you," Nella said, handing over the portrait. "I guess most babies look alike, huh?"

"Looks like a boy, all right. I just wonder if he looks too old," Deborah said. She didn't know much about watercolors, but she remembered from painting with Erin when she was a child that if you didn't have the right paper, the paint just rolled off. She traced her finger along the ridges and wells in the paper where the paint had settled. The baby's eyes were closed.

"It's a baby. That's how babies look." Nella was sorting through the canteen order.

Deborah shook her head. "I wish she had a picture. I guess you've seen what her daughter looks like, though. The one comes on visiting days."

"Yeah, but she's what, almost twelve? I just sort of used the shape of LaJavia's eyes and then gave the baby a lot of curly hair, so you know he's black."

Deborah saw that Nella's teeth were nearly all rotten—a sure sign of meth use. She knew the girl had run off her own family by stealing from them, too. It was why she needed to earn canteen money. Bets made sure that Deborah had plenty of canteen money and sent quarterly packages full up with stuff. She held the portrait close to her chest.

When she got back to her cell, Deborah borrowed a pencil from one of her bunkies and wrote a note to LaJavia on the back of the painting.

"Nella done a good job for you. Looks just like LaJavia's kid," said a new bunkie, who'd got put in their cell a week earlier. She was black and didn't think much of Deborah's relationship with LaJavia. Told them both that what LaJavia needed was a prison husband, not a prison mother.

"Nella's a fucking junkie," Deborah said, knowing this new bunkmate was also in for selling meth.

The girl backed away from Deborah, muttering under her breath. *She could be trouble,* Deborah thought. She considered adding a warning to the note she'd left for LaJavia, but instead, she slid the picture into a large envelope and put it on LaJavia's bunk. In her small, tight handwriting, she'd written, "Don't open until I'm sprung."

CHAPTER TWENTY

Fools

The simple pleasure of sitting at the kitchen table eating dinner together brought Deborah immeasurable joy. After eating, she usually sat on the porch and sometimes was joined by Anna, Bobo nipping at her heels, and Bets. Her daughter preferred to watch some televised singing competition and her mother disappeared with the phone into her bedroom. Glancing across the sweeping view, she saw that the olive trees looked to be on the verge of flowering.

"I was thinking about throwing Erin a surprise party," she said one night in late March.

"For the baby?" Bets asked.

"No. It's her birthday on Wednesday," Anna said.

"It snuck up on me, too," Deborah said. The last few days that she'd been home had moved by with incredible speed. Even the hours she spent working with her mother at the store seemed to be no more than minutes.

"She doesn't like big to-dos," Bets said. "All those pranks when she was in school—"

"There wouldn't be pranks," Deborah said quickly, wanting to make sure she stayed in charge. "Just cake and maybe a few friends of hers from high school who live around here."

Anna and Bets exchanged a sour look. "I'm not sure who she'd want to see. And she's never been good with surprises. You remember the year she turned twelve and that Parker boy—"

"You know I don't remember any of this," Deborah said, convinced that Bets had been trying to hurt her feelings.

Bets laid a hand on her knee. "We just want what's best for her, same as you."

"It's been so long since I've been able to give her anything," Deborah said, rocking a little faster in her chair.

"When you were with her, you were a good mother," Anna said. Her chair moved back and forth so slowly, Deborah couldn't be sure if she was moving it or the wind.

After a while, Erin came to the screen door. She was sniffling and her cheeks were tear-stained. "That show is all schmaltz, but it still gets to me. They had to pick ballads to sing tonight."

Deborah and the other women murmured their agreement of the difficulty of listening to love songs. "Come, sit with us."

Bets, who'd been humming a few bars of "Always," broke off and began talking about the night Erin was born. They'd all thought Deborah was pranking them when she called from the boardinghouse to say she was in labor. Callie took over telling the story. "Hand to God I thought it was an April Fools' Day joke," said Callie. Deborah remembered her family's inaction when she told them about her water breaking. Carl had been too drunk to wake up. She'd lain next to him, feeling the contractions strengthen and become more regular as the hours from midnight to dawn passed.

Callie became the hero of the story, telling Erin how she had run every stop sign and the one red light in town to get her to the hospital in time. Deborah didn't want to hear this, didn't want to have her mother be praised. It only reminded Deborah of how her mother couldn't stand to be alone in the same room with her. How she hadn't visited Chowchilla one time since she'd been locked up, and how on all of the birthday and Christmas cards she received, Bets had obviously signed her mother's name, writing "All my love, Mother" in a script too close to her own. As Callie spoke, Erin had crept onto the porch and was now sitting with rapt attention at her great-grandmother's feet. The dog curled itself against her hip. It was clear to Deborah that this was a story her daughter hadn't heard before.

"Where was Daddy?" Erin asked.

There was a long silence. Anna coughed and the creak of the rocking chairs filled the porch. "He was at a rodeo," Deborah said. "Made it to town that afternoon. I wouldn't let anyone else hold you until he got there."

"I'd forgotten that," Anna said. "You were quite persistent, too, got outta bed and yelled at that nurse for reaching to pick Erin up."

The party had been a surprise, though Anna had been right about Erin not wanting to see old acquaintances. Those who'd remained in Kidron had married young and were either in the midst of bitter divorces or happily pregnant with their third or fourth child.

Deborah needed her daughter's expression to say: I feel loved and look how many people care about me. Instead, she realized, watching her daughter's eyes, that what her expression held most of all was bewilderment. She'd made the mistake so many mothers make of thinking that what they want is what their daughters need.

Most of the presents were baby-related items and a few albums and sheet music from those girls who'd been in choir with Erin. The only personal gift had come from a quiet man, who'd married one of the choir girls. In high school, he'd been charged with making videos of all the performances, and he and his wife had spliced together all of Erin's solos and put them on a single DVD for her.

"We made one of my singing when we first got pregnant. I thought it would be fun to show the kids how me and their father met. Of course, they hate watching it. They tell me it's boring."

The husband grabbed his wife around the waist. "It's not boring."

After everyone had left, the women gathered around the table in the kitchen. Deborah's mother cut herself another slice of the enormous sheet cake. "Who's going to clean this place up?" Callie asked.

"Not me," Erin said, leaning back from the table and rolling down the stretchy fabric of the maternity jeans she wore. "I'm partied out."

"Sorry about that," Deborah said to her daughter. "I guess it wasn't what you wanted."

"It was lovely, just lovely," she said, picking at the icing on the leftover cake.

"Have another piece," she urged. "There's so much left over." Erin hadn't eaten much of the cake. "You sure you're not hungry? What about you, Grandma?"

Bets pushed the Happy Birthday paper plate toward the center of the table. "When you get as old as I am, nothing tastes good for more than a bite. I used to love steak. Thought there was nothing better than a well-aged filet, but then I turned eighty and all my brain says when I eat is 'not this old thing again.' Even took to trying exotic food, but it's the same. No pleasure in it anymore."

Anna laughed. "I tried switching to spicy food when that happened to me, but it tore up my insides pretty bad."

"Isn't that something," Deborah said. She turned to her daughter and mouthed, "What's wrong?"

Erin shook her head. "We've just had a long day and the burger I ate at lunch is giving me indigestion."

Idle chatter started and stopped among the women, and for the first time in decades, Deborah had clarity. Looking at the women around her, she could see her past, present, and future. She had so much more life in front of her. Forty-two wasn't that old. She could still start a family, go to college, start her own business. Why did being in this damned home make her feel like her life was over? It was one problem when she was behind bars and had no choices, no opportunity to keep growing. But not now; the world should be wide open to her.

Anna excused herself to use the bathroom and Callie looked up from her third slice of cake. She slowly licked the pink and blue frosting from her fork while her glazed eyes looked at a spot above Deborah's head. The emptiness in her gaze seemed to enter the room itself.

"I should check on Anna," Bets said.

"Bets is depressed," Erin said when her great-grandmother had crossed the threshold of the kitchen.

"Has she done anything about it?" Deborah glanced toward her own mother, to see if she was listening to any part of their conversation.

"You know how she is. Won't even take an aspirin for a head-ache. It has to do with Frank, you know."

"Frank's a bastard," Deborah said. She and her grandfather had never gotten along. "You've all been building him up in your minds, ever since he started losing his. But I remember him from before, when he was mean to me just because my presence meant his little girl wasn't little anymore."

"Nobody else seems to think that," Erin said. "It's more than that. You haven't been around. You haven't seen the way he is in the nursing home. He's different."

Deborah didn't want to talk about her grandfather. "Did you at least enjoy the party? A lot of work went into it."

"Don't you mean to say you put a lot of work into it?" Erin asked. Her daughter had inherited her directness from Bets.

Callie snorted. "Never could fool her," she said, still looking above their heads.

Deborah ignored her mother. She lowered her voice and said to her daughter, "You talk to the father of your baby yet? Tell him when the due date is? Invite him out for the birth?"

"The party sucked," Erin said. She picked up what was left of the cake and dumped it in the trash can before leaving the kitchen.

"She never thought she was really coming back here," Callie said from the end of the table. "I used to be like that, and yet here we both are, stuck in Hill House with the kind of people we can never escape."

"You have a real problem, Mom. Just keep your mouth shut."

"There's the little girl I know. Do you know you were always mean? Even as a child. If your feelings got hurt, you'd lash out at people. One time, you couldn't have been more than eight, you pushed your brother down the stairs because I'd told him I liked a drawing he'd done of the olive trees. Broke his arm in two places. For two days you stubbornly insisted that he'd fallen on his own, even though we all saw it happen. And then, when you finally admitted it, you told me it was my fault for not loving you enough—"

"Shut up. Shut the fuck up." Deborah stood up and pushed at the table until it pinned her mother to her seat. "You are as good as a damned junkie. Do you hear me? A junkie. You've always been a junkie. Those pills—they let you escape the hard stuff around you and leave you with what? Nothing."

"I can't breathe," her mother said, making a dramatic show of pushing back against the table.

The commotion drew all the women back into the kitchen. In a moment, Bets had unpinned Callie from the table and Erin had wrapped both arms around Deborah and started pulling her into the living room. Anna repeated the Lord's Prayer in a thin, reedy voice.

"You never loved me," Deborah shouted toward her mother as Erin wrestled her onto the couch. "Nobody has ever loved me."

CHAPTER TWENTY-ONE

Mother and Child

Nobody ever spoke directly about the fight. For the rest of April, everyone made an effort with Deborah. The house was icy with politeness. She told herself that Erin was the only one who mattered. In a normal world, Bets and Anna would have already passed on, their funerals would have been well attended and their memories frozen by banality. *Never speak ill of the dead.* If that were only true, then this schism with her mother wouldn't matter. Lots of women hated their mothers. She just didn't want Erin to be one of them.

She tried to give advice. When Erin winced in discomfort, she said, "Make sure you're sleeping on your side. It'll help with the back pain during the day."

Watching her daughter write out her birthing plan, Deborah shared with Erin her own birth story. Explaining that the women in their family had an easy time of it. "It goes quick for us, and none of the kids have gotten stuck. With you, they barely had time to give me the pain meds. It was just a few quick pushes, and there you were, a long, skinny baby, head not even a little deformed from the birth canal, and a little rosebud mouth."

Silence.

"You mewed. It was sort of a joke with the nurses because your cry was so small and seemed to say 'I hate to inconvenience anyone, but I'm hungry.'"

Erin looked at her through the bangs she was growing out. "I'm not doing meds. It's bad for the baby."

As they closed in on the baby's due date, everyone began to tread a little lighter in the house. Ears listened for any sound that Erin was in labor. Deborah watched her daughter sleep in the afternoons on the worn couch in the living room. Sometimes, when she woke up, she seemed to forget the unhappiness between everyone and her face was full of joy.

"You know," Deborah said one late afternoon in May when she came in from working at the Pit Stop, "I did all this planning and worrying about being pregnant and giving birth, but it never occurred to me to visualize what my life would be like when you were actually here. Maybe it is because I was so young."

"It's not just you," Bets said. "Every woman I know makes that mistake with her first."

"And then we vow to never do it again," Anna said, the corners of her eyes crinkling.

Callie came through the front door, leaning heavily on her good leg. "Helluva day," she said. They listened as she stomped through to the kitchen and ran the faucet. Deborah guessed she needed water to wash down the handful of pills she'd just swallowed.

Whatever playfulness had been in the room evaporated, and each of the women turned back to what had been occupying their interest. Deborah watched her daughter watch the singing competition and listened to her mother's giggly voice as she spoke to that doctor in Pennsylvania.

∽

The next visit with Ms. Holt did not go well. Deborah felt ambushed, first by the random drug test and second by the parole officer's suggestion. "I think you and your mom need to have a face-to-face."

"Did I tell you my mom's a junkie?"

Ms. Holt pursed her lips. "I understand she has a prescription for Vicodin. Same as your prescription for Paxil."

"I didn't get it when I was a kid. You know, it took being in prison, where I saw junkies day in and day out. The pill poppers were the worst."

"Don't be so hard on her. Deborah, I think you need to understand the harder you are on people, the more they're going to expect out of you. And meeting expectations, that's something your whole family needs a lesson in."

"Still," Deborah said. She pressed her tongue to her bottom teeth. "How long until you get the test results back?"

Ms. Holt narrowed her eyes. "Do I have to be worried about this test?"

At that moment, there was a sharp knock on Ms. Holt's half-closed office door. Turning around, Deborah saw her mother in the doorway, and then before she could react, Ms. Holt had motioned her into the empty chair across from Deborah.

"Erin's in labor," Callie said.

Deborah looked at Ms. Holt for permission to leave. "Fix it," she said, and then waved them out the door. They spoke only courtesies to each other during the hour-long drive back to Kidron. Her mother asked if a particular radio station was okay, Deborah suggested turning on the air-conditioning. They said they hoped Erin's labor was easy. The late-afternoon sun bore down on her mother's side of the car. No matter how the visor was adjusted, the sunlight seemed to bounce around the interior of the car, making it difficult to clearly see her mother's profile. She listened to her sing along quietly to every ballad that played on the radio. There were times when her mother's voice caught with emotion over one love lyric or another, and Deborah thought about patting her on the leg, or making some physical gesture that would give them both the assurance that happier times were ahead, but she couldn't bring herself to reach out.

Bets ran toward them when they stepped off the elevator. "You've got to talk some sense into her. She won't do it and the doctors keep telling her she has to."

For reasons that Deborah didn't fully understand, her daughter had decided that Bets should be her birth coach. Erin claimed it was because Bets had delivered all her children at home without the aid of pain medication, but to Deborah, it was ridiculous to pick a woman who'd made those choices not because she shared Erin's ideology but because there hadn't been a proper hospital in Kidron when Bets had her children.

Callie took both Bets's hands in hers. "Slow down, Mom. What is going on?"

Not wanting to wait for an explanation, Deborah sprinted toward the room Anna was pacing in front of. Inside, Erin argued with her doctor, a small Korean woman, who shouted down her daughter's objections by repeating the phrase "the baby's in distress."

"I'm not having a C-section," Erin said, pushing away a metal tray next to her bed. Her thick black hair was damp with perspiration, and her heavy bangs were clumped along her forehead in small sections like badly applied mascara.

"At least not yet," Deborah said, stepping between her daughter and the doctor.

"Mom!" Erin said, and Deborah thought she started to cry, or maybe she had already been crying. Either way her soft gray eyes darkened to the color of ash, and she held her hand out.

For the first time since she'd left Chowchilla, Deborah felt like she had a purpose. She thought about how she'd had to carry herself all those years in prison so that the other women knew to leave her alone. She straightened her shoulders and jutted out her chin and then narrowed her eyes at the doctor. "You will give us five minutes to discuss our options. We're going to ask you questions and you are going to answer them, without prejudice. My daughter doesn't want medication, and she doesn't want the baby cut out of her."

"Yes," Erin echoed. "No cutting."

Before stepping away, the doctor explained that while monitoring Erin's contractions, the nurse had noticed a troubling pattern. The doctor held out a receipt-size slip of paper and pointed at it. "You see here that with each contraction the fetal heart tones dip below the baseline, and then are taking a long time to return to normal."

Deborah wasn't sure she understood, but she nodded to the doctor to continue. Behind her Erin began to hum as a contraction overtook her.

"She's contracting fairly regularly, about every three minutes, and she's dilated to five centimeters. But this pattern, it worries me." The doctor looked around the room and then motioned to Deborah to move closer. She lowered her voice. "It can mean the cord is wrapped around the body of the baby."

"The neck?" Deborah asked, darting her eyes back to Erin, who had turned on her side after the contraction passed.

"No, no, no. But the torso or the legs or most often the shoulder and the chest, like a sash. It puts stress on the baby. It's a risk, and one we can avoid if we do a C-section. We get in, we get the baby, we get out."

"Can we have our time now?" Deborah asked the doctor.

"Time. I need to call the anesthesiologist if we're going to do this, and since he lives in Redding, it'll be at least an hour until he's here. If the baby's heart tones continue to be distressed, we'll be doing the surgery without anesthesia."

"Just a few minutes?"

A nurse sidled up to the doctor and spoke in low tones, passing along another strip of paper. They looked at it together, and then with a curt nod of her head, the doctor left the room.

At the door of the room, Anna talked with Bets and Callie. They seemed to be waiting for Erin to invite them in. In the hospital bed, Erin sat with her knees up, and her face was flushed and pale at the same time. Deborah motioned the other women in and they gathered around Erin, each offering advice or words of support.

"Try the next contractions on your hands and knees," Bets said. "Got through the hardest part of labor with two of my boys that way."

"Poor baby," Callie said, rubbing Erin's back. "It'll all be over soon and we'll have our little girl here."

Anna said, "Do you know how to make God laugh?"

Reflexively, Deborah answered, "Make a plan."

With some difficulty, Erin changed positions and then Deborah and Callie stationed themselves on either side of the bed. Her humming grew louder, the pitch rising with the intensity of the contraction and at the peak she let out a musical chirp.

"It's not so bad," Erin said, leaning forward onto her arms and pushing her head against the mattress. "Grandma, tell the doctor I can do this. I can get my baby out. I really can."

Callie tucked Erin's hair behind her ears. "You don't have to."

"She wants to," Deborah said from the other side of the bed.

"You're in no position to say anything about this," Callie said.

"I'm her mother," Deborah said, the words faltering as they left her mouth. "I am," she said with more force when she saw that Anna and Bets were shaking their heads.

"This is not the time or the place," Bets said, stepping forward and kneeling in front of the bed so that she looked Erin right in the eyes. "Sometimes the most courageous acts are ones of submission."

"There are other options," Deborah said. "There have to be."

Erin banged her head rhythmically on the mattress. "I don't know. I don't know. I don't know."

Anna rapped sharply on the wooden door. "Stop all your nonsense," she said. At once the women in the room turned to her. She trembled like a leaf about to be blown from a branch. "What is the baby telling you? Listen."

Erin dropped to her side and curled herself around her stomach. She clenched her eyes shut and covered her ears with her palms. Both Callie and Deborah stepped back from the bed, leaving a buffer of emptiness around the girl.

They waited.

The doctor came to the door of the room. She waited.

An image of a chain of paper dolls cut so that the space between each joined arm created a heart came into Deborah's mind. After a moment that felt like a day, Erin started her humming again. When the contraction had passed, she looked up at the doctor. "We're going to do this."

Over the next few hours, the nurses fluttered around Erin with grim faces. They tore off strips of paper from the fetal monitor and took them back and forth on their charts. The doctor inserted a tube to pump fluid into the uterus, explaining that it would relieve some of the pressure of the umbilical cord, if it were indeed wrapped around the baby's body. Bets gave charge of coaching to Callie and took Anna to get coffee. Deborah worked to make sure her daughter had a peaceful labor. She kept the lights dimmed and the music volume adjusted and unpacked Erin's overnight bag into the small chest of drawers in the room. Unpacking the baby's first outfit, Deborah realized that her daughter didn't think she was having a girl. The small layette was white with a blue ribbon threaded around the collar.

"This is pretty," she said to her mother, holding the outfit up. Another contraction hit and Callie leaned over her granddaughter as she pushed and smoothed her hair. "You are the strongest woman I know."

"So you don't think it's a girl?" Deborah couldn't help asking after the contraction had passed.

Erin groaned and then said something in Italian that to Deborah's ears sounded like "Shut the hell up."

"I think she's ready to push," Callie said.

Their complete dismissal of her made Deborah feel useless. She folded the clothing and slipped out into the hall to look for the doctor and the rest of her family. Anna put a hand on her shoulder before going into the room, and Deborah understood that it was her great-grandmother's way of forgiving her for all that had happened between them.

Two nurses entered the room rolling a cart affixed with a clear bassinette and an assortment of hospital equipment. It reminded Deborah of the media carts she'd transported to and from the prison library. The doctor nodded at them as she entered and said to Erin, "Everything is going to be just fine. You keep pushing. The baby's heart rates are no worse than they've been, and we've got our neonatal specialist on his way in. Just in case."

Bets put her arm around Deborah, and they watched from the doorway. "You were right to stand up for her," she said.

"One last big push," one of the nurses said to Erin.

Her daughter's scream as the baby emerged was not altogether different from some of the notes she held when she sang her arias. The musicality of her voice seemed to hold the room in a spell for a moment, and then chaos erupted.

"Heart rate dropped," said the nurse who'd been standing by the portable bassinette.

"Come on, come on, come on," the doctor said, pulling the baby out and clamping the umbilical cord.

"You did really, really, well," Callie said to Erin.

"It's a boy," Anna said.

"Is he okay? What are you doing?" Erin said. She lay back on the hospital bed, tears streaming down her cheeks.

"It's a boy," she said.

CHAPTER TWENTY-TWO

Coming and Going

$\mathscr{E}$xcept for Callie, they'd been made to wait outside Erin's room once the baby had been delivered. They looked at the doors. The clock ticked, and again Deborah became aware of time. She wanted to step outside and breathe in air that wasn't institutional-ized. It was May, and that meant all of Kidron would smell faintly of olive blossoms, and the pollen from the bunchgrass would tickle the back of her throat. She wanted to be on better terms with her mother so she could ask her to go home and make mashed potatoes and roasted beets. The potatoes in prison had been instant and the beets canned. She felt time speeding up again, and she tried to con-tain these thoughts and those about her daughter before the clock ticked again.

It was not like the soaps that Deborah had watched in prison. No doctor, no nurse, no attractive person in fitted scrubs burst through the door to rip off a surgical mask and exclaim that the baby was alive. Instead nearly an hour later, Callie stepped through the large double doors and told them the baby was fine, that Erin was fine, and that everyone needed sleep.

"Thank God," Deborah said. "Can I see her? Can I see my grandson?"

"You realize," Callie said, taking a step toward Deborah, "that this is all your fault?"

"No," Deborah said. "I was just doing what a mother—"

"But you're not her mother. She has Anna, who held her hand on the first day of school, and Bets, who taught her to ride a bike, and me. Do you know what I did for your daughter?"

"It isn't my fault," Deborah said, looking behind her for support. Bets slumped awkwardly in the plastic waiting chair and Anna turned her bright eyes on them both.

"Have it out and get it over," Anna said. "Set it on fire and see what's left after it burns. This back and forth is going to destroy us all and we'll be right back where we were."

Her mother hardly waited for Anna to finish speaking. "It is your fault. You shot her daddy. Do you understand that? All of this is because of you. She had no chance of getting married and living happily ever after. You did this to her. And then you couldn't leave well enough alone and let the doctor do what was needed. You decided to take her side now? Why now?"

Deborah was at a loss for words. She looked desperately for help, for kind eyes. The other people in the waiting room, including Bets, had their heads down. She looked at her mother. She was damp and her clothing wrinkled. Her roots needed to be touched up and her hair lay flat against one side of her head, from leaning in close to Erin to coach her through childbirth. For once, her eyes seemed to be clear and focused, but her hands were shaking.

Deborah closed the remaining distance between them. She spoke forcefully, nearly spit the words out at her mother. "It turned out okay. What's wrong with you? That you had to come out and find a way to make it all my fault? I spent my whole childhood trying to make you see me, see that all that was wrong with you, I wasn't one of those things. You're the one who's broken. You're crippled and not just because of your leg."

"Take responsibility. Just admit that you are at fault for some damn thing in your life. Do you see me limping around, begging for sympathy? Playing people because I was dealt a shitty hand?" Her mother grabbed her by the shoulders and started shaking her. "Why are you so selfish? Where did I go wrong with you?"

Deborah shoved her mother with enough force that Callie fell backward onto the linoleum floor, scattering several of the plastic chairs. A man who'd been in the waiting area since they'd come in with Erin yelled at them to knock it off. Deborah advanced on her mother, who had trouble standing back up because of her leg. She could have helped her mother up, but Callie scuttled away when she offered her hand. Deborah kicked at her mother, who screamed, and the man who'd yelled at them stepped between them. Deborah screamed and grabbed blindly for something to throw. Picking up one of the waiting chairs, she flung it across the room into the portable stand with a coffee urn sitting on it.

The crash seemed to awaken the rest of the hospital.

A security guard stepped off the elevator and lumbered toward them. Bets wrapped both her arms tightly around Deborah and whispered "shhhh, shhhh, shhhh" into the crown of her head. The man helped Callie up, settled her into a chair, and immediately a nurse knelt next to her, asking if she had any pain.

Deborah struggled against Bets. The old woman was not as strong as she'd been and she easily broke free and moved toward her mother. "I'm hurting. What about me?"

The security guard caught one of her flailing arms and twisted it behind her back. In a moment he'd secured her with plastic cinch cuffs. "I'm taking her outside," he said to nobody and everybody. Then he whispered into her ear, "Calm the fuck down. What are you trying to do causing a big scene like this? What are you thinking, messing up my hospital like that?"

She relaxed against his grip and nearly fell. She felt the energy drain out of her body and into the linoleum of the hospital, which smelled of the same industrial supply wax they'd used in Chowchilla.

Deborah and the security officer watched the sunrise on the bench in front of the hospital's circular driveway. Because the sun came up behind the northern Sierra Nevadas, the arrival of the sun always happened first in shadow. It was a cloudless day, and the sky didn't give them much of a show, transitioning from murky blue to orangey yellow with little gradation.

"Should be here any minute," the guard said.

They were waiting on the Kidron Police Department to send an officer out to take down a report of what had happened. The hospital wanted a record of the events so that it could file an insurance claim on the damage to the waiting room. "I don't think my mom will press charges," Deborah said, as much to herself as anyone.

The squad car's tires rubbed against the concrete curb with a squeaky wail as the officer pulled up. A small peach of a man in a brown uniform stepped out of the car. He was round and blond, closer to fifty than thirty, but still solidly middle-aged. His hair had a tinge of pink to it, which made Deborah think he could catch fire at any moment. His eyes were a muddy brown, and he had small Kewpie doll lips. He didn't look at her, but glad-handed the security guard.

They greeted each other with familiarity, and the guard explained the fight that had taken place a few hours earlier. When he questioned her, the officer stood a distance from Deborah. She was taller than him by half a foot, and she felt he was trying to maintain a sense of superiority over her. She tried to explain to him that they'd all been tired and overwhelmed by the emotional experience of the delivery. "I'm sure my mom will tell you it wasn't a big deal. Not big enough for these," Deborah said, lifting her hands as best she could. They'd remained tightly cuffed behind her back.

The small officer rocked back and forth on his heels. "You say you're on parole?"

Deborah felt her stomach heave. She nodded, trying to make herself appear smaller by dipping her knees and sagging her shoulders.

"Hmmm." He frowned and made note in a skinny notebook he pulled from his back pocket. "Lemme go see how much damage you've done." The officer hitched up his pants and entered the hospital.

"What were you in jail for?" the security guard asked.

"I killed my husband."

The guard slid away from her on the bench.

"Shot him with a gun I stole from my grandfather."

"You don't sound sorry about it," the guard said.

"I thought I was, but I think now what I am is sorry for all the other stuff that happened afterward."

"You're not helping yourself, you know that?"

She rose from the bench and paced the sidewalk. "You think I'm going back?"

The guard pried a piece of gum from the arm of the bench. "I'm not sure why you got out in the first place."

The doors to the hospital opened with a mechanical *whoosh*. Bets stepped out, shading her eyes against the early morning light. She addressed the guard briskly in the tone that many older women were able to use to successfully guilt younger people into action. "She's not fighting you anymore. Go on and let her out of those plastic restraints."

Using a utility knife from his pocket, the guard slit the plastic from her wrists. Deborah felt the cold of the blade against the back of her hand. Her arms were numb and felt useless dangling at her sides. Bets put her hand on the guard's shoulder and leaned down, speaking quietly. Although Deborah couldn't hear them, she heard the urging in Bets's voice and was unsurprised when the guard rose from the bench and announced his intentions to find some coffee and check on the policeman's progress upstairs.

"Being a mother is as full of tragedy as it is triumph," Bets said. "If I had to do it all over again, I'd put more distance between us. Having us here, always together, hasn't allowed for any fondness to grow between us. Callie and I've always had a difficult time. She was never the child I expected her to be and she's never forgiven me for letting her know that. I, I—"

"Grandma, this isn't your fault," Deborah said, her numb arms sharp with the pinpricks of pain as the circulation returned to normal.

"It is. She's the way she is because of me, and you two are just the wrong sort of fit. I don't understand how God could put two people together who consistently bring out the worst in each other."

"At least God gave me you," Deborah said, reaching her still tingling arms out.

They embraced. An ambulance with only its lights on pulled into the driveway and two paramedics unloaded an elderly man, who turned his head and gave them a watery smile as he rolled past them. Deborah became aware of the sounds of Kidron waking up—more cars hummed along the surface streets around the parking lot. A few of the nightshift nurses had gathered in the smoking cupola at the edge of the parking lot.

"Are you leaving?" Bets whispered into her ear.

"How bad is it?"

"Bad. The hospital administrator wants you arrested, but Anna talked Callie out of pressing any charges, and she told them she just fell over. If I weren't so old, they probably wouldn't have trusted leaving the two of us alone. But you know how easy it is to underestimate Anna or even myself."

Bets pressed her keys into Deborah's hand. "There's money in Anna's sock drawer and in the coffee can on top of the refrigerator. Callie never locks the safe in her office if you can get—"

"I'll be fine. Tell me about Erin's baby."

They stood together for several more minutes, and she listened to her grandmother describe the two perfect dimples on her grandson's cheeks and the way he crossed his fingers while he slept.

SELECTED E-MAILS EXCHANGED BETWEEN
CALLIOPE AND AMRIT

From: Amrit Hashmi a.hashmi@pittsburgh.edu
Subject: Congratulations and Condolences
Date: May 21, 2007 8:48:12 AM PST
To: Callie olivescallie@hotmail.com

Cham-Cham,
I would tell you that a fruit slips and falls into milk, but how can I explain this to you. It is to say that you must not think of your daughter's leaving as all bad. There is so much joy in your house now and we cannot always see the good that will come of actions that appear to be harmful.

How is the baby? I will have to admit that I, too, was hoping for a girl, but perhaps this little boy (Keller is it?) will prove me wrong, or right. Again I'm back to the fruit slipping into milk.

It is difficult for me to understand the relationship you have with your daughter. My wife and her mother were like sisters and I think even more so as we came to admit we were never going to have our own children. I once asked her if she'd gotten along with her mother when she was a teenager (you know we married when she was just nineteen, so she never knew much outside her parents' house) and she told me that all daughters fight with their mothers. So maybe you and Deborah are just reliving the fights you couldn't have because she's been away so long. I'm sure wherever she is that she's safe.

The research is going well, I think if we continue on the pace that we've set that I should be back for a follow-up visit in early July. I know we've talked about this before, but you, your family, is turning out to be exactly what I needed for so long.

I am writing to you from work, or I'd be more bold in my declarations. The laboratory is too sterile and our visit in March feels so long ago. I will look forward to our conversation this evening, when I can be the other man. The Amrit who you bare your soul to.

xxA

From: Callie olivescallie@hotmail.com
Subject: RE: Congratulations and Condolences
Date: May 22, 2007 7:21:45 PM EST
To: Amrit Hashmi a.hashmi@pittsburgh.edu

Darling,

If you were here I wouldn't have so much trouble getting out of bed every day. (Or maybe I would, but at least it would be for a good reason.) Nobody here knows what to say to anyone—especially Erin. She had such hopes that having her mother here would solve all of her problems. I guess it is better for her to realize she needs to work out the situation with Keller's father head-on and stop dodging his phone calls.

The baby is perfect. I wish you'd had children, then you'd understand what I mean when I tell you how much peace holding a newborn can give you. Erin thinks he cries so loud and nearly panics each time he opens his mouth, but his cry is so small and unselfish, that listening to it makes me feel better. Like I understand that he's just crying out for food or because he wants to be warm or held and that's sort of why we're all crying. Or at least why I'm crying.

I haven't been able to face the Pit. I tried yesterday to go in. You'll laugh at me if I tell you that it's just too cold, but for us Californians it is. There's so much that Nancy won't take care of if I'm not there. The place will get dirty, and she has no idea how much the money that Deb stole is going to hurt the store. I should try to put it back myself, but I don't have it and I can't ask Anna for it. I know I should be able to, but I don't want her or Bets to know what my daughter did. It was bad enough that I couldn't just let her be, that I had to pick a fight with her.

I wish I could be the woman you thought I was and I wish you'd tell me what a cham-cham is or at least promise to show me when you come back to Kidron.

xxC

From: Amrit Hashmi a.hashmi@pittsburgh.edu
Subject: letter
Date: May 23, 2007 10:32:19 AM PST
To: Callie olivescallie@hotmail.com

Cham-Cham,
Your letter arrived yesterday. I cannot begin to write down all the ways that I feel about you, but please know that it is more than my interest in your family. My lovely Padra who died so many years ago never had what we had. You must understand that, your husband, too, gave you some but not everything. I am overwhelmed by the emotion and I don't trust myself to even say this to you on the phone. My first wife and I, we were strangers when we met and we had the passion of youth on our side that blinded us to how little other connection we felt.

But you, with your letter. I won't write it, but to answer your question, yes we have so much more together than I've ever had before. And as much as I want to be with you, there is work to be done. Important work, research that will change so much for you and your life. I can see the message light on my phone blinking and the e-mail will not stop dinging at me. I will see you soon and we will have a heart talk. One that will explain what is between us.

xxA

From: Callie olivescallie@hotmail.com
Subject: too long
Date: May 27, 2007 9:58:43 PM EST
To: Amrit Hashmi a.hashmi@pittsburgh.edu

Darling,
Every night after we talk, I think of a dozen other things that I should have said to you. It is sweet to hear your voice, but it all feels so insubstantial. I lied earlier. I didn't get out of bed the entire day. I said it so that you wouldn't think me weak, but I just took my pills and drifted in and out of sleep. I reread the letters you've

sent me and I looked at all the magazines in the house. My mother tried to get me out of bed. She started nice in the morning with homemade cinnamon rolls, but by the time she went to bed, she had resorted to idle threats. Anna told her to leave me alone.

Tell me more about the sequencing. I don't understand any of it, but I do hope that some good comes from it. If not for us, then for somebody else. Do they have some disease that our DNA could cure? Do children age rapidly like that dumb movie with Robin Williams? Can you cure that? I should try to understand more of what you're doing.

Please come soon.

xxC

From: Amrit Hashmi a.hashmi@pittsburgh.edu
Subject: research
Date: May 30, 2007 6:13:29 AM PST
To: Callie olivescallie@hotmail.com

Cham-Cham,

Forgive me for not responding earlier. As I said on the phone, there is so much to be done before I can come for my visit and explain it all to you better. You maybe know about ambrosia? It is a drink for the gods that the Greeks said if man took even a sip of he could attain immortality. We have an Indian word for this drink—it is *amrit*. A common enough name, but one picked by my parents for sentimental reasons. They told me that the best way to ensure immortality was by having children. My mother used to take my face in her delicate hands and kiss me all over—declaring that I was the perfect mix of my father and her and that it was my job to make my own children who would be a mix of my parents and also of me and my wife.

But you know about this sorrow. There were no children. We found out that I could never give Padra the babies she wanted when we were in Spain and I had first started working with this idea that an organism could achieve biological immortality.

You can see where this is going. There are so many little steps from you and your family to ambrosia. But I believe it is possible. I know that if we can figure out why people age and why some people age far slower than others, that we can find a way to extend our lives. Do not tell anyone this. The study of aging is so new and fraught with moral dilemmas. To others I talk about cures for the diseases of age, but we all know, we all understand, that if we can cure the things that kill people, then we can cure death itself.

I could tell you so much more about sirtuins and the keys they hold to keeping our cells young, or about the idea that so much of what goes wrong in the body is completely attributed to inflammation. But what good will that do you? What I want to do is good old-fashioned science. I want to study you and your mother and her mother and find out what makes you age so slowly. Maybe it is proteins or maybe it is some mechanism that we haven't found yet, or don't have the capability to find, but that is what I'm doing, what I'm looking for.

I miss you with all my heart.

xxA

Calliope in Summer

CHAPTER TWENTY-THREE

Sole Survivor

A full month passed before Calliope set foot in the Pit Stop. She tried in the days just after Deb's escape to return to the store, but every time she worked up enough energy, the cold stopped her dead. Nothing made her leg hurt more than chilly weather. That excuse and others allowed her to spend weeks sitting with Erin and her baby boy, Keller, on the porch, watching the north wind stir the leaves in the orchard. At first, Anna and Bets tiptoed around them, but gradually their patience waned. She and Erin made promises to each other. "If I wake up and can't see my breath, I'll . . ." they'd say and rattle off a list of all that had been left undone. Nature gave them until mid-June, when the sun finally warmed up and the talk in Kidron turned from Deb's escape to fruit set.

The warmth rejuvenated Calliope—her smiles came easier, and she needed fewer pills to control the pain in her leg. After two or three sunny mornings, she began to wake up buoyed by the possible. With this attitude, she arrived at the Pit Stop well before Nancy, who'd been acting as manager during Calliope's absence.

The morning sun streaming into the front windows exposed a film of filth that had settled over much of the store. The Pit Stop needed a good cleaning. Calliope examined each square foot, making note of the grime between jars, dust underneath shelving, and scuff marks on the linoleum flooring.

"I see you took the poster down," Nancy said as Calliope inspected the few cobwebs that occupied the front corners of the store. At the request of the police, Nancy had put the wanted poster with Deb's picture up in the window. If Calliope had been there, it wouldn't have gone up, but Nancy often mistook herself for the owner and made decisions that weren't hers to make. She was sure she'd eventually find an excuse to hang the posters back up.

"It felt right," Calliope said, rubbing away the last traces of tape on the window with her fingernail. "She's never going to be found."

"Nobody's looking all that hard. She not only broke her parole, she stole from us. Do you know how much she took? How much was in that safe? What'd you tell the police—some smaller number, I'm sure," Nancy said, putting on the glasses that hung from a chain around her neck. The cashier, although she was the same age as Calliope, managed to look years older.

"We told the police everything we could. Erin's taken her mother leaving again hard. She hasn't left the house in weeks, and then I keep finding her asleep in the living room, the baby at her nipple and an atlas open on her lap. She'd give the world to not have had her momma run, and a little more to at least find out where she's gone to."

"That granddaughter of yours has been through too much for one lifetime," Nancy said.

"I should have warned her about Deb—about how you can't let someone else failing to live up to your expectations ruin you. I spent most of my life feeling like I was somehow responsible for my daughter, that I was as guilty of killing Carl as she was. And then when she ran, somehow this time she took all of that guilt I had with her. I just worry she left some of it behind with Erin."

"She's got the baby now. That should help," Nancy said, looking over the top of her glasses in a way that made Calliope feel like the pain pills were letting her mouth run on. Nancy had been around a long time, and Calliope was sure she had her own thoughts about the Keller women.

"Do you feel that way about your grandbabies?" Calliope knew asking this was mean. Nancy didn't have any children of her own. She hadn't married until she was in her late fifties, but her husband, an Elvis impersonator, had six or seven kids of his own.

"We feel how we feel," Nancy said, with a tremble in her voice that could have been emotion or the suppression of a cough.

Calliope nodded. Nancy's stepchildren were all bastards, born by women stupid enough to think that sleeping with a man who looked like Elvis was near enough to the real deal. Nancy treated all his kids like they were hers, but they didn't always reciprocate. Over the years, she'd seen Nancy try to make amends for her husband, spending most of her salary on gifts for them and the grandchildren. Mr. Elvis, as Calliope thought of him, was retired now and only put on the jumpsuit to do a monthly show at the American Legion up in Redding.

"How are things with you and the doctor?" Nancy asked, as if sensing Calliope's thoughts had turned to relationships. In the years since Calliope's husband had died, Nancy had become a confidante. The cashier knew about the few flings, one-night stands, and affairs that Calliope had gotten herself mixed up in over the years. She heard details Calliope was too ashamed to share with her family, especially her mother. Bets's morality was rigid and passionless. Nancy, despite being reserved, listened to Calliope's confessions as if they were teenagers. And yet, this time, Calliope held back many of the juiciest details of her relationship with Amrit.

She and Amrit had made love on the night he first arrived in Kidron. From the moment she'd heard his voice on the phone, Calliope had known she would sleep with him. Seeing him, that first day, sitting near him on their too-soft couch that rolled people toward one another, heightened her desire. During their excruciatingly polite lunch conversation, she'd elicited his room number and then after her mother and Anna had finally gone to bed, she drove to the motel, put on a fresh coat of lipstick, slipped on four-inch heels, and knocked on his door. She never once considered the possibility of rejection.

Amrit had been married for thirty years to a dutiful wife. They'd had no children, and she'd died quite unexpectedly from an aneurism the year she turned fifty. He told Calliope this and more after the fifth time they'd made love. That day he'd confessed that he and his wife had never been together unless they were in their own bed with the lights off. Calliope laughed, and then realizing that he might misunderstand her joy, she took his hand and confessed that although she'd been with too many men in too many places, what she felt with him was entirely different. While they spoke, he traced the outline her hardened nipple made against her thin silk blouse, and before their stories were finished, they'd undressed and made love in the front seat of his rental car in an abandoned field with a view of Mount Shasta.

The passion Calliope experienced with Amrit made what she'd felt for her own husband, and for the other men she'd slept with, seem like mere excitement. After he returned to Pittsburgh, she found she couldn't drive anyplace without getting lost. Landmarks she'd used her whole life to mark intersections took on new shapes to her eyes. The elm at the corner of C Street and Polk now looked like two trees twined together, and the house with the blue door at the corner of Main and F Street seemed to morph from a two-story ranch to a slatternly Colonial in the space of just a few days.

The relationship was more than physical. He'd called while the plane was moving from the runway to the gate and told Calliope he thought he'd fallen in love with her. Still, she'd not confessed this to her mother or grandmother, or even Erin, who she thought, now, would have understood the relationship. She'd visited him twice so far, both times making up excuses about wanting to see two of her children who lived in the Northeast. She'd flown into New York to spend Christmas and a few days with her eldest son's family and then claimed she needed to attend a conference in Pittsburgh, so she could spend the rest of the week with Amrit. In March, she'd flown to D.C. to visit her middle son and claimed an allergy to a cat so she could stay in a hotel in Alexandria with Amrit, who drove down to meet her.

Before her relationship with Amrit, Calliope could never understand how her daughter could have loved her husband more than her own child. But what Amrit awakened inside of Calliope made her aware of the possibility of such selfishness. There were times, like when they were in the hotel elevator and she couldn't stop herself from pressing against him until they were both breathless. At that moment, getting caught didn't matter, being embarrassed didn't matter—she needed him too much to stop. But Deb was gone, and she'd never get the chance to explain to her daughter that she was finally beginning to understand why she shot Carl.

There was no one else to tell. She felt that if she kept it to herself, it would be safe. Nancy, because she was privy to Calliope's affairs, was dangerous. She feared that if she told Nancy any of the truth of her feelings, that the woman would somehow make her feel foolish, point out that there was no difference between Amrit and the contractor she'd slept with a few years ago, who'd only wanted to convince her to sell the Pit Stop to his brother so he could replace it with a Jack in the Box franchise. So Calliope had told her own family almost nothing, and admitted to Nancy only that Amrit was something new for her old bones.

Nancy took her glasses off and said, "It is difficult to stay in love over long distances." She spoke in such a way that Calliope began to wonder why her cashier had married late and who she'd loved before she found Mr. Elvis.

"Who mentioned love?" Calliope asked.

Their conversation was interrupted when a young family came into the store, filling the place with conversation. Calliope smiled at Nancy and then went to the storeroom, calling out to her stock boys as she went, "Roberto. Pedro."

They stopped stacking boxes and shuffled to her. She motioned for them to follow her and started to explain to them in Spanish about the mess. She wasn't fluent, and as she walked she stumbled over the words. She felt her mind spin, like loose gears, and then catch when she found the first word she needed. *Sucios.* Filthy.

She stopped to point out the grime that was apparent on the nearly empty shelves and leaned heavily against one of the poles that distributed the weight of the roof. She'd gone too long between Vicodins, and the throbbing that had been present since she woke had turned into a stabbing pain. The older boy looked at his younger brother and then cleared his throat.

"We can speak English, if that's easier for you," he said. His brother nodded.

"And honestly we'd be happier if you called us Robert and Pete. My friends call me Petey, but I don't like that so much."

His brother laughed and punched his arm. "You should call him Petey."

The muscles in Calliope's thigh began to strain to keep her upright. Most people didn't understand her pain. They were used to healing—to scar tissue knitting itself over wounds and the gradual ebb of pain. The tissue in her leg, after the crash, became infected.

The doctors kept carving off bits of her calf, claiming to have gotten the last remnants of dying tissue and muscle, only to have to go back weeks later and take more. When they were done, there was a fist-size concavity on the outside of her lower leg. The pain had never ebbed.

"It's okay if you want to speak to us in Spanish," said the younger boy. He looked worried, and Calliope thought that she must be grimacing.

"I didn't realize," she said, trying to recall what her backroom manager had said when he suggested he hire the boys. "When Juan hired you—"

"Keep speaking Spanish to Juan. His English is awful," Robert said.

"And he evidently can't keep a clean store either." She sent Pete to get a bucket of soapy water and showed his brother how dirt hid in the crescents of space between the jars and cans.

"They should make rectangle containers," the boy said, grabbing a rag from his brother.

She took a stack of inventory logs to her office, which was an elevated space near the front of the store. Calliope was short and had spent her life looking between people in crowds. After her husband, Greg, died, she'd had the walls, which used to go to the ceiling, lowered. The Pit Stop had been his idea, the location hers. In her childhood, the building had housed a Lucky's. Greg never liked that no matter what they did to the place that it still felt like a grocery store, but Calliope always felt at home there. By the time she reached the office, she could no longer hide her limp. She pushed the swing-gate set into the half-walls that surrounded her office and eased into her ergonomic chair. There was a small supply of pills in her desk. She fished one out and swallowed it dry.

From the space, she could see the entire store. The tasting bar took up the middle portion of the store, and the aisles around it were divided by country of origin, with the largest section devoted to California and, specifically, Kidron. The far corner of the store housed a small lunch counter, and around the perimeter of the store were the novelty items—olive soap, olive wood, postcards, and kitschy olive-serving devices. They didn't sell as well as the olives themselves, but the markup on them was high. Plus, many of the items were from local artisans, and she sold those on commission. Louisa Ramirez, with her olive wood roses, did well for herself. She had to come in every three days or so to restock the delicate flowers. Lucy Talbot's *Olive You* platters weren't doing so well. Calliope couldn't remember the last time she'd sold one. She'd have to consider offering Louisa some of Lucy's space.

The truth was that in the last few years, the Pit Stop had become a money pit. The spring storms had been especially bad for business. The rain kept those on I-5 in their cars—stopping only for gas and a quick spin through a drive-thru for lunch. On years when the winds from the south were gentle and the flowers stayed on the trees, visitors felt they had time to spend. They drove along the streets near the orchards and lingered in Calliope's store, asking questions about olives and growing techniques, and always those conversations led to purchases.

It used to be there were very few retail places to get specialty olive oils and products, but the Internet had made what Calliope had to offer less exclusive. She sometimes saw customers scan a bottle of oil with their phones to compare prices. She'd lost contracts with some of the local suppliers, who now found it more lucrative to sell their olives themselves. Despite all of this, she couldn't shake the feeling that a turnaround was coming. What was it they said? There are no second acts in life? Well, Calliope knew for a fact that the women in her family not only got second acts, but sometimes even thirds.

While waiting for her laptop to start, she flipped idly through the front section of the *San Francisco Examiner*. She sold copies at the store, and the out-of-date ones were always laid on her desk. The news was no different than it had been before Deb's escape. It was like betting on all the horses at the track; the paper had no idea what would retain its importance, and so it reported on elections that would be forgotten and businesses that would close. The story, the one that would change Calliope's history, was tiny—just the briefest mention in the columns of a section entitled "News Around the World." Hong Wu, the oldest living person in the world, had died two days earlier at home in the Shinxing province. His daughter, the article stated, was inconsolable.

"Anna's the oldest," she shouted. The boys, who were elbow deep in soapy water cleaning the shelves, looked up at her. Nancy shook her head and said, "I'll be."

CHAPTER TWENTY-FOUR

Origins

"Do you believe in miracles?" Calliope asked Anna the next morning.

"What's not to believe," Anna said. She stood up, twisted side to side at the waist and then bent down and touched her toes. "Used to be I could do the splits, but my bladder isn't what it was when I was a hundred."

Erin laughed, and at the sound of his mother's voice, the baby tried to mimic what he'd heard. Bobo responded with short high yelps.

"It's like a circus in here," Calliope said, shifting uncomfortably in the deep couch. Next to her, Bets, in an uncommon gesture, put her arm around Calliope's shoulder and pulled her close. They slid together, pushed by the couch, and for a moment, she felt like a girl curled up on her mother's lap.

"Makes it feel like a home again," Bets said.

Calliope let herself be enveloped by the warmth of her mother's love. Their relationship had borne too many strains over the years, and such intimacy was rare between them. The truth was, for the first time in Calliope's life, Hill House was beginning to feel like home. Over the last few weeks, she had started to believe in miracles. The news about Anna not only had the potential to save the store, but it was also sure to bring Amrit back to Kidron. It had been many years since so much had gone so right for Calliope.

"I've got something to show you," she said, pushing herself off the couch.

"Don't tell me you can do the splits," groaned Erin. "I'm still recovering from childbirth and shouldn't be subjected to old ladies running circles around me."

"We're not all old," Bets said. "Just Anna."

Laughter echoed around the living room and followed Calliope down the hall. She couldn't remember the last time her mother had been in a joking mood. The bottle of oil, which she'd lovingly wrapped the night before, stood on her nightstand. She couldn't wait to share her plan with Anna and with the others. She closed her bedroom door, and out of habit, knocked twice on the frame for good luck. *Don't want it too much,* she thought. The women were still giggling when Calliope walked back into the room, and she felt like joining in their revelry. She called out to Erin and then slid into a near perfect center split.

"Once a cheerleader, always a cheerleader," she said.

"What is that?" Anna asked, pointing to the bottle. "Champagne?"

"No. It's your oil." Calliope placed the bottle in Anna's hand.

"Mine, huh?" Anna said, struggling to untie the delicately curled ribbon that held the paper in place.

Calliope was as obsessed as Anna with longevity, but unlike her grandmother, she needed explanations. How was it possible that Anna could still hear so well, or that she was able to walk unaided? Her yellow-brown eyes were rimmed in red, but her sight was strong enough to scan the headlines in the newspaper. "For years I've watched how carefully you strip the trees of the last of their fruit and press the oil. I know there's something to it, something you may not even know yourself."

"So much of what I do is just out of habit," Anna said.

"But those habits, those are what keep you so youthful," Calliope said.

"There's nothing special about me," Anna said, sliding the bottle from its bag.

"There is. There's something special about all of us." Everyone turned their eyes toward her, and their expectation made Calliope backtrack. "I mean, I just feel like there has to be or why else would Amrit have come so far to study us?"

"I don't think we should make too much of this," Bets said. Erin disagreed with her, and the two argued back and forth for several minutes.

Calliope took some satisfaction in knowing her mother would soon be proved wrong. Finding out why the Keller women were special had brought Amrit, and now it might even be able to bring much more. Her instincts told her that Hong Wu's death was just the beginning. Once the press met Anna and discovered their family's beautiful unbroken line of firstborns that stretched over six generations, people would be clamoring to find out their secrets. That was the way the world worked—people wanted explanations for the oddities in the world. They wanted to know what made supercentenarians able to live so long.

Before Hong Wu, the title had changed hands every few months and during one brutally hot summer in 2002 the title of world's oldest person had been held by fourteen different people. And then she discovered Jeanne Calment, the *doyenne de l'humanité,* as her French countrymen called her. She'd held the title for nearly a decade and when she finally died at age one hundred and twenty-two, she also held the title of oldest person ever. This "elder of humanity" had lived an extraordinary life. When Jeanne was thirteen, she sold Vincent van Gogh a fistful of colored pencils when he came to her father's fabric shop. She remembered the painter as a dirty, smelly, disagreeable man and found his work to be of a similar nature. By the time she was in her eighties, she'd outlived all of her family, including her grandson, who died in a motorcycle accident, and her husband, who ate a dessert topped with canned cherries that were later found to contain botulism. Jeanne had eaten the same dessert herself but was only mildly sick from the canned fruit. In reading about this extraordinary woman, Calliope was fascinated by two items. The first was the way in which the press celebrated her. Once she became the oldest living person, reporters from as far away as China showed up in the small French town. She entertained them with witticisms, like "I've only got one wrinkle and I'm sitting on it." She gave advice. "He who hugs too much, hugs badly." She philosophized. "I've been forgotten by a good God." She was their darling, and what she said delighted them. Her accounts of history were given more weight than any text, and it was said that the press would take her version of the construction of the Eiffel Tower over Mr. Eiffel's own written words if it came to that. Calliope, who'd had her own brush with celebrity in the aftermath of the plane crash, envied the decade-long thrall Jeanne held over the press.

The second item that Calliope paid particularly close attention to was Jeanne's prescription for longevity. It included the usual tropes about enjoying life, living for the future and not the past, but in addition, Jeanne gleefully told reporters that she enjoyed three vices every day—one unfiltered cigarette, one glass of port, and a piece of chocolate—and that she was able to wash all these evils out of her body with a big dose of olive oil. She not only cooked with it, but she also used it as a moisturizer for her face, and every night before bed, she swallowed a tablespoon of it.

Taken together, these two facts made Calliope realize her family was sitting on a potential gold mine. For the last thirty years, the Keller women had sold their olives to a neighboring orchard that processed them for canning. In exchange for the olives, the neighbor took care of the orchard and gave them 60 percent of what he made after his labor costs. It was enough money for Anna and Bets to take care of themselves and the house, including the cost of Frank's care. However, there were always olives left behind, and in a good year a grower, especially one wanting to use the olives for oil, could leave the fruit on the trees through January. Most years, after the harvest was finished in November, Anna would wander into the orchard and glean what she could—using those olives and her father's handpress to make her own oil. This *olio nuovo,* as the Italians called it, was revered for its bright, peppery taste and health properties. This year, while everyone else had been preoccupied with Deb's parole hearing, Calliope had hired a few locals to strip the orchard bare of the leftover olives.

Olive oil is notoriously tricky and *olio nuovo* is even more volatile. She'd arranged to have the oil pressed at one of the facilities on the outskirts of Kidron the day after the harvest, which coincidentally had been the day Deb was up for parole. If she'd not had them pressed immediately, there was a danger of fermentation. Once the oil was pressed, it was filtered into large steel drums and left in a cool dark cellar to settle. No matter how fine the sieve, there were always bits of olives that slipped through during the pressing, and fresh olive oil, like the sort Anna pressed, had to be consumed quickly. Fresh-pressed oil was more green than gold, with an aftertaste of pepper. The oil took on a gold hue after it settled. In late March she tasted the settled oil to make sure nothing had gone wrong in the process. There was always a chance of an oil turning during settling, a chance that the bright bite of fresh oil would turn to a fustiness as it settled, or worse that the room would not have stayed cool enough and she'd have gallons and gallons of rancid oil.

Her oil, which she'd been calling Sixth Generation, was beautiful, with an assertive olive flavor with a hint of pepper and a buttery finish with a bright, almost citrus note. She hired the stock boys, Robert and Petey, to help her bottle the oil and attach the labels advertising the oil as a special family blend from the Keller Orchards. By the time the baby was due, Calliope had more than five hundred bottles at the ready. Her plan was to present the oil as a gift to everyone when Erin had her baby. But then Deb pulled her disappearing act, and Calliope's plans for the oil had gone with her daughter.

Like all fats, olive oil has a tendency to turn rancid. She had, at most, until the beginning of fall before the oil would go bitter and be good for nothing more than fire-starter. Before they had electricity at Hill House, Anna and her mother, Mims, used rancid oil for light. Anna said they gave off light that was almost as bright as what you got from whale oil, but that the edges of the light were blue and afterward the air tasted like olives.

In the living room, the women had turned their attention back to the bottle. Anna moved the bottle around in her hand and ran her fingers over the embossing on the gold label.

Bets got off the couch and moved to where she could peer over Anna's shoulder. "So, you've actually done it."

"It's already on display at the store, and I've brought you over a dozen bottles to pass around when the media come calling," Calliope said.

"Media?" asked Erin.

"Of course."

"—Now we don't need to start that already," Bets said.

Calliope ignored her mother and kept speaking, turning so that she faced Anna.

"It's your oil," Calliope said. "I mean, not exactly, but I had it pressed from the olives in our orchard, and I can tell you there was nothing left to glean this year."

"How extraordinary," Anna said. "It looks so expensive. I'm used to just pouring it out of that old wine bottle I keep in the back of the cupboard. This is too much."

"No." Calliope worked hard to restrain her excitement. "The oil is what's going to save the store. You'll see. We can put it out when the reporters come and then you can talk about how you have the oil every day. I think—"

"What exactly is your plan?" Bets asked, talking over Calliope.

"People are going to want to buy this, and where there's demand and limited supply, there's money to be made." Calliope turned to face her mother. "I know you don't—"

"I don't want to hear about this foolishness. I've been worrying about you and that store for months. You are living in some other world."

"Grandma Bets," Erin said. The baby started to squirm in her arms.

Bets closed her mouth and compressed her lips until they were a thin line of disapproval.

"I can't believe they'd actually send anyone out to interview me," Anna said. "Maybe they would have years ago before there was the Internet and phones that you can see the person you are talking to, but I'm afraid the world has moved past people like me. Poor Hong Wu got no more than a paragraph."

"They'll come," Calliope said. She was sure of it. What Anna said was true, but she also knew that their family had more story than Hong Wu. They were more than a flash in the pan. Amrit had told her as much the last time they spoke about his research.

"How much are you going to charge?" Bets asked. She'd taken the baby from Erin and returned to her seat on the couch. Erin stood in front of the bay window and stretched, arching her back and leaning from side to side.

"Fifty dollars an ounce."

"That's insane," Erin said, almost laughing.

Anna laughed, too, but she seemed to understand what Calliope was driving at. "You underestimate the fear of dying. People will give all they got to buy a few extra years. That's what Callie's selling. Years, not oil."

CHAPTER TWENTY-FIVE

Frank

Twice a week Calliope visited her father at the facility. In the beginning she'd accompanied her mother on her daily trips to see him, but that had been too difficult for everyone. He was easily frustrated, and trying to figure out who two people were and why they'd come to visit was enough agitation to send him into restraints for the rest of the day. Also, when she and her mother were alone together, they had nothing to say to each other. The coldness had intensified since their disagreement about the oil, and what Calliope wanted most was to be able to talk to her father about her mother. He used to know all the secrets to thawing out Bets, but now he didn't even remember who his wife was.

Driving from Hill House through Kidron, she began to think of a way that she could unlock her father's memory—if not of her mother, then of the orchard. Anna's father had shown Frank most of his secrets, and it was only the two of them who knew the species and crossbreeds that made up the varieties of fruit in the orchard. It would be greedy of her to expect another miracle, and yet it didn't keep her from hoping that her father would have a moment of lucidity. She wanted more knowledge about the olives, some bit of information to feed to the reporters. No matter what Bets said, they were coming. Calliope believed it.

She tried to see Kidron as outsiders would. There existed a haze of ruin over many of the buildings. Lots of the stucco houses were missing bits of plaster, leaving the chicken wire framing to show through. Others were covered with splotches of yellowing water stains. The hitching posts along the main sidewalks had all been painted primary colors as part of the town's centennial celebration seven years earlier. Their garish brightness drew attention to the colorlessness of the rest of the city. Her home was a dry, dusty town with too many people on the other side of fifty.

They'd lost the hospital about fifteen years earlier, but Golden Sunsets kept building additions and annexing property until it stood alone on a block near the edge of town, which had once been considered Kidron's medical district. The facility's sole architectural feature was that each wing had been painted a different tone of yellow. She guessed the intended effect had been to evoke a sunset, but in reality it looked like a day care, which she supposed in a way it was. Her father had been a resident for two decades.

He managed to look old and young at the same time. His white hair was exactly as it had been his whole life, thick and bold, and his facial expressions were those of a young man in his prime. His body seemed strong and he moved more easily than most of the other patients, but his skin was leathery and covered in age spots. It hung off his arms and chin and cheeks, where the fat deposits had just melted away.

"Frank," she said and held her hand out to him with her palm down. She'd learned from earlier visits that calling him Daddy, as she longed to do, only upset him.

"*Ma chérie,*" he said, his lips grazing the backs of her knuckles. These were the sorts of affectations he'd acquired since moving to the home. Such changes made Calliope suspect that he had wanted a different life.

It was early and he'd not fully dressed for the day. Around his neck he wore a dark purple scarf as if it were an ascot. "You look well," she said.

"What news have you come with today?" Frank asked, leaning forward in his recliner.

His ears were long and the lobes wobbled when he talked. "Plenty of gossip around Hill House," Calliope said, pulling her chair closer.

"Ahhh, the Keller women. They're always getting into trouble." His eyes brightened at the mention of the house; he never failed to remember it.

She told him about Anna being the oldest and about the oil—changing enough of the details that he wouldn't connect it to himself. Time had stopped for her father and she'd learned it was dangerous to remind him of his current age. Still, she wanted so badly to make him understand about the Sixth Generation oil. She needed someone to take her side, and her father even when she was little took her side.

The year she turned twelve, she clung to him like a burr on a dog's coat—desperately afraid that she wouldn't be allowed to roam the groves once she became a woman. Her mother had been on the lookout for the change in Calliope that summer, prompting her to stay out of Bets's reach. A few weeks into June, to keep the peace, her father put her to work grafting branches of a new species of olive that could be used to produce oil onto an acre of Anna's trees. The habit of taking her into the groves carried over into August, and by the end of the summer at the end of a long day, they would emerge from the groves together, with Calliope riding piggyback. Her brothers were either working for pay on the Lindseys' orchard or too little to be of any use.

"I worked in that orchard," Frank said when she described the trees that she'd taken her olives from to make the oil. "I used to carry my little girl around with me and feed her bits of jerky I kept in my overall pockets."

"Yes," Calliope said, drawing in her breath.

"You were my daughter's teacher, right? Or maybe the boys'? Did you have the boys in your class? They're all away at school now and my little girl flies airplanes."

The boys had never come back from college. They moved to the towns where their wives grew up and put down roots deep enough to keep them out of Kidron. They were in their sixties now. The youngest, Johnny, had been killed in Vietnam. Every few Christmases, Bets and Calliope visited them, but they were always ready with excuses to keep them from coming home to Kidron. Calliope thought it was because they didn't love their father—Frank was harsh with them.

"Your daughter? She's a flight attendant?" She tried to keep her voice even. It was greedy of her to ask, but she was desperate for a connection to her father.

"Flight attendant? I think they just call it a stewardess. But I'll tell you she's smart enough to fly that whole plane. The only thing she loves more than flying is the orchard."

"Tell me about the orchard," she said. The time she spent at her father's elbow gave her the ability to lose herself in the vineyard. She often felt as if she were treading on holy ground when she was in the grove, stepping into the shaded spots among the trees. Calliope left Kidron behind when she walked the orchard—felt that she was translated to some higher plane where the world was as expansive as space and the fruit of the trees was as innumerable as the stars in the sky.

Listening to her father speak, she heard him describe the same feeling. Gratitude overwhelmed her—this gift of his had kept her sane the last forty years she'd been confined to Kidron. She was sure her mother married Frank because he knew how to make their family's olive orchard better. Before his family arrived in Kidron, they'd worked the trees in Italy. The summer before she went to flight school, he had finished grafting the farthest corner of the orchard with Bouteillans. No one believed that olive oil was worth producing. That had been the idea early on in Kidron, to produce olive oil, but the first settlers soon discovered that the olives that grew well there didn't produce enough oil to make their investment pay off, and no matter how effectively they worked, how many efficiencies they adopted, they couldn't price their oil lower than it could be imported.

He stopped talking and looked at her closely. "I'm a terrible host. You've come to me for advice. I've just talked on and on and never once asked you what your problem was."

Calliope told him about how people wanted California oil now. How table olives were out of fashion and many of the orchard owners were playing catch-up and just now grafting oil-producing varieties onto their stock. Calliope described this new breed of American who cared about buying local, pesticide-free products. He reached over and picked up her hand. He held it like they were both children. The intimate gesture was devoid of intent. Calliope stopped talking and looked closely at her father, hoping for a glimmer of recognition in his eyes. Occasionally this happened, but he was never in the present. If he recognized her, it would be from a time before he started to forget. There was no familiarity.

"There's money in oil," he said.

"No one's ever found oil in this part of California," Calliope said.

He laughed, and it was like rain after a dry, dusty summer.

"That's a good one. You're a sharp lady. Sharp enough that I'll tell you my secret." He put his head close to hers. "Bouteillans. I've got acres of them over on my wife's land. Best cultivar for oil. Thirty-five percent yield, and they're big enough for table production if you don't want to wait for the oil. Of course, no one believes me because even for Bouteillans, that's too high. I used to think I'd invented a new breed, but I had some young guy from the agriculture college come out and test 'em. They were just what I said they were. I guess it's the land or the trees that makes them special. I never could tell. I'll cut you some if you want to graft some of your acreage."

"Liquid gold," she said.

Her father smiled. His shock of white hair, which he kept swept back and was quite vain about, fell over his eyes. "There's a trick to it though. You can't harvest in October; you have to wait sometimes until Christmas or maybe even as late as New Year's. And if you get an especially cold snap in October, then the oil production will be through the roof."

This much she knew from watching him work in the orchard all those years. One of her favorite memories was tied to this late harvest. She tried to get him to speak of it. "I remember one of your kids telling me about your oil. They found bottles of it in their stockings?"

Frank narrowed his eyes. She didn't know if it was because he was suspicious of her or because he couldn't remember. "Wasn't us. Oil spoils too quickly. Sounds like a fool thing to do. We put oranges in the kids' stockings, filled out the toe better than anything else."

She remembered the oranges. She'd hoped he'd tell her about that first Christmas when the Bouteillans were ripe enough to harvest. He'd had to glean what was left after the harvest in the fall because Anna had refused to let him keep a full crop on the trees. Christmas eve, she'd watch as her father, as prideful as he'd been when one of his sons was born, set up an elaborate tasting of his oil for their mother.

She tried again. "Can you tell where the oil came from by tasting it?"

Frank's eyes darted around the room. "Why are you asking me about oil? I thought you were here to see if I'm fit to go on outings."

She'd lost him. This happened quickly with her father—a look out the window or a question that made his brain work too hard could reset him. She was someone new to him now. She knew enough, had been in the situation often enough, to recognize the best option was to leave as quickly as possible.

"You're fine, Mr. Wallace. I'll tell Dolores that you are healthy enough to leave for the occasional day trip." She extended her hand to him, and he rose to shake it.

"Guy will be so pleased. He's wanted for ages to go to the casino."

Frank followed Calliope out of his room and called loudly for Guy. She stopped and talked with Dolores at the front desk and watched her father greet his friend with a kiss on either cheek. Guy, who'd had a stroke, was in a wheelchair, and he reached up to Frank for a hug. "They're getting close," she said to Dolores.

"It's nice that they've found each other. They're so much alike and I gotta say Guy was pretty depressed until he met your father. He's good with him, calms him down."

"Dad said he wanted permission to go on a trip. Do I need to sign anything?"

"Naw. Your mom took care of it when she was in here earlier."

"So, she knows about Guy?" Calliope asked.

The nurse shrugged. "Who knows anything these days?"

What Calliope remembered about that particular Christmas eve was that her mother had never come home. Before Johnny was born, Bets disappeared a couple of nights a month. Frank called it running out. She remembered that year her father had laid out finger-size bowls of different olive oils and pieces of bread. "Got a treat for your momma," he'd said after he finished reciting *'Twas the Night Before Christmas* from memory and tucking the children into bed. Calliope told him she was worried, and he leaned close and whispered for her to say a prayer. "Your momma always comes back, but we can't give her everything she needs. That's why she runs out."

Calliope came down the stairs at midnight, but instead of sending her back up, he called her down and asked her if she was ready for an adventure. There were five bowls of oil on the table. He had her taste each one, talking about the different qualities of the olives. Some were fruity and others bitter, like the rind of an orange. When they were done tasting, he asked her which one was his. She tapped one of the bowls on the table. Her father roared his disapproval. "Look at the color," he'd shouted. "That one's crap—the color of a muddy pond. Look at this one." He held up the bowl in the middle. "It looks like liquid gold."

Calliope thought the color was more like a beam of light coming through a cloud. She'd always wished she'd taken more time picking, remembered that the middle one had fruity undertones, while the rest of the samples tasted greasy or soapy and had the aftertaste of rot. But at that moment, she'd been so tired and all she wanted was to finish her father's test and go to sleep so she could wake up the next day and see her mother cooking pancakes.

Instead of sending her back to bed, he opened the hall closet and pulled the rope of a trapdoor that was hidden underneath the shoe rack. He handed her one present after another and told her to put them under the tree. Up until that moment, Calliope had still believed in Santa Claus.

CHAPTER TWENTY-SIX

Selling

*B*ets found Calliope alone in the kitchen cleaning the stove.

"Nobody sees those crumbs but you," Bets said.

It was the first time she'd spoken directly to Calliope in weeks. "The ants will find them and then we'll have to call that horrible pest company again," Calliope said.

"I'm not trying to start a fight. Why do you always do this?"

"Do what?"

"Think that every word out of my mouth, out of Deb's mouth, is somehow an attack on you?"

"I don't know what you're talking about," Calliope said, wiping the last of the crumbs into her hand and then leaning against the stove, taking the weight off her bad leg. Cleaning was like meditation to her. The smell of lemons and vinegar and the sight of a bare expanse of countertop unlocked her mind, allowed her to be open to ideas. Just now she'd decided to add olive oil to the tasting bar at the store. She glanced at her mother and saw that when she relaxed her face and thought no one was watching her, she looked to be on the verge of tears. This vulnerability was new to Bets. As a child, Calliope remembered Bets being strong and distant, like granite. Her eyes had the same black flecks.

"You okay?"

"It's been a long week. Knowing my mother's the oldest person alive makes me feel older."

Calliope raised her eyebrows at her mother. She'd felt invigorated by the news, it made her feel younger, and her life seemed to stretch out in front of her. If Anna were alive and well at one hundred and thirteen, then Calliope hadn't lived half her life yet. For the first time since she'd returned to Kidron after the accident, she felt like she had time to leave. It wasn't a jail, and the fear that had kept her there, held her back, was evaporating, like rubbing alcohol. "You don't look older," she said and joined her mother at the table.

"What about this oil?"

"Don't start this again."

"I'm not. It's just that sometimes you remind me too much of Frank and of Uncle Wealthy, and it worries me." Bets blinked slowly and then breathed out her question. "Is it the real thing? Does it do what you say it does?"

Calliope knew she could tell her mother the truth. People had been telling Bets secrets as long as she could remember, but Calliope didn't want to burden her.

"It's not fraud," she said.

"Those are your daddy's olives, right? I remember when Frank told me about them. I could never see what was so special about them, but I didn't have the touch you did in the groves."

"Why do you think Anna's lived so long?"

Her mother looked like she was about to tell her one of her long-kept secrets. "Your grandmother's a unique woman. What does that boyfriend of yours say?"

Calliope felt her cheeks get hot and it angered her that she could blush at her age. "He thinks a sequence of our genes doesn't turn off properly."

"That's a reason I'd buy. But what makes our genes special?" Her mother said this as if she already knew the answer.

"Mutation," Calliope said.

Bets shook her head. "You've got to give this oil up. It's quackery. It is one thing to market it to those idiots who are willing to pay so much more because we sprayed the trees with lemon juice and garlic instead of dimethoate kill, but you know the oil has about as much to do with Anna's longevity as the prayers she says at night."

"I need the money," Calliope said. She wanted her mother to understand this, to feel the practicality of her decision. After all, she hadn't claimed the oil would add years to people's lives, only asked that Anna mention that she has a bit of it with bread every night for dinner.

"Sell the store," her mother said. "You might make a little money."

"What would I do?" asked Calliope. She was stunned by her mother's suggestion. She'd always thought of the store as her nest egg, as her retirement plan. She was still paying off the loan, and she wasn't able to save much of the salary she paid herself. If she could just have a good enough year to pay the loan off, she could turn the management of the store over to Nancy and live off what she would have paid on her mortgage. She'd need at least ten more years to have enough money to live on, and that didn't take into account her extended life expectancy.

"It wouldn't be enough," she said.

"It's holding you back," her mother said.

"What's holding you back?" Erin asked. She'd appeared in the doorway without either one of them realizing she'd been listening. They stared at her and she added, "The baby's finally asleep, just finished feeding him. Anna's out like a light."

"Don't let Anna know you've accused her of sleeping," Bets said.

"You know Grandma, she just rests, and when her eyes are closed, she's just replaying some part of her past," Calliope added.

Erin pulled up a chair. The girl was tired. Calliope remembered her first months of motherhood when she was bone weary and that the lack of sleep had set her nerves on edge so that the littlest slight would send her crying and screaming. She blamed it on her leg. One of the reasons she married Greg was because he let her scream at him for hours and never reacted, just kept doing what he'd been doing whether it was watching television or whittling his pieces of wood until she wore herself out and started crying. And here it was forty years later and a habit she couldn't break.

"Mom thinks I should sell the store," Calliope said. She thought that Erin would take her side, would immediately see the legacy of the store, but instead she nodded in agreement.

"That place is killing you," she said.

"Gives you too many excuses," added Bets. "You should have been there for Deb's hearing."

Erin started to talk in bits and pieces that were hard to follow. Half-finished remembrances about her time at the store when she was younger and a funny story about olives and mice poop that she never finished telling. Across the table Bets smiled at Calliope, and she knew that they were both remembering how hard the early months of motherhood were.

"I always thought you'd leave someday. The whole time I was here doing my growing up I knew that you had that one good leg of yours out the door and that one day I was sure to wake up and find that I was left to just Anna and Bets to raise me." Erin yawned and then before she put her head on the table, she said. "Why didn't you leave?"

Looking at her granddaughter, Calliope felt as worn-out as she ever had. She didn't know what to say and had never known that the girl knew that she felt trapped in Kidron. This past summer had been the first that she hadn't planned to leave. That was how she'd kept sane over the years, by planning her escape, but this year, her own daughter had beaten her to it. Walked away from another lifetime in prison, and that had taken away Calliope's desire to run, but it hadn't made Kidron feel any less like a cage than it had when she arrived at age twenty-two in a half-body cast wheeled up to Anna's house and set in the front living room on a bed that Frank had moved down so that she could look over the olives as she convalesced.

Her mother leaned across the table and said, "It's time to close up shop. I'm going to bed." She shook Erin awake and whispered that she'd better be in bed soon, because little Keller was likely to be up and hungry in just a few hours.

CHAPTER TWENTY-SEVEN

Proof

The next day, a research assistant working for the company that published the book of world records requested Anna's birth certificate. In the midst of promising to fax a copy, Calliope looked up to see Bets shaking her head and mouthing what looked like, "We don't have it."

"Just a minute," Calliope said to the assistant and covered the mouthpiece of the portable phone.

"There's no birth certificate," Bets said.

"Then we'll get it from the courthouse," Calliope said, waving her hand, as if erasing the problem.

Bets opened her mouth and then closed it. "It doesn't exist."

Calliope had the sense that her mother had wanted to say more, that behind that short sentence was a hoard of secrets.

The researcher grew impatient. "Ma'am? Ma'am? I've got half a dozen other claims to sort through. Can you just call me back at this number when you have the proof?"

"Of course," Calliope said, placing the phone back on the wall. Her leg throbbed with pain. She called out to Anna, who was sitting on the back porch with Erin and the baby. Some of the anger and the urgency she felt must have come through because in a moment all the women of the house were settled around the kitchen table.

"I thought you knew this already," Bets said.

Erin moved the baby to her shoulder and rubbed his back. "This is the problem with this family. You think whatever you know everyone knows."

"But I've told all of you this before," Anna said.

"Your stories are about Kidron, not Australia," Calliope said. "I just assumed that Mims and Grandpa Percy came over as newlyweds."

"I don't understand why it makes a difference if Anna was born in Brisbane or Kidron. It doesn't change her age," Bets said.

"It does matter." Calliope pushed her chair back from the table. "It'll take months to get any records out of Australia, and who even knows if they kept this sort of information?"

"You've always been such a pessimist," Bets said. "Even as a little girl, you couldn't unwrap a present without pointing out potential flaws. The doll's hands were too fragile. White sweaters never stay white. So-and-so broke his leg trying to learn to ride a bike. It's no wonder that plane crashed on you. You've been asking for it your whole God damn life."

Calliope wished her mother were wrong. She wished that someone else in the room would disagree with her, but the long silence told her how right Bets was.

"I just can't get him to burp," Erin said, switching her son to her other shoulder.

"Let me," Anna said.

Erin handed over Keller. "There are other ways, you know."

When no one responded, she continued. "We could look at the census records or figure out how Anna ever got a Social Security card. We've got boxes of old papers in the attic. There's got to be proof lying around here."

By lunchtime, the women were surrounded by boxes. Bobo yipped and tried to pee on every bit of cardboard, but Calliope had three potential pieces of paper to prove Anna's age. Right off, Anna had produced a yellowed slip of paper, which had been fastened to her dress the day they arrived at the immigration facility near Los Angeles. The paper, with its loopy handwriting, stated that a girl, age four, had arrived with her parents, Veda, or Mims, as she had always been called, and Percy Davison, to the United States on March 1898. They also had Anna's Social Security card and her driver's license, which had expired.

With shaky hands, Calliope called the researcher back. He listened patiently to the descriptions of the proof, and then sighed heavily.

"Ever heard of Carrie White? Or Shigechivo Izumi?"

"No," Calliope said, sitting down heavily at the table.

"If you ask Carrie's relatives, she lived to be a hundred seventeen, but their only proof was the age listed on the intake form at the sanatorium her husband dropped her off at when she was in her thirties. Izumi was thought to have died at a hundred and twenty, but it turns out that his family submitted his older brother's birth certificate as proof for his age. The two siblings had the same name."

"But we have more than enough. I'm sure Hong Wu didn't have a birth certificate. His whole family was washed away in a flood."

"True enough. The immigration paper is good, but the other two are just fruit from a poisonous tree. That is, they could be legitimate, or they could be based on incorrect information. If I were making this decision, I'd want more. Tell me your grandmother's story again," the man said.

Calliope recounted what she knew of Anna's history and then

motioned for a pen and paper as the researcher gave her a rapid-fire list of documents that could supplement the ones they'd found.

Calliope looked down at the scrawled list. "We need more proof."

Erin made everyone lunch, and then they started looking for further evidence that Anna Davison Keller had been born on January 18 in 1894. Erin called a second cousin who was working Wealthy's land in Alaska to ask if there were any journals or letters from her great-great-uncle stored away up there. Bets visited the courthouse and the library, looking up what public records of Anna did exist. She'd seemed the least interested in learning what Anna remembered of her time in Australia. Erin peppered Anna with questions, and Calliope, too, found herself caught up in the stories Anna told. For the first time in years she listened close as Anna reminisced.

"They grow olives in Australia?" Erin asked. She had Keller on her knees and was playing peek-a-boo with him. "That's why Grandpa Davison came here, because he knew how to grow olives?"

Anna laughed when Keller laughed. She seemed as amused by the game as the infant. She started to tell a story about a giant tortoise, as if she were reading a picture book to the baby. "There once was a curious girl who liked nothing more than exploring."

As she continued, Calliope felt as if she'd heard the story before. She thought it might be the cadence, but when Anna held up her hands to show the size of the tortoise, Calliope realized she'd heard this story and a dozen more like it the summer she was recovering from her accident. Every night that year had ended with Anna telling her a fairy tale about a curious little girl in a curious land. There was a story about the tortoise, one about a sick little boy, a girl who lived in a tree, a kind washerwoman, and others that she could only recall emotions about. The stories seemed lost in her memory.

"Why that curious girl is you," Calliope said, interrupting the big finish. "I've just now figured it out."

Anna shrugged. "I guess they are me. I doubt there's much truth left in them. I've added to them over the years in telling them to all the children, grandchildren, and . . ." She faltered, and Calliope saw she was trying to figure out how many *greats* to add to get to Keller's generation.

"Great-great-great-grandchildren," Erin said. "Now that sounds like a fairy tale."

There were more stories as the afternoon wore on. In Brisbane, the family had lived around the corner from the Botanical Gardens, and for a nickel, any child could ride on the giant tortoise that was said to have been one of the specimens Darwin collected during his voyage to the Galapagos Islands. Wealthy told Anna the tortoise was king of all the reptiles.

Erin interrupted her. "Did you ride it?"

Anna nodded. "I don't know where I got the nickel, but I climbed on its back and the creature walked me around the paths of the gardens. I kissed its nose before I got off."

Calliope turned to Erin. "She's told me this before, only it started with once upon a time in a land far, far away and that kiss gave the child the gift of a long life—to live as long as the tortoise, who was already a century old when the girl kissed it."

Bobo tilted his head, as if to weigh in on the conversation. Anna scratched his ears and grinned at them. "Every tale has a bit of truth in it, or it wouldn't be worth telling."

"You can't possibly remember that," Calliope said. "You couldn't have been more than two, unless your parents lied and you are older than you're supposed to be."

Erin opened one of the boxes and as she pulled out leather binders that smelled of decay, she begged for another story.

"I don't remember much more about Australia," Anna said. She took the book Erin was holding and turned it right side up. "Daddy's ledger. Kept track of crop yields."

"Tell us something about Kidron then, what it was like when you first got here."

"Dusty," Anna said, coughing as she fanned the pages of her father's ledger. She passed the book to Calliope. The pages were brittle, and bits of them broke as she thumbed through them. "Useless."

"We need something of my mother's," Anna said. "Daddy liked numbers and details. He could tell you how big an olive was going to be just by looking at its flower, but he wasn't good with people. He always said he married Mims to take care of the people in his life."

Erin, who'd left to put the baby down for his afternoon nap, sat down on the floor in front of a box marked MIMS. She hummed to herself as she unpacked a wooden doll and a small wreath under a glass dome.

"That's made out of human hair," Anna said, extending her finger toward the wreath.

There were two shades of hair in the finely wrought flowers and knots that formed the wreath, one a copper-gold color and the other a yellow so light it appeared white when Calliope held it up to the light. While Erin questioned Anna about how such a decoration was made, Calliope tried not to think about it. She pictured the long strands of hair greasy with dirt and oil that she pulled out of the drain of the tub, and the thought that Mims had spent hours tying it into knots and winding it around wire made her sick.

A date was carved at the back of the dome, which was mounted on a piece of walnut. L AND C 1893 TO 1895.

"I wonder who they were," Erin said. "Do you know, Anna?"

Anna shook her head. She reached for the wreath, which Erin held, and ran her fingers over the letters. "I remember Mims had this in her bedroom. It hung by the portraits she kept of us and later of our children." She closed her eyes, and Calliope thought she looked like she might be remembering something, but when she opened them, she just said that no one had the time to work at such intricacies anymore.

Erin adjusted her nursing bra. "I can see why you'd do such a thing. We have so much to hold on to now. I've probably taken a thousand pictures of Keller already. I can't imagine not having that to go to, to remember what he was like as a baby. Why, when Mims was a girl they didn't even have cameras."

"I have all my children's booties," Anna said. "Knitted them myself. Of course your mother only wore hers that first night. She kept kicking them off. Liked to go barefoot, and I didn't have the patience to put them back on again. Mims kept telling me she'd get a cold and I'd lose her. That was a real possibility back then you know. We lost babies who got sick."

Calliope had a difficult time thinking of her mother with bare feet.

"Proof," Erin shouted. She held a sheaf of paper that had at one time been folded into thirds. "I've got her name here, her age, and the year and month they set sail for America."

"I wonder why we have that," Anna said, turning the ship's manifest over in her hands. There was a list of more than 250 people who'd sailed on the *Una*.

"It meets the requirements," Calliope said, looking at her list.

Erin had taken up a piece of paper and was making her own calculations. She looked up at Calliope and shook her head. "This is all so confusing. Wanna order a pizza for dinner?"

Bets came home from the library just before their dinner arrived. She had photocopies of the town's census records, which first listed Anna as a resident at age six during the 1900 census and in every survey after that. She also had a photocopy of the immigration papers the Davison family had filed when they arrived in San Francisco. "You won't believe what you can get on the Internet these days," she said, pulling all the toppings, including the cheese, off her pizza.

Calliope looked at her mother and laughed, forgetting about their fight that had been going on for weeks now. She pictured Bets as a baby, kicking her shoes off, and the image made her squeeze her mother's arm and whisper that she loved her.

Early the next morning, Calliope found Erin in the kitchen. The sun was just beginning its rise but hadn't yet climbed high enough for them to see its light. Instead, the sky around the hill was blush-colored. "I think I'm doing something wrong," Erin said. "I've been up half the night trying to figure this out. You're good with numbers."

Erin slid the pieces of paper she'd been working with over to Calliope. The ship's manifest listed four children with the Davison family. In addition to Anna and Wealthy, there were two other names: Louisa and Charlotte. They were listed as being three years old. Calliope tried to understand what her granddaughter had been figuring. She had Anna's birthday of January 18, 1894, the date the ship left Australia June 13, 1898, and three other dates on various sheets of paper.

"Do you see?" Erin asked. "If Mims were pregnant with Anna in May of 1893, then she still would be pregnant with Anna when these twins were born."

Calliope worked out her math on the scraps of paper. She wanted to talk about these girls Charlotte and Louisa and what had happened to them. Erin's math was right, but she didn't take into account any variables. "Not all pregnancies go nine months," Calliope said. "Twins are almost always early, there's not a lot of room for two."

"But at two months? It seems like back then they wouldn't have survived."

"Without the exact birthdays, we can't tell. Anna could've been born two weeks early and the twins conceived at the end of March."

Erin put her head down on the table. "I guess you're right, there's just something about it that doesn't make sense. I wanted to prove that Anna was born in January."

"You did," Calliope said. "She's at least as old as she says she is, and heck, maybe older."

They were laughing when Anna came into the kitchen, followed by her dog. "What's all this?" she said, looking around at the papers that covered her table. Erin explained what she'd found, including the mysterious twin girls on the manifest.

Calliope watched her grandmother's face change as Erin spoke. Anna's eyes clouded, and the muscles in her jaw slackened. She eased into one of the kitchen chairs and fingered the yellowed papers. "I never thought that was real. They'd come to me in dreams and sometimes I'd wake with their laughter still in my ears." She shook her head. "What a silly thing to say. I should tell you that I always knew that. But I'm not sure I did."

"None of us ever had a sister," Calliope said. She was shaken at the change in Anna, the way she'd seemed to age in front of them.

Anna said, "I would have liked to have them here in Kidron. I used to ask Mims about children, pester her, for siblings. She'd tell me that after Violet, she was like a chicken gone broody, she's just interested in sitting around on the eggs she's already got, not laying new ones."

Keller's small mewing cry came from the bedroom and Erin smiled. "I've gone broody," she said and went to feed her son.

Bets entered the kitchen fully dressed. "Why are we talking about chickens?"

The dog barked and pawed at the back door.

Anna, who had been reading and rereading the passenger manifest, slid it over to her daughter. "I had sisters," she said.

Bets let the dog outside. "Who wants oatmeal?" she asked and started gathering the pot and the milk.

"Do you think we'd be different if we had sisters?" Calliope asked. She remembered as a child that she'd desperately wanted a sister to even the odds against her brothers. For a while, she'd tried to make Lucy, who lived at the bottom of the hill, her best friend, and they became blood sisters, but it wasn't the same as having another woman in the house.

"I don't know how it would be much different than what we have," Bets said. "There's enough women in our family."

It surprised Calliope that Anna disagreed with her. "The woman who's your mother or your mother's mother is different than a sister," she said. "Look at your brothers, the way they bonded to each other, shared the same growing-up experience."

"But they don't have Daddy around, so they had to cling to each other, to that growing up," Bets said, stirring the oatmeal.

Anna shook her head. "You'll understand it better when I die. That despite how age has equaled us, we're not equals, and that's what you have in a sister, an equal."

Bets thumped the wooden spoon against the side of the pan. Calliope looked up from the table and saw that her mother had her back turned to them. She pulled the spice cupboard open with a violent tug and shoved jars and bottles aside until she found the cinnamon. More to the wall, than to them, Bets said, "You're never going to die. You're going to live on and on and on and on."

"I just might," Anna said. Her mouth had tightened and her lips were turning white as she compressed them.

The cap came off the cinnamon and a splash of it fell into the oatmeal. Bets yelled and then turned sharply toward her mother. "You don't even want to die. You're too greedy for that. Can't let go and let any of us have a life that you're not a part of."

"What's wrong with wanting to live? That's what God put us here for," Anna said.

The oatmeal started to burn. Calliope moved to take it from the stove, but hesitated when her mother threw the wooden spoon against the wall. She walked right up to Anna's face and said, "Then live! Just don't expect me to follow along."

Anna poked her daughter in the chest. "So go ahead. Die. Stop talking about it and give it up."

Calliope gasped.

"What in the blazes is going on in here?" Erin asked, taking the burning pot of oatmeal off the stove. "The baby's sleeping. You're both being so morbid."

"It's just all so exhausting," Bets said, taking a seat at the table. Calliope took up her mother's hand and stroked the back of it.

"It's going to be okay. We'll all be okay," Calliope said, not meeting anyone's eyes.

Anna took out a kitchen towel, wiped the oatmeal off the wall, and then bent to pick the spoon off the linoleum, where it had landed. Calliope hadn't seen them become angry with each other like this in years. Maybe even a decade. The year Anna had turned one hundred, they'd stopped talking to each other for several weeks. Bets didn't like to be mothered. Calliope wondered if it had always been this way, even when Bets was too young to take care of herself. She knew that her mother hadn't mothered her. She'd never felt clucked over, or smothered. Part of the urge she had to run away came because her mother never seemed to care what she was doing or how she'd been. Frank had cared; it was her father who had taught her the important lessons in life.

In many ways Frank had been like a mother and a father to her, and yet he'd ignored his sons. He let Bets mother them, and she had; she treated them like little princes all in need of being served, waited on them as if they had some disadvantage in life.

Calliope felt cold. She stood up and kissed Anna on the top of her head and then went to start another batch of oatmeal. She spoke quietly to her mother, not wanting Anna to overhear. "How did you know about the twins?"

"I didn't," Bets said. She took the cinnamon off the counter and stirred it into the new pot.

"You weren't surprised," Calliope said. "It was like you expected that we'd find something like this and you're so angry about it. You've been angry about everything lately."

"I'm angry about a century's worth of small annoyances," Bets said.

"They're still small annoyances," Calliope said. She took four bowls down from the cupboard. "You don't get mad unless some-one's found out one of your secrets, so what is it this time? What do you know?"

"I don't know anything," her mother said, taking the oatmeal to the table.

They ate in silence, passing the slip of paper with the ship's manifest around to one another and wondering aloud about Charlotte and Louisa. They gave them characteristics and family traits. Lottie, they called her, would have had Mims's gray eyes and her dimples, and Louisa would have had red hair instead of gold. Calliope listened as Anna spoke about Mims and her father. Bets was quiet and Erin asked questions to fill the silences. Calliope wished she, like Erin, had known her great-great-grandparents. To hear Anna describe them, Mims and Percy Davison were as alive as any of them sitting at the table. Listening to Anna's voice, she heard a slight Australian accent. She finally understood that if it weren't for some genetic miracle, or health craze, that she wouldn't know Anna, wouldn't have had so much time with her own mother, and all the sisters in the world wouldn't make up for that.

CHAPTER TWENTY-EIGHT

Independence

The night before Amrit returned to Kidron, Calliope asked Petey and Robert to hammer a FOR SALE sign into the small strip of grass that fronted the Pit Stop's parking lot. Nancy, the cashier, hovered over them. She didn't conceal her resentment.

"Did you tell your family about how serious the doctor is about you?" Nancy asked. She lit a cigarette and smoked it, standing in the open door of the store.

"Can't smoke inside," Calliope said.

Nancy shuffled her feet so that they were on the outside of the doorframe. "You didn't tell them did you?"

"Nothing to tell," Calliope said. "Got any plans for July Fourth?" She listened to Nancy's yammering and wished she'd thought to bring a level. The boys had eyeballed the sign and called it straight, but to Calliope, it still had a slant.

One of her third cousins owned a real estate office in Kidron and had listed the property, promising not to charge a commission. Still, the property and business were worth less than she'd thought.

Petey wiped his face with a bandanna while Robert gathered up the tools.

"What if it never sells?" Nancy asked. "Will you just shut it up? What if someone wants the store, but not the business? This is prime real estate. I think they'd buy it for your sign alone."

Calliope looked up at the metal billboard that stretched up out of the back lot of the Pit Stop. It rose nearly fifty-five feet, bringing it in perfect placement for drivers on I-5. Far enough from the exit that drivers had time to change lanes. "I'll sell what I can. I got time enough to wait. Why you worrying? You don't need this job."

Nancy's husband was on disability. "Everyone needs a job," she said, tapping her ashes onto the cement stoop. "Even if you've got a man, you need a job."

Calliope locked up the store and turned off the lights on the billboard. She waved good-bye to the boys and walked Nancy to her car. It had been a strange month. The *Guinness* people had accepted the census records and the ship's manifest as proof enough of Anna's age and had officially anointed her the oldest person in the world. Anna then spent a week receiving visitors from major news outlets—appearing on *Oprah,* via satellite, and talking on the phone with Regis. Anna told Oprah about the olive oil, and in a matter of two days, Calliope had sold out her entire stock and made enough money to cover all the missed mortgage payments on the store.

She'd confided in Amrit that she'd felt less excited than she thought she would. "I've found other things to worry about, like my mother, or that Deb will get caught." She looked at her watch. He would already be on the plane from Pittsburgh to San Francisco, which meant it would be the first night in six months they hadn't wished each other good night. She turned the car on and drove toward Hill House. It would be good to see him again. When they spoke, she had trouble picturing his face. He was a fleshy, robust man with a beard that did nothing to cover up the roundness of his cheeks, his voice with its slight accent was deep and powerful. She'd turned down the volume on her phone so that his voice didn't alarm her. She had it so low now that when they talked, he sounded like he was whispering, something he did in the bedroom. It had been too long since she'd seen him.

The lights at Hill House were off and Calliope expected to find everyone on the porch watching the sunset. She walked up the gravel path that led to the back of the house and found it was only Anna in the rockers. "What's the doctor going to tell us tomorrow?" Anna asked, holding out a wrinkled hand.

"He won't tell me. Says it wouldn't be fair to you."

"That's a smart man you've got," Anna said. She motioned for Calliope to sit in the chair next to her. "Your leg always hurts after such a long day."

"I should take another pill. Amrit's coming in later tonight, and I told him I'd meet him for a late dinner."

"Your mom thinks you take too many of those pills," Anna said.

"Just 'cause they didn't have medicine when the two of you were in pain, doesn't mean I should suffer. I've had enough of suffering."

"Your mom and I are of the mind-set that suffering is rewarded," Anna said, compressing her lips.

"You know I don't believe that anymore. How could I after what happened?" Calliope gestured to the sky, which had started to darken.

"Unbelief's no reason to stop paying attention to God," Anna said. They were both quiet a long while and Calliope heard the now familiar noises of her mother helping Erin give Keller a bath. A yellow and gray bird came to rest on the porch railing.

"It's a Bullock's oriole," Anna said. "I haven't seen one in years. Or maybe I just haven't been looking."

Calliope didn't speak until the bird flew away. She saw in flight that the bird's chest was a deeper shade of yellow, more like saffron and less like lemon and said as much to Anna.

"It's a male. They have their own song," Anna said.

"Wouldn't the females have their own song, too?" Calliope asked.

Anna looked at her and laughed. "My daddy taught me about them and I guess I never thought about it. But what was special for him about birds was the way the males looked better, sang better, than the females. He didn't care about the hens, unless he found their nests and could see their eggs, and then he appreciated all the tending as he said."

There was so much that Calliope didn't know about the men in her family. The stories passed around at holidays and funerals were about the women. Even her brothers talked about their mother—they didn't have stories about Frank. A consequence of showing favoritism, she guessed. She had never felt like sharing the moments her father had given her. But now with Bets as silent as ever, and her father's mind gone, she understood that it would be left to her to pass on her father's stories.

In World War II, her father had served aboard one of the smaller vessels that had been stationed in the Pacific. She remembered being in the orchard with him while he talked about what the ocean looked like without any land around it. In the stories he told about himself, Frank was a joker, playing the other shipmen for laughs, setting traps that strung up the new mates by their ankles. He'd showed her one day how to set a snare that would tighten around a man's ankles and swing him up into the sky. She'd tried for months to catch one of her brothers but ultimately only succeeded in pulling the family mutt up by his hind legs.

Calliope told this to Anna. "Was he like that?"

Anna nodded. "Frank had made everyone laugh, even your Grandpa Mike, and he was one helluva son of a bitch."

"Grandma!" Calliope had rarely heard Anna swear.

"Used to say *bitch* all the time. Was a farm term. Somehow it got all mixed up with those other words, but it was what my husband was."

"You've been alone a long time, know how to stand on your own two feet," Calliope said. She wanted to ask Anna why it was so much easier for her to be alone, to be celibate.

"I hear you're in love again. With that doctor fellow," Anna said.

"I guess." She would have agreed with Anna, but just then, hearing the way she said it made her feel foolish. They weren't in love; they were lovers, and now it seemed ridiculous to Calliope to think of her and Amrit being in love. What they were was lonely.

"I never needed that foolishness after Mike died. But it was different then. It was different for a long time. Seems like it only stopped being different a few years ago."

Calliope thought about how it'd been when she'd returned home from the accident. How most of the men who courted her wanted her because she had money and land. They wanted to be in charge of her, of her family. Greg Rodgers had been different— he'd been in love with her since he was the fat boy whose parents owned the theater. She used to giggle over him when she and her girlfriends went to the movies, took advantage of his crush to get free concessions. "I guess it's only been different for Erin, and she had to go and fall in love with someone who's old enough to be her father. So old he treats her the way men used to treat women. Just like her mother. There's been too many bad men in our lives."

"Don't talk that way. You've got good brothers and good sons. Deb made her choices, Erin made hers. Your father wasn't that way. Frank never treated Bets as anything but an equal, and he didn't marry her for the land. You understand about him, don't you?"

Calliope shrugged. She wasn't ready to talk about her father.

She didn't want Anna to stop talking. "How've you done it, Grandma? How have you been celibate all these years?"

She expected Anna to blanch at the question, but instead she threw back her head and roared with laughter. The noise brought Bets and Erin to the porch, and Calliope, after resisting for several moments, joined Anna in her mirth.

"What's so funny?" Bets demanded. She shook her head at them.

"Discretion," Anna choked out and then chortled.

Erin sat down in another rocker. "I wish you'd tell me. I need a good laugh. All that baby makes me want to do is cry out of frustration or joy. I'm tired of crying."

CHAPTER TWENTY-NINE

Lovers

*S*he met Amrit at the hotel just before midnight. Calliope felt like a teenager sneaking out of the house after everyone else had gone to sleep. Walking down the long corridor from her room, she'd held her shoes in her hands until she reached the porch. The conversation with Anna had lightened her mood, and instead of wearing a sensible outfit, she'd put on the only bra she owned that put most everything back in its rightful place and a half slip instead of underwear. Over this ensemble, she'd pulled on her raincoat and sprayed herself with perfume. She put her overnight bag, packed with sensible pajamas and a change of clothes, in the backseat and thought how when she was younger she never gave a thought to the outfit being sexy. The perks of youth were that the body was enough. It didn't need to be pushed up, smoothed, or hidden in the dark—now she tended to keep her nakedness under wraps until both parties were too far to turn back.

Calliope understood that the world would think her ridiculous. But she didn't care, it was possible for a sixty-six-year-old woman to have sex without absurdity. Just look at Raquel Welch or

Sophia Loren, beautiful and well into their sixties. Even Elizabeth Taylor, overweight as she was, clearly still had sex.

The motel was not far from Hill House. It was, because of the nature of Kidron, of the interstate variety and served as a stopover for drivers who found themselves too sleepy to make it over Mount Shasta in the dark. There were a dozen other cars parked behind the motel. Callie put on red lipstick, adjusted her bra for maximum lift, and cinched the waist of the coat tightly. She stood for several moments watching shadowed figures move behind the curtains of the hotel. As a stewardess, she'd slept with a fair number of pilots— all of them older and most of them married. It was strange to think she was older now than most of those men.

Amrit opened the door at her first knock. She smiled and opened her coat.

"How very American of you," he said. His voice was like it'd been on the phone: throaty and low.

She leaned in and smelled his neck. His hand came to her breast and he squeezed gently, slipping his thumb inside the lace of the bra. She moaned, and all thought of her sagging, wrinkled, and puckered body left her mind. Calliope was transported to the first time she'd let a boy touch her breast. The feeling of power and submission she felt as the warmth and fluttering started in her belly and spread like fire through her body. She was greedy to let that fire burn, to feel it in every part of her. She knew from the other times that Amrit was a man of irksome patience. She pulled at his belt, and he took her hands and put them on his face.

"Kiss me first," he said.

He had soft, full lips and tasted of cloves. She had to stand on her tiptoes to reach his mouth. His tongue pushed gently into her mouth, which she opened wider. *Yes*, she thought. *It's all yours. I'm all yours.* He pressed against her and she could feel him against her soft stomach. He nibbled at her neck and then bit her shoulder gently, pulling at the straps of her bra with his teeth.

She let her hands move down his broad back and then pushed herself against him until he walked backward with her in his arms toward the bed. She knew his wife had not been an adventurous woman. He'd called their lovemaking adequate, and because of this, Calliope had some confidence with him. They fell onto the bed together.

"Naughty," he said, his breath coming quicker. "Such a naughty American woman."

He withdrew from her and ran his hands along every inch of her, telling her what he loved about her collarbone, her elbows, and even her legs—kissing the scar tissue on her calf.

The guest in the next room banged on the wall and told them to hurry it up. She lay back and pulled him on top of her. She opened her eyes wide and watched Amrit's face as he made love to her. He was smiling, and she could see in his eyes a hint of what he'd looked like as a young man. She had a vision of the two of them coupling when their bodies were young, and she knew they would be together until death claimed them. She bit his shoulder to quiet her screams and let the joy wash over her entire body. She turned toward him to find him smiling. "I've missed you," he said.

He'd awakened before her. Calliope had not, after all, put on her sensible pajamas, and she felt the rough texture of the sheets brush against her skin. Her arm was asleep and she'd drooled all over her pillow. He opened the bathroom door, and she expected to see him in a towel, still wet from the shower. Instead, as the steam escaped around him, he stepped toward the bed cinching the knot of a plum-colored tie. "We should see your father first," he said.

"You are being terribly old-fashioned," Calliope said. "Daddy won't even know who I am, let alone that you're trying to ask his permission to shack up with me."

"It's more than that. I want him to understand that you're going away. That you, whoever you are to him, will be in Pittsburgh now instead of Kidron. Plus I'm dying to meet the famous Mr. Frank." Amrit winked, as if he knew something about her father that she did not.

"What did my mother tell you?"

"Nothing that I can tell you," he said, reaching over to pinch her cheek.

Calliope felt a new awareness of the decrepit state of her body. "I'll get showered and dressed," she said, wrapping the sheet around her and taking it to the bathroom with her.

They discussed her father's medical history on the way to Golden Sunsets. Amrit wanted to know all the technical details, the story of how Frank was initially diagnosed with Parkinson's and then Alzheimer's and finally Lewy body dementia. "It's all the same to me," Calliope said. "Dad can't remember what he wants to, what we want him to."

"It must be hard," Amrit said.

Calliope shook her head. "Dad and I, we've got a pact. When I was sick for so long, I tired of people coming in with sad faces casting their worries all on me. I got into it with Mom after I'd been back for about two weeks. Told her I didn't want to hear how sad she was. She wasn't the one with two broken arms, a broken leg, and a lung puncture."

Amrit patted her leg. "How awful."

She stopped the car hard at the stoplight. "That's it. That's what I'm talking about. No sympathy, no special treatment. Just treat me like you would if I were normal. That's what I do for Dad. Mom can't bring herself to be that way, and that's why he can get so violent with her. When she's there, he knows there's something wrong with him."

The light turned green, and Calliope waited for the cars to clear before making a left into Golden Sunsets' lot. "It makes every visit an adventure," Amrit said.

"Yes. That's it exactly. You don't know who you'll be until he talks. So get ready to play along," Calliope said.

"Athena," Frank said when he saw her enter the rec room. He was seated next to his friend Guy, who despite being thirty years younger than her father looked a good deal older. Calliope didn't mind it when her father confused her with his sister.

"Franky," she said and extended her arms. The embrace was awkward. Her father's fedora fell to the floor, and then Amrit stepped on it. He stammered an apology as he bent down to pick it up.

"It's been too long," Frank said, looking at her closely. "You look good. There's a new gleam in your eyes. Is it this man you've got with you or are you going on a trip?"

"Both," Calliope said, and Guy laughed. She liked her father's friend, who was in the wheelchair because of a stroke. When he was around, her father's confusion seemed humorous. With Guy, he was quick to laugh, whereas before, the dementia had made him angry and the intensity of his emotion frightened Calliope.

Amrit extended his hand to both Guy and Frank. "I'm taking her away from you. Asked her to move out east with me to Pittsburgh."

"Well now," said Frank.

Guy grasped for Calliope's hand and squeezed it tightly. "Good for you. You need this," he said.

"Don't believe I've ever been to Pennsylvania," Frank said. "What kind of racket you got going on out there?"

Guy winked at Calliope. "Don't you recognize him?" he asked

Frank. "This here is one of the premiere exotic animal veterinarians in the world. Got his start working with the elephants in India and then Ringling hired them."

Amrit opened his eyes wide and started to disagree with Guy.

Calliope, wanting to have fun, talked right over his protestations. "Oh yes. We're going to start a sanctuary for exotic animals. They'll be lions and tigers and bears."

"Oh my," said Frank, and all four of them laughed like they were children.

Calliope watched as Amrit relaxed and followed Guy's lead. It was difficult to believe that Frank was the same man who'd nearly beat her mother to death. It had happened just three months after Deb had been sentenced for killing Carl. Although her father had been deteriorating for several years, the sudden progression of his dementia startled them all. Calliope worked sixty hours a week and still lived in the small house on Butte Street, where she'd moved when she'd married. During those months, there had been a period of silence between Calliope, her mother, and Anna. The coldness between them had solidified into ice when she refused to help with Erin.

If it hadn't been for Frank nearly killing Bets, she isn't sure the coldness between them would have ever thawed. She was closing up at the Pit Stop when a neighbor who lived at the bottom of the hill called. Nancy, who had just started working there, picked up the phone, and Calliope remembered watching the woman's ruddy complexion turn yellow. "Something awful has happened to your mother," Nancy said, and then she nearly commanded Calliope to go to Hill House. "There's bad trouble," she said, shoving Calliope out the door.

The cops who met Calliope at the bottom of the hill told her that her father had broken her mother's arm and then run into the orchard with his shotgun and started shooting the trees. "They won't leave," the policeman said. "The women and your grand-daughter are hiding in the back room and refused to budge. We got men looking for Frank."

She drove as fast as the wind would carry her to the house, hustled everyone into the car, and drove to the hospital. Her mother was undone that day. Bets's shirt was torn and bloodied, and her hair, its careful chin-length bob, was ratty and disheveled, leaves stuck to her clothing. On the way to the hospital, Anna prayed. It was not the formal scripted prayer that Calliope remembered from her childhood, but a naked pleading that mostly consisted of *please God, please.*

Erin sat in the front seat of the Camaro next to Calliope. "Bang," the little girl said. She was holding her Strawberry Short-cake doll, the one Bets had made to replace the doll she'd had when her father was shot. She pointed her fingers at the doll's head and again said, "Bang."

Joy Fielding had been at the intake desk that night. Even in high school, she had been bitter. Her mouth was small and hard, small as an olive pit, and her lips were so pale they were almost yel-low. She and Calliope had gone to school together but had not been friendly. Calliope realized, watching Joy exhale with irritation at the sight of her family in the flickering fluorescent lights, that the Keller family was getting a reputation for trouble.

She sent Anna with Bets and stayed in the waiting room with Erin. Calliope wondered what the girl thought about guns. They'd always been present in Calliope's life; her father had hunted, and so had her husband. There had been the wars and all of them had grown up playing at cowboys or bank robbers, pointing their fin-gers at one another and saying, just as Erin had: Bang.

Erin was a strange child. They'd expected to have to be deli-cate around her—walk on tiptoe and whisper about Deb, but she'd accepted her father's death more easily than they expected. She wasn't one of those children who were silent about their tragedy. That first year she spent living with Anna and Bets, she talked about it constantly: telling the clerk at the bank that her mother was in jail, asking the stock boy at the grocery store if he'd ever fired a gun, and pestering them all with endless questions about her parents.

Erin looked up at Bets. "Why'd Grandpa Frank shoot the trees?"

"I don't know, sweetie," Calliope said. Her leg ached and she wanted to get down on the floor and play with Erin, but she was afraid she wouldn't be able to get back up. She reached her arms out to the girl and pulled her close. "I think Grandpa Frank is sick."

"He's funny," Erin said. She crawled into Calliope's lap and began to playact with her Strawberry Shortcake doll and another one she'd pulled from a basket in the corner of the waiting area. The found doll was grimy and had most of its blond hair pulled out. Its eyes were supposed to open and close, but one of them was stuck shut. Erin made the dolls talk to each other.

"Who are you?" asked the one-eyed baby doll.

"I'm me," said the strawberry doll. "You know me."

"Who are you?" Erin raised the baby doll in the air so it looked down at the other doll and then she had it ask again.

Calliope kissed her granddaughter's head. "He knows who you are," she said. "He forgot for a little while, but he'll remember."

At that moment, the police brought Frank through the hospital doors. He'd been handcuffed to keep him from attacking the people who were trying to help him. Calliope couldn't help herself, seeing her father in handcuffs muttering incoherently. "Daddy," she screamed.

"Daddy," echoed Erin.

Frank looked at them, but Calliope could see that he didn't know who they were. Erin had dropped the baby doll to the ground and hugged her Shortcake doll tightly. "That's your daddy," she said and patted Calliope's cheek.

"My daddy," agreed Calliope.

"He's gone," Erin said, and Calliope didn't turn to look to see if the child meant that he'd been taken back to an examination room.

Her granddaughter curled into Calliope's shoulder and began to suck her thumb, and even though her leg felt like it was on fire, she rocked back and forth until the child had fallen asleep. Two weeks later, after her father had been moved into Golden Sunsets, Calliope moved into Hill House with her mother and Anna.

Calliope glanced over at her father and realized he was asleep. Guy was talking on and on about his grandson, who was an understudy for Lumière in the traveling production of *Beauty and the Beast*. She reached over and tapped his knee, and Guy laughed. "It's the entertainer in me, I feel a constant need to tell stories to keep you young folks interested in us. I just keep forgetting that unless the story is about hunting or fishing, Frank will fall asleep."

"How's he really doing?" Calliope asked.

"He's fine," Guy said.

"You are wonderful with him," Amrit said. "I never would have come up with that elephant story. How long have you two been together?"

Guy looked quickly at Calliope and then shook his head.

Amrit blushed. "I mean how long have you been here?"

"Too long," Guy said.

They'd never spoken openly about their relationship, but Calliope observed the intimacy between them, and although she didn't want to know more, she knew that they were not just friends. "Honestly. The staff tells me he's doing great for a man his age, but you've been by his side for more than two years now. You'd see the little things, like today how his hands were shaking more than normal. Or that he looks less pale and more yellow."

Guy's face softened. He gazed at her for a bit, and Calliope could see that he was relieved to be able to talk openly with her. His voice, when he began to speak, was less hoarse and had more warmth in it. She felt like she'd just watched a clown take off his makeup.

"You see a lot of death in a place like this. You get so you know what it looks like when the body starts turning itself off. That's all old age is really, a bunch of gremlins running around your body, turning stuff off, slowing down the mechanisms that have kept us going." He paused and scratched his arm. "I came in here too young. It'll be years before my body shuts itself down. Frank's has started though."

Calliope cried. "And here I am, telling him that I'm leaving."

Amrit took her in his arms.

"He was happy for you and I have to say it is about time that you do leave," Guy said. "I could never figure out what was keeping you in Kidron."

"I should stay if he's only got—"

"—got what? Two weeks? Five months, you know how this is. He hasn't recognized anyone in such a long time. There are days when he walks right past me in the hall. I have to roll after him. Call out his name and remind him that I'm his anchor in this place."

They sat together feeling unsure for several minutes. Amrit rubbed her back. Other patients shuffled by and Calliope listened as they spoke with their friends, with their loved ones who were visiting. When she felt strong enough, she stood up and then leaned over to hug Guy. "You're good for him," she said and then, "No. You've been good to him. Thank you."

She shook her father's arm until he woke up. She saw it then, how he didn't recognize anyone around him or the place where he was. His eyes were wide with fear, but he knew he shouldn't tell them that he didn't know, that he couldn't remember. She watched as he looked up at her, and she saw what came to his mind was not recognition, but familiarity, routine.

"Hey, tumbleweed," he said. It was the nickname he'd given her as a child when they worked out in the olive groves together.

"Oh, Daddy," Calliope said, and hugged him tight.

As she left she heard him talking with Guy. "That's my daughter?" he asked him. And then "I have a daughter?" His voice was thin and high and she heard Guy trying to soothe him, to reorient him to the world he lived in.

CHAPTER THIRTY

Bets

*T*he morning visit with her father had exhausted her. The day had started sunny, but just after lunch, clouds had swept down from Shasta and the temperature dropped ten degrees. Calliope pulled into the driveway of Hill House and thought about how her life was going to change. She wanted to talk to her mother first and alone. There were emotions she wanted to share about her father and Guy. She just wanted to say good-bye to Anna, because although she could live another couple of years, the end was nearing for her. Being with Amrit and watching Erin with her new baby had made Calliope fearful of regrets. She had regrets about her husband's death, how it had come so swiftly and so silently and there had been no time for good-byes.

Her mother opened the door before she could reach it. "Where's Dr. Hashmi?"

"He'll be here soon. I took him to meet Daddy earlier this morning," Calliope said. "You wanna go for a walk?"

She looked up at the sky and then back at Calliope. "It looks like a good time to get out of the house." As she came down the stairs, she buttoned up the old house sweater she wore and took her plastic rain cap out of the pocket.

"It's not going to rain," Calliope said.

"It might," Bets said.

They walked along the path that led from the front steps to the orchard and then took the overgrown road that would bring them to her daddy's trees. It wasn't any darker in the orchard, the trees barely topped out at five feet. The light, however, was different. It was absorbed and then diffracted by the leaves. The gray of the leaves was much more pronounced in the cloudy weather. The magpies warbled as they walked down the path and then their calls softened as the birds settled into their presence in the orchard.

"I sold out of the oil pressed from Daddy's olives," Calliope said as they reached the bench that their father had built from limbs he'd pruned. He liked to use green wood that he could wet and twist into shapes. The seat was made of an old tree that had been hit by lightning. Her daddy had sawed it himself and then oiled and sanded it.

"People are the same," her mother said. "Always looking for the easy answer, ready to believe in snake oil but they'll tell you why it's not snake oil."

"It can't hurt them," Calliope said. "It isn't like we know why Anna's lived so long, or you, or Daddy."

"False hope is a dangerous weapon," her mother said.

"Hope is hope." Calliope wanted to change the subject. "The vain deserve a little false hope; besides, I think I'm through with all that." She'd had an offer on the store, and it was enough to leave the oil behind, to leave Kidron behind and move east with Amrit.

Bets grabbed her hand. "I'm glad. I didn't want to tell you it was wrong, but it was. I was afraid someone who was truly sick would buy it. You have no idea the lengths I would have gone to if I'd thought there was a way to make you heal after your accident.

And now there's your father. I'd give the whole of this to bring his mind back."

She told her mother about her most recent visit to Golden Sunsets, about how her father had mistaken her for his sister. She told her about Amrit and the way her father had responded to him. Her mother laughed and she looked younger. Calliope wanted to ask Bets about Frank's relationship with Guy, how long she'd suspected that he preferred men, but she didn't know how to start.

"They hold hands," she said.

"Guy's a good friend," her mother said.

Calliope wanted to push her, to ask her about their marriage, about her brothers, but she knew that one of the talents her mother had was keeping secrets. If she pushed her today, as she had a dozen other times in her life, her mother would just get up and leave. Busy her hands with work. There was a certain catch in her mother's voice when she brought up Guy that told Calliope what she wanted to know. Her mother wasn't oblivious to the change in her father, and it made her wonder if it was actually a change at all. What could a man have done in the 1940s if he preferred men? It wasn't as if there were parades, anthems, coming-out guides. It still bothered her to consider this, that there was a less than genuine feeling between her parents, that their love wasn't real, that it was wrapped up more in practicality and convenience than in fate or romance.

"Amrit and I are in love," Calliope said this quickly, and then without pause, she asked her mother to tell her the story of how she and her father had met.

"We always knew each other," she said. "You know this."

"But there must have been a moment when you looked at him and realized that he was more than someone who worked in the orchards."

"No. That's what there was to love about him, he'd always been there."

"Then tell me about the day he proposed? Did he know that you loved him?"

Her mother turned and looked back at the house. "Anna's going to be wondering where we are. We should head back."

Calliope wanted to hear the story again from her mother, the one she'd told them growing up—how Frank had swept her up out of the orchard and carried her away on his horse like she was Guinevere and he Lancelot. How they rode to the river and he'd told her that he couldn't live without her. Her mother always ended the story, which was unusually sentimental, by saying that the war made them all stupid. Calliope had cherished that story growing up. She'd nursed it in her head until her parents were fated to be together. She magnified moments between them, how her father always brought her mother small wildflowers he'd found in the orchards and knit them into flower crowns.

It was the sort of love she'd been looking for her whole life, desperate for during her marriage. And now she suspected that it had all been the product of her imagination, that her mother and father had been nothing more than friends who had a family together. She heard the words her mother said earlier echo in her mind. *He was always there.*

Bets stood and started to make her way back to the house. Calliope still hadn't told her she was leaving. "Mom," she managed and then she started to cry.

"Deb's fine," Bets said, stepping back to the bench and rubbing her back. "She's just fine. Before she left I gave her money and directions to one of Uncle Wealthy's old cabins in the Cascades. I'm sure that's where she is, and when she's ready, we'll go find her."

This revelation caused Calliope's confidence to collapse. She'd truly believed that her mother didn't know where her daughter was, that Deb had left on her own. The tears ran down her face and dripped down her collar. Her leg began to ache and after a while, she was forced to blow her nose on the edge of her blouse. She was finally angry enough to say what she'd come to say.

"I'm leaving." She reached for her mother's hand.

"But you just got here," her mother said. "And you haven't said hello to Anna yet."

"No. I'm leaving Kidron. I've had a reasonable offer on the store, and Amrit wants me to move east with him. Back to Pittsburgh."

"Oh."

The silence was not a good indication. Calliope knew this, remembered from her childhood that a quiet mother meant anger with consequences that could never be seen ahead of time. When her brother Jimmy had eloped it had fallen to Calliope to tell their mother. She'd nodded at Frank and then stayed in her room for two weeks.

"I'll come back, of course," Calliope said, her voice an octave higher than she wished it to be.

Her mother looked at the sun sinking toward the horizon. She spoke without blinking. "You'll come back. It'll just be for a funeral."

CONFIDENTIAL

2007 MacArthur Fellows Nomination Dossier

Prepared By: Redacted

Proposed Nominee: Amrit Hashmi

Area of Research: Genetics with specific focus on the longevity gene and a stated research goal of helping humans achieve biological immortality.

Location: University of Pittsburgh

Geographically, this is a strong location for us because it offers us an opportunity to diversify our award locations.

Publications and Awards: Appended

RESEARCH SUMMARY

For the last two decades, Dr. Hashmi has worked to understand the genetic mechanisms of aging and longevity. Initially, his research interests centered on the *Turritopsis nutricula,* commonly called the immortal jellyfish. As a response to adverse conditions, the *Turritopsis* undergoes a reverse aging process and changes from a mature jellyfish to a polyp, which is the species state of infancy. In this way, the jellyfish can avoid death and just continue to repeat the cycle of growing young and then old again in indefinite cycles. This ability, which is a form of biological immortality, has not been found in any other species.

While many others in his field have continued to focus their efforts on researching and understanding the conditions of aging in lesser organisms, Dr. Hashmi is among the few who has advanced to studying the genetic makeup of specific humans. When the near completion of the human genome project was announced in 2000, Dr. Hashmi shifted his attentions entirely to finding the longevity gene(s). He claims the fastest route to stopping the aging process in humans is to understand what sets apart the small percentage who are able to live well into their tenth decade with better physical and mental health than those who are thirty or forty years younger. He launched a worldwide effort to document every living human being over the age of 110. He's been criticized by his peers for not including anyone a century or older, but the correlation of his data suggests that superior medical care in the last twenty years has artificially inflated those numbers. His focus on supercentenarians means that fewer than 1,000 people worldwide meet his qualifications for inclusion in his studies.

Because of this low number, in the last year at the urging of the National Institution on Aging, which partially funds his research, he has focused his efforts also on the offspring of these supercentenarians. This helped Dr. Hashmi move toward identifying general biological markers that control aging in the body. Rumors in the research community purport that Dr. Hashmi is close to finding the specific sequence of genes. Last year he started working with a 112-year-old Northern California woman and her direct female descendants. One of his research assistants told us that there is some indication that each of these women has a mutation that prevents degradation during cell division. In most humans, the telomeres, which are part of the DNA that occur around the edge of chromosomes, shorten with each division. Their contention is that there is almost no shortening in these women.

RESEARCH APPLICATION

What sets Dr. Hashmi's study apart from others is his contention that the longevity gene does more than keep us from aging. He contends that there are many other elements at work in supercentenarians that not only extend their life, but also fight off deadly conditions like cancer, diabetes, obesity, and heart disease. In addition, these genes working in concert with other inherited traits in these genetic superagers help them to maintain physical integrity in areas where the elderly often see degradation, such as hearing, eyesight, dental care, flexibility, and other mobility issues. Dr. Hashmi thinks big and he thinks beyond his discipline. He believes his research could change the way we treat not only general wear and tear on the human body, but illness in general. He claims that the only age-related difficulties that won't be treatable in fifty years are those caused by environmental damage. In the immediate future, identifying the specific genes will enable researchers to extend human life by an average of thirty years.

CONTROVERSY

To date no specific drugs or even targeted gene therapies for use in humans have resulted from any of the research on longevity. While Dr. Hashmi's research, which focuses on the production of a specific class of proteins, shows the most promise for targeted therapy, there are still many who claim that the increased levels of these proteins in Dr. Hashmi's superagers is nothing more than a symptom of longevity. Despite this, no other researcher in this field has even posited a cause of the slowed aging in Dr. Hashmi's superagers. To his detractors, Dr. Hashmi points out that the children of superagers also live to be older—indicating a genetic connection to aging.

In addition to the questions of scientific accuracy, some have raised ethical and practical questions that surround extending life. Questions about overpopulation arise when considering expanding the current life span by as few as twenty years, which essentially adds an extra generation to the world's population. However, it is important to point out that just two hundred years ago a human being's life expectancy at birth was only forty-five years. Today, most residents of first-world countries can reasonably expect to live nearly twice that long. These advances in longevity were a direct result of scientific advances in food production, vaccination, antibiotics, and a better understanding of what keeps humans healthy. Dr. Hashmi's research is a natural extension of those scientific frontiers. Just as humans have adapted to their new reality over the last two hundred years, the ensuing generations will alter the pattern of their lives to reflect a longer life span. Also, this may be moot, as everyone is hypothetically opposed to extending life spans until faced with the loss of a loved one or their own deteriorating health.

PERSONAL ASSESSMENT

Although born in India, Amrit Hashmi has lived in the United States since 1940, when his father was recruited to work at Oak Ridge as part of the nuclear experiments. He became a citizen in 1949 along with his parents, although he does retain his Indian citizenship and returns fairly often for visits with his extended family. His first marriage was arranged and he and his wife didn't have any children. She died more than ten years ago.

Dr. Hashmi is a dynamic speaker and passionate about his research. Some other researchers have been put off by his zeal for his subject matter. In his spare time, he volunteers with a youth organization in the Pittsburgh area that teaches underprivileged children to fly kites. One of the members of that organization said that a few years ago Dr. Hashmi designed a curriculum for their afterschool program that taught the basics of geometry and spatial recognition through building kites.

Personally, I find his research not only compelling but boundary-pushing. His area of expertise is young in relation to many of the more established disciplines, but it may be that because it has been previously overlooked, the study of aging will yield tremendous society-altering results. So far the field, without even knowing the exact and varied mechanisms of aging, has managed to find ways to extend life in the laboratory. It is admirable that Dr. Hashmi seeks to bring that same approach to humans themselves.

RECOMMENDATION

Dr. Hashmi should be awarded a MacArthur Fellowship in the next three years.

Bets at the End
of the Season

CHAPTER THIRTY-ONE

Trust

*E*lizabeth had never enjoyed being called Bets, but nicknames had a way of sticking when you least expected them to. It'd been her Grandpa Percy who called her Bets. Bitty Bets because until she became a teenager, she was a foot shorter than all the other children her age. Elizabeth thought about this as she ducked her head under one of the branches in the orchard on her way back up to Hill House. In all of her ninety years, she'd never lived anywhere else, and unlike the others, she'd never wanted to leave. She watched the dry summer breeze blow across the orchard and stir the glaucous leaves. Her hands were still shaking from her fight with Callie. The girl must know Elizabeth's secret. She was sure her boyfriend had told her, had betrayed what she'd confessed to him in confidence. She should never have trusted Dr. Hashmi.

She steadied herself on the porch railing. Inside Anna plunked out a series of commercial jingles on the piano while Erin hummed along. The baby let out a gurgle of excitement each time the music swelled, and his laughter made the dog bark. They were oblivious to all the confidences Elizabeth held, not just her own, but others'.

There had been small secrets disclosed by her siblings and her play-mates, admirations, petty thefts, but her first big secret had come the summer she turned fourteen, when Grandma Mims told Eliz-abeth the truth about Anna. It was Mims who'd marked her as a secret-keeper, pointed out that Elizabeth looked trustworthy—with eyes set evenly and so roundly that the corners melted into high cheekbones and a voice that was soft and at such a decibel that there were those around her who couldn't hear her speak.

She slid her hands along the railing, and a small sliver of wood embedded her palm. She sat in the rocking chair and pinched at it with her fingernails, thinking about her grandmother. It seemed like two lifetimes since the old woman had died, but Elizabeth felt her presence now, had felt it in the grove arguing with Callie. She knew that when Dr. Hashmi arrived, there would be revelations, and then there would be change. Elizabeth wasn't ready for either. She dug at the splinter until her palm bled.

When it became clear that Mims was dying, father asked Eliz-abeth to come in from the olive fields and take care of her grand-mother. That had been the summer he'd dropped Bitty from her nickname. Calling her Bets, she saw now, was an attempt to delay the obvious—that she was growing up. That July she'd been taken to the department store in Red Bluff for what Anna called wom-anly wears.

Mims had been a large woman, but that summer she lost fifty pounds and her skin hung on her like sheets on the line. She'd seemed so old then to Bets, as wrinkled and gray as Anna was now, although at the time Mims couldn't have been much more than sixty. When Elizabeth lifted Mims's arms to bathe her, she had to push aside folds of skin to clean between them. It reminded her of patting dry the chickens after they'd been plucked. They both averted their eyes during these moments. At other times, when Elizabeth read to Mims from the book of Tobit or Esther, a conspiratorial feeling emerged between them. Mims had grown up Catholic but became a Lutheran to please her husband. The first night Elizabeth had sat with her, she'd asked her to go next door to the Lindseys' and borrow their mother's Bible. "I need a little of my girlhood faith," she'd said by way of explanation to Elizabeth.

One night after Mims's eyes closed and Elizabeth got up to go to her own room, her grandmother let out a whimper. Elizabeth tried to soothe her, but she became more distraught and finally she said, "Your mother is not my daughter."

The entire story unspooled from Mims. The time spent in Australia and how on the night they were forced to leave, that her husband had told her about his infidelity with the girl who came into town to help with the laundry. That bush woman's child, the little four-year-old girl who had freckles, was also his child. "He wouldn't leave Brisbane without her," Mims said. "I watched, stood by as he took Anna from her mother's arms. I grabbed tight to my own children as he did this, as if I were protecting them from being taken."

Elizabeth wondered that her mother didn't know. Days after learning the story, she studied her mother and saw that she looked nothing like Mims. Anna had skin that was the same color as the bark of the olive trees. Her hair was dark with a hard wave that resisted all attempts to pin it back. She had mannerisms of her father, but where he had the high, chubby cheeks of the Irish, Anna's cheeks stretched from her eyes to her chin, and her heavy mouth gave her face the appearance of a bulldog when she was angry. She had her father's eyes, in shape, but they were yellow-brown instead of blue. Elizabeth knew she looked like her mother, her own skin was lighter and the wave in her hair more manageable, but side by side they were the same—especially now that she'd started to take on a woman's shape.

The story came out in bits as Mims's illness lingered. Elizabeth didn't know what to do with her secret. She was afraid of her grand-father, who she'd always thought of as a hard man. Now that she knew he'd taken Anna from her real mother, she stopped talking to him. He didn't seem to notice that she answered in nods instead of yes, sirs. One afternoon as she helped her mother knead biscuits, she asked Anna about her childhood, about Australia.

Anna was brisk and efficient in the kitchen. "What I remember most is wanting to leave. If you want to learn about kangaroos and wallabies, you should ask your Uncle Wealthy."

She pushed her mother, asked her about her earliest memory of Mims. Anna pursed her lips and folded a biscuit in half. "She didn't cry. The day Violet was burned up in the school fire, I remember her slapping Daddy when he cried, but not Mims. She said God gave them either what they deserved or what they could handle."

"But Mims cries all the time," Elizabeth said. She was alarmed that when her mother had said this, there was a hint of satisfaction to the story.

"She's gotten old," her mother said with a wave of her hand. "You get near the end of your life and you start regretting. But when you're young you can't waste time on tears."

At that moment, Elizabeth's father had come into the room. "That's the Scot-Irish in you," he said and grabbed his wife around the waist. Anna stiffened and then rested her shoulder briefly against his shoulder. "You aren't telling my baby girl to toughen up, are you? You save that talk for the boys. I'm pretty sure one of your sons was wailing about a splinter this morning."

"Oh hush," said Anna, tossing a bit of flour at him.

Mims died in July. It was at her funeral that Elizabeth thought to talk with Uncle Wealthy about the secret. He had been nearly eleven when they came over on the ship—old enough to remember the sudden addition of a four-year-old to his family just before they left for the United States. Wealthy was a speculator. "Trying to live up to my name," he'd said if someone asked him about his current project. He bought and sold land, originally trying to second-guess the railroads and then spent most of his time in Texas buying and selling leases in search of a well plentiful enough that he could retire.

At the funeral, he arrived wearing the largest hat Elizabeth had ever seen. He had a mustache, and his red hair had started to turn white. He entertained the children by making shadow puppets on the walls outside the home in Kidron. Elizabeth didn't know how to start a serious conversation with an adult. She felt that if she asked him outright, she'd be betraying a secret, so she asked him sideways questions like she had of her mother. *Tell me about Australia. What's your earliest memory of my mom? What did you do when you were on the boat?*

On his second day there, he asked her if she wanted to go for a ride. Her father kept a few horses for when the roads became too muddy to drive in, and they saddled up two old mares and headed down to the river. They talked a little as they rode, mostly about how different the land was in west Texas, and he tried to teach her a few words in Spanish. When they could see the river, they stopped their horses. He didn't look at her as he spoke.

"What did Mims tell you?"

"She isn't Anna's mother."

"She's wrong about that. Mims was every bit a mother to Anna."

Elizabeth stumbled over her words. "I mean she told me that Grandpa stole my mother from her real mother."

Wealthy sighed. "I'm not sure he stole her, but what he did was wrong. He should have brought the laundress with us, paid for her passage to America, too."

"I don't know what to do," Elizabeth said. The water was muddy. It always was back then. There weren't any dams and reservoirs to keep the silt from flowing down from Mount Shasta.

"Forget it. Knowing that Mims isn't your grandmother changes nothing."

"Does my mother know?"

"She knows and she doesn't know." Wealthy dismounted from his horse and led it to the river to drink.

It took Elizabeth many years to understand what her uncle was telling her. Wealthy never did live up to his name, but every time he hit big, before he poured it into another speculation, he bought a few acres of land around the family orchard in Kidron, so that by the time Elizabeth married and her brothers went off to seek their fortunes, there was enough land for everyone to feel safe. Wealthy died in 1943 mining a claim in Kiwalik Flats. Two of Elizabeth's brothers and a score of nephews and cousins had made the trek to western Alaska to mine the claim. It was there, like Wealthy himself on the verge of paying off. A month after his death, Elizabeth received a nugget in the mail that he'd fashioned into a necklace. It was five ounces of gold and looked like a hardened lump of oatmeal.

Elizabeth's palm had stopped bleeding, but a bit of the splinter remained. She unhooked the necklace she'd worn most of her life and weighed the gold nugget in her hand. There had been no note with Wealthy's gift, and as she turned it over in her hand, she understood that it was payment for keeping secrets.

CHAPTER THIRTY-TWO

Bunyip

The hard crunch of tires on the gravel drive brought Elizabeth from her memories. She saw the geneticist with
his unkempt black hair and round face peering at her through
his windshield. In her periphery, she saw Callie step out of the
orchard and move toward the car. The piano had stopped playing.
A wave of panic rushed over Elizabeth. For the last few months,
she'd avoided considering what Dr. Hashmi would find when he
looked at her blood, at her children's blood, but seeing him again
the fear rushed at her, and she felt submerged. She had to talk to Dr.
Hashmi before he spoke to them all. She stepped quickly down the
stairs and waved at him to stop.

He rolled down the window. "You are excited," he said.

"No. We have to talk before you tell the others what you know.
Can we go someplace? Or maybe just talk in the car?" Elizabeth
opened the passenger door and got in. Callie arrived at the car at
that moment.

"Mom, what are you doing?" she asked.

"The good doctor forgot one of his papers at the motel, and I need the fresh air. Told him to take me for a drive." Elizabeth gestured to Dr. Hashmi to back the car up and waved to her daughter and her mother, who'd come onto the porch.

"We'll be right back," Dr. Hashmi said and gave a sort of a nod to Callie.

They didn't speak until he'd turned onto the main road from Hill House.

"Where to?" he asked.

"No place, anyplace. There's a field about two miles down with an access point that only a few of us know about. I'll tell you when to turn," Elizabeth said. Her palm had started to bleed again, and she wiped it on her gray trousers.

She directed him to park under one of the oak trees that dotted the field. "This used to be an orchard, but some fool got the idea that it would be cheaper to lop off the trees every year rather than prune them. Called it coppicing," she said.

"Didn't work?" asked Dr. Hashmi.

"Broke him. The trees didn't regenerate as fast as he thought."

She rolled down her window and put her seat back far enough that she could stretch out. These compact cars always felt like she'd stuffed herself into a box. Dr. Hashmi pulled some papers from a folder he had in the back of the car and shuffled them.

"I'm guessing this is about the blood work," he began.

She cut him off. "You ever hear of a bunyip?"

He shook his head. Elizabeth stretched out her legs and rested her feet on the dashboard. "When we were younger, Mom used to warn us about a creature that had the skin of a seal and the mouth of a crocodile. Said it hid in water. We liked to come down here before I had breasts and swim in the mud holes. They were cold as hell." She looked out the window and pointed to a small clearing past two oak trees and several other stumps. "There's one that pops up there. Vernal pools they called them back then."

"Yes. I know about these. They come in the spring when the water channels get overloaded with melting snow," said Dr. Hashmi. He did not appear to want to hurry Elizabeth's story up, just nodded at her to continue.

"I never went in the water. I'd come down here with my brothers and watch them strip to their skivvies and jump in with yelps and hollers. But I couldn't do it because I just knew that that bunyip was waiting for me to put my toe in the water."

"Surely there's no such thing as a bunyip," said the doctor quietly.

"No. No. It's just a made-up monster, some beast held over from my mother's childhood. It's just that when you get older, get to be as old as I am, that you wish there were bunyips. What can hurt me now are the monsters I made myself."

"It's not as bad as all that," he said.

Elizabeth wanted it to be over. She turned to him and said the line she'd been practicing since the day he came to draw her blood. "You've found me out." The words weren't lighthearted and funny as she intended. Instead, she blinked away tears and the words fell like stones into a pond. Each one making its own ripple.

He handed her a sheet of paper, and she saw that Callie's name was typed at the top of it. "The lab, as part of my research, analyzed the DNA your family provided, not just for longevity but also to group them by similarity in profiles. I wanted to see how being directly related to Anna affected the results. Basically, these tests also revealed paternity. There are fifteen DNA markers we use to determine paternity." He pointed to numbers on Callie's sheet and read off numbers he called *alleles* and discussed *locus*. Elizabeth wasn't listening.

She knew what he was saying. Callie was her daughter and Frank's daughter. It had taken them four years to conceive. Four years of Elizabeth lying in bed and praying for her husband to touch her. She'd wanted a large family, like she'd grown up in. But Frank didn't want her.

The geneticist pulled out the sheets of paper with her boys' names on them. Matthew, John, Mark, Luke. The four gospels. The names were an apology to God. Her boys had all sent samples of their blood to Dr. Hashmi. This collection of samples from all the direct descendants was what had taken the doctor so long, he explained. He paused before continuing. "These results exclude Frank as the father and, I was surprised at this, they show that it is highly probable that each of your sons has a different father."

What must he think? Elizabeth looked at Dr. Hashmi, who was intently focused on his pen—clicking the top of it repeatedly. "Can we keep this from them?"

He cleared his throat. "In my experience." He stopped and then reached out to take her hand. "Ms. Bets. This happens more often than you'd expect. I can keep your secret, and unless one of your sons or their children is particularly knowledgeable about genetics, you won't be found out. I wonder that some of them don't already know. I mean, if you look at the odds of you and Frank having a blue-eyed child, and you have three sons with blue eyes."

She interrupted him. "You'll keep this from them then?"

He nodded. "But if it were me, I'd want to know about the bunyip."

"Wouldn't you hate her though?"

"Who?"

"Your mother."

He shrugged. "Hate's a thing you can get over."

"I don't have enough time left for them to get over it."

"You have more time left than I do." Dr. Hashmi hugged her then, and whispered "Tell them" into her ear.

She opened the car door and stepped out into the field. The grass was dry, and as she walked, grasshoppers leaped ahead of her steps. "I need a minute," she called to Dr. Hashmi. He waved her off, reclined his seat, and closed his eyes.

She wished she could be with Frank. She needed him to have a lucid moment to talk with him honestly about what she'd done, about what she'd asked him for permission to do. She thought about her boys and knew that if she dared tell them, they would forgive her.

The drive back to Hill House was far too short. She saw Callie sitting on the front stoop drawing letters in the gravel with the tip of her shoe. Elizabeth let Dr. Hashmi get out first. He leaned down and offered a hand to Callie. When he pulled Callie to her feet, she stumbled into him and they embraced for several seconds, exchanging low whispers. Her daughter wouldn't forgive her. Allegiance was more important to Callie than water, and no matter what her reason, she'd blame Elizabeth for the disloyalty.

"Feel better?" Callie asked, holding her hand out. Elizabeth had expected her daughter to be holding on to some of the anger from their earlier fight in the groves, but Dr. Hashmi's presence seemed to have erased the tension that had been between them. Her daughter had not been this temperamental since she was a child. Elizabeth, for the thousandth time, wondered what her daughter would have been like if that damn pilot hadn't committed suicide by flying his plane into that mountain. She embraced her and breathed in the scent of her hair, which smelled like lavender and the dirt around Hill House.

"Too tight. Oomph," Callie said and pulled away, but for just a moment, Elizabeth had felt her daughter return her embrace.

She'd been the wrong kind of mother to Callie. Even before the crash, she'd not mothered her in the way she needed. She felt that she owed it to Frank to let him have her, raise her the way he wanted. They both knew the others wouldn't be his and that he'd feel this. Her husband had been superstitious and taught Callie all his rituals. Frank had always been in awe of Elizabeth's family. He watched as their vineyards prospered in years when his family's withered. He'd been there to see Anna appear to stop aging as his own mother lost her mind. Her mother-in-law had died not because she'd gotten old, but because she'd wandered away in the middle of the night and fallen into an irrigation ditch. The old woman never recovered from the pneumonia she caught that night.

Callie was as much Frank's daughter as the boys were Elizabeth's. Without the imprint of their father, they became what Elizabeth wanted them to be. She fostered them with her uncle Wealthy in the summers—sending them to work wherever his next big find landed him—Sedona, Walla Walla, and finally western Alaska.

"You look funny," Callie said.

"I was just thinking about your brothers."

"They're just in a different stage of their life. Remember when they were all having their babies. That one year, when was it? In 1968, when between the three of them they had three babies. They couldn't stop calling you then—asking for advice and reassurance that they were doing what was right. You'll see them soon."

"It was hard to talk with them after Deb disappeared again. I hated making those calls because I never know how to talk to them about you or their niece and it always leaves us with such sadness and distance." Elizabeth, without realizing it, had brought up the sore spot between them.

Callie furrowed her forehead. "It's nobody's business where Deb is. Or why she left—especially my brothers. They were never kind to her—to us."

How could the happiness her daughter had felt just a moment earlier be so easily obliterated? "No, that's not true, they just want what is best for—"

"Nobody wants what's best for me. You all blame me for the way she turned out. I know they think it is my fault. Do you realize that neither Mark nor Matt has sent me a thank-you card for any of the presents I sent for birthdays, graduations? Their photocopied Christmas letters are full of how well their children are doing. Who graduated from college, who was elected mayor, how many times they've sailed around Africa. And they're just like you, they think the smartest thing Deb did was leave again. Run away from her problems and leave us with our own."

"There was no choice. If they find her, she'll go back to prison until she dies."

Dr. Hashmi cleared his throat.

"That's what she deserves." Callie was absolute in this statement.

"Should we go inside?" he asked.

"Not even Erin believes that. And out of all of us, your granddaughter should have the last say," Elizabeth said.

It was because of Erin that Elizabeth and Callie kept peace. Invoking her now brought the argument to a close. They both knew there was nowhere for them to go with their anger and that it would be best to move on to another subject.

Callie slid her arm around Dr. Hashmi's waist and walked up the steps. Leaning on him, her limp was less pronounced, and Elizabeth watched her daughter's shoulders relax as they walked in the house together.

CHAPTER THIRTY-THREE

Disclosure

When Dr. Hashmi and Callie entered the living room, there was silence for an uncomfortably long time. Then a flurry of activity erupted; cookies were brought from the kitchen, tea offered, and the women settled themselves around the doctor, who'd brought a large bag and a computer with him.

"I'm going to make you all famous," he said, rubbing his hands together. "Do you know what makes us old?"

"Time," Elizabeth said.

"Yes, but no," the doctor said.

Callie jumped in with the answer he wanted. "Deterioration."

He smiled at her, and Elizabeth could see that his interest in her daughter went beyond scientific curiosity. When Dr. Hashmi had first come to talk with them, he'd spent many hours describing the different effects of aging. His interest was in longevity genes. Or rather, he believed that aging was controlled by genetics. He now unfolded an easel and then pulled several large poster boards out of his bag.

He set the first one on the stand with a flourish. Bobo charged the tripod, and as the doctor reached to steady his poster board and Anna called the dog to her lap, Elizabeth wondered if he knew that the picture, with its row upon row of colored bars, meant nothing to them. He pointed to a small section near the last third of the board. "This is the Anna mutation." He circled it repeatedly with his pointer. "You all have it."

Callie clapped. Elizabeth, along with the rest of her family, was silent. Callie was the first to venture a question. "What does it mean? This mutation?"

"Everything," he said. "You are aging environmentally, but not genetically."

"But what does it mean?" Anna asked. She was shaking a bit and Elizabeth reached across the table to hold her hand.

"Stay out of the sun, eat right, keep exercising, and you could be the first to make it to a hundred and fifty," said the doctor.

"I don't want to live forever," Elizabeth said.

"Well you probably won't," said Dr. Hashmi. Elizabeth imagined that the weight of their earlier conversation settled into his shoulder, and he shook his head as he spoke. "I was just trying to say that in ideal circumstances someone with this genetic mutation, who avoided all environmentally degrading substances, could potentially not age. You"—he looked at everyone in the room—"have all been exposed to—"

"—the world," Erin said, finishing his sentence. She held her baby close, almost shielding him from Dr. Hashmi.

"The remarkable thing about this mutation is that it is only present in women, and a daughter can only inherit the mutation if her mother has it. So little baby Keller will have a normal life span, but any daughters you have could claim immortality. Especially now, because we know."

He reached for a cookie and took a long drink of his tea. Low conversations started and then stopped just as suddenly as each of the women thought about Dr. Hashmi's pronouncement. Elizabeth clenched her fists. She couldn't look at her daughter or her mother, who she knew felt differently than she did. Erin grinned like one of those contests on the reality shows she watched.

Anna was first to address the group, the first to open up the discussion with question after question about the mutation, where it had come from and what Dr. Hashmi and his team wanted to study.

"It would have come from Anna's mother, and quite possibly from her mother's mother and so on. We know this is not a recent mutation, but one that happened hundreds of years earlier," Dr. Hashmi said, pulling out more posters to point at. Elizabeth realized, listening to them talk, that Anna hadn't owned up to knowing Mims wasn't her mother.

Elizabeth cleared her throat. "The mutation didn't come from Mims."

"Of course it did," Callie said. "Mom, you just have to follow the logic. I got it from you, you got it from Anna, and Anna got it from her mother, Mims."

"No," Elizabeth said.

The dog pawed at Anna's chest and licked her cheek. She pushed him down and looked at her daughter. "It doesn't matter, does it? We can't know for sure."

Dr. Hashmi had no trouble following the conversation. It was almost as if he'd anticipated this turn. "There are some unusual markers in your DNA, for someone of western European descent," he said.

"What about aborigines?" Elizabeth asked. "Would our DNA make more sense if Anna weren't Irish?"

"Papa was Irish," Anna said.

"What are you saying?" Callie asked. She turned to the doctor. "Amrit, what are they talking about? Is this the information you wouldn't tell me? Is this why you told me to ask my mother about her secrets?"

Elizabeth looked at Dr. Hashmi, imploring him not to give away the other secret. Then she turned to Anna, "Do you know this, Mom? Do you know that Mims isn't your mother?"

Anna smiled. "Sometimes tall tales have a bit of truth to them. Was it your uncle Wealthy who told you? I knew and I didn't know." She closed her eyes and leaned back into her chair. Erin and Callie whispered furiously to Dr. Hashmi, asking him for verification and more.

Elizabeth touched Anna's arm. "It's your story to tell."

"Then get me something a bit stronger than tea to drink," she said, setting Bobo on the ground. The dog sniffed at her feet and then trotted over to his bed and settled into sleep.

Erin went to the linen closet, where they kept a bottle of scotch wrapped in the winter sheets. When she returned, she poured a little in everyone's tea glass except for the doctor, who refused.

Anna told them her story. She told them how much she'd hated her father for taking her, but how Mims made it hurt less by loving her so much. She described the image she held in her mind of her mother—a tall woman wearing a dust-covered handkerchief over her hair. "I try very hard at night when I fall asleep to see her face, but nothing is there. I think that her eyes must have been brown and that her nose must have been like mine." Anna reached up and ran her fingers along her own face. She cupped her full cheeks and tapped her finger against her broad triangular nose. Her bottom lip was much larger than her top, and at times, when she relaxed her face, it looked like she was pouting.

During the secret telling, Dr. Hashmi sat on his hands. Elizabeth thought he looked like a man sitting on too narrow of a seat, and at every pause in Anna's story, he moved his lips, as if he were about to speak. Finally, when Anna had settled back into her chair and Callie and Erin had exhausted their questions, the doctor stood up and paced the room. "There's a chance that your mother could still be living."

Anna shook her head. "That would take a miracle."

"But don't you want to find out?" Erin came over to Anna and knelt beside her chair. She'd come to the same conclusion as the doctor; Elizabeth could see it in her eyes. She'd always been hopeful, willing to believe that the best was waiting to be found. It was what had driven her to get her mother released, and Elizabeth knew that her great-granddaughter now had a new quest.

"I, I don't know enough about her," Anna said.

Elizabeth thought about all that Wealthy had told her more than sixty years earlier. "Your brother said that she wasn't more than fourteen when she had you. Wealthy said that she was hired to work for your parents from the orphanage and they didn't keep girls past that age. She was pregnant the next year."

"Still, she couldn't be alive. Nobody lives to be older than a hundred and twenty."

"She'd be a hundred twenty-eight," said Erin. "Give or take a year."

"That's an impossible age," Elizabeth said, considering what the weight of another thirty years would do to her mind.

"It is not impossible," said Dr. Hashmi, placing his hand possessively over Anna's.

"It is," said Elizabeth, standing and then sitting quickly. For the first time, she'd seen a glimpse of ego in the doctor's mannerisms.

"I think. No, we think Anna, even with all the environmental aging, still has another thirty years left." Dr. Hashmi spoke so quickly he missed the nonverbal conversation that was happening among the women.

"What else did my brother tell you?" asked Anna.

Elizabeth looked away from her mother. "Mostly I know what I know from Mims."

"That's a long time to keep this to yourself." Anna's tone had changed from friendly to parental, and Elizabeth felt as she had as a girl when she'd been caught lying about having done her chores.

Callie came and stood between Anna and Elizabeth, as if in anticipation of refereeing their fight. "We could go to Australia. Try to find out. It might be a goose chase but—"

"We have to go," said Dr. Hashmi. "Or rather I have to go. If she is alive, or if there are other relatives with the mutation."

Elizabeth ignored her daughter and the doctor. "She didn't know how much you remembered and she didn't want to make you unhappy. Wealthy felt the same way. If you knew, why didn't you say anything?"

"Father told me that if I was sure I didn't belong to the family that he'd send me back to Australia. He told me it was a dream and that Mims was my mother."

Erin immediately took Anna's side. "You didn't believe him," she urged.

"How could I? The memory of him ripping me from her arms was too real to be a dream. I could smell her, I tasted her tears."

"And you never asked Mims?" Erin said softly.

"I was afraid she'd stop loving me. So I let Mims be my mother."

Dr. Hashmi opened his small laptop computer and began typing furiously. "Where did you say your parents were from? What part of Australia again?"

"You know this," Elizabeth said, suspicious of how much of this had been staged. She peered over the doctor's shoulder. "Brisbane."

He scrolled through page after page of records. "We keep a record of anyone who claims to be older than a hundred ten. There are more than you'd think, but then the world has more than six billion people on it. You get reports like this one from a village in

Somali. A pair of women claiming to be mother and daughter, but no one knows which is which and they're so old no one in the village remembers them as anything but crones. They think they are a hundred twenty and a hundred and six, but we don't know."

He highlighted a row of records and then clicked. They all opened quickly, filling up the screen of the tiny machine. "Twenty-one unconfirmed supercentenarians in Australia. And, oh my, eighteen are women."

"So?" asked Callie.

"That's much too high," he said.

"What?" asked Erin.

Dr. Hashmi sat next to her with the computer on his lap. "It's typical to have more older women than men. Women take better care of themselves; they don't fight in wars, or take risks at the same rate as men. But this percentage is too high. Makes me think we might find a mutation like Anna's. One that is only present in women."

Callie drifted over to them. Elizabeth watched as her daughter put her hand on the doctor's back. It was a gesture of ownership. Knowing her daughter, Elizabeth was sure that she was proud that he'd discovered this mutation and so quickly connected it to Anna's past.

Elizabeth went to her mother. "I'm so sorry."

"Folks have always trusted you," Anna said, putting her hand on Elizabeth's head. "Tell me what you know."

Despite her age, and the discomfort it caused her, Elizabeth put her head in her mother's lap. She unspun every bit of information she'd tucked away about Anna's lineage. When she was done, she stayed with her mother and watched Callie, her own daughter. It had been decades since she'd seen her happy. She stood next to Dr. Hashmi, leaning toward him and putting her weight on her good leg. He was talking excitedly about the science of genetics and longevity and his hands, moving as he talked, looked like he was conducting an orchestra. Her eyes were bright, and Elizabeth thought she could see a slight flush that crept from her daughter's collarbones to her cheeks.

She thought about the other secret she and Dr. Hashmi were keeping from Callie and wondered if she were told that she was Frank's only biological child whether she'd be able to keep her happiness. She wanted to ask her mother if she thought she should keep quiet about it, especially now that Anna had discovered the whole truth about her mother.

Anna didn't look happy—for the first time Elizabeth could remember, her mother looked old. She began to think that Dr. Hashmi had been wrong about how much time her mother had left.

"Mom?" Elizabeth said. Her voice seemed to bring Anna back from where she'd been.

"I'm fine," she said. The color returned to her cheeks and the yellowish cast disappeared from her face. "We've got a trip to Australia to plan."

CHAPTER THIRTY-FOUR

Leaving

The day Callie left with Dr. Hashmi, it rained. It had not stopped raining in the month since her departure. Wet summers were an abnormality in Kidron, and glee about plump olives had turned to dismay at the signs of blight that began to appear on the drupes in August. Elizabeth liked the grayness and the drizzle. It suited her mood.

"Cheer up, sourpuss," Erin said, coming into the living room. "Weatherman says it's supposed to be sunny today." The baby rested in a fabric sling Erin had tied around one shoulder.

"Bring that baby of yours over here. He'll cheer me up." The boy was nearly four months old and Elizabeth couldn't believe how large he'd gotten. "I think his father was part sumo wrestler."

"His father is all of five foot six," Erin said, sitting down in the recliner opposite Elizabeth. "He's going to meet us in Australia."

"Oh?" The baby grabbed at her nose.

"I guess after his wife was done being mad, she decided she wanted to meet Keller. They never had kids of their own."

"Be careful," Elizabeth said.

"I'll keep an eye on everyone," Anna said, coming into the living room. "Besides it'll be good for the child to know who his father is."

Erin blushed. "I think I just got a little crazy for a while. Now it seems so foolish to have made such a fuss over a man who didn't love me."

Anna laughed. "We've all been a little crazy about men. Just be glad you've got more of us in you than your mother. That was crazy."

"Grams!" Erin said.

"I'm starting to think that we take our tragedies too seriously," Anna said. "What's God going to do? Hand the Keller family a little more smite? He should've figured out it doesn't work so well on us."

Despite herself, Elizabeth smiled. The news about Anna's paternity had made everyone less cautious. She bounced Keller on her knee, talking nonsense to him and thinking about what it would feel like to be in Hill House alone this winter. She'd decided not to go to Australia—it would be too much time away from Frank. She hadn't missed one day of visiting with him since putting him in Golden Sunsets.

"Don't jostle him so much. He just ate and he tends—"

"Aaaak." Elizabeth held the baby away from her and let him finish spitting up on the floor. Her pantsuit was stained with sour milk. She handed the baby to Anna, who was laughing.

"You never were good with babies. Don't get me wrong, once they could walk, you were the best mother I've ever seen. But you barely tolerated them as infants."

"I'm sure you can see why," Elizabeth said, leaving the room to change. She was supposed to meet Callie's Realtor that morning to give him the keys to the Pit Stop. Her daughter had ended up keeping an online version of the store and selling the land and the building to an entrepreneur who wanted to open a roadside church for truckers. She changed into her plum pantsuit and gave Keller a kiss on the head before leaving.

"Auntie Bets," called the Realtor as Elizabeth stepped from the car. The boy was young, and distantly related to the Kellers. His mother was the cousin of one of the girls who'd married a nephew of Elizabeth's. Relationships in Kidron were complicated. She waved to him, flashing the keys to the store, which were in her hand. The man who was purchasing the store had his back to her and was peering in the windows. Wanted posters with Deb's face on them were still posted on the doors. The man wore a plaid shirt with the sleeves rolled to his elbows. He had hairy forearms and a tattoo that reminded Elizabeth of Popeye.

"It finally stopped raining," said the Realtor. "It's been a hard summer to sell stuff. No one around here wants to go out if their feet are going to get wet."

"I guess I had an advantage then, not being from around here," said the man. He extended his hand to Elizabeth. "Name's Dennis. Well, they said you Keller women look young. I gotta agree you don't look a day over sixty."

Elizabeth relaxed. "Thank you. My husband often mistakes me for his nurse, and she's not even fifty."

They laughed and Elizabeth offered to unlock the store and show him the fixtures that were part of the sale. The fluorescent lights flickered when she flipped the switch. The air was stale and smelled of burned coffee. The merchandise had been packed and shipped by Callie's stock boys the week before. She gestured to the shelves and the register. "These are all yours, although I'm not sure what you'll be needing them for."

"The Lord doesn't have anything against me selling a few necessities to my congregation," Dennis said. "I was a trucker myself for a lotta years. There's some stuff we'll buy no matter where we see it."

"Do you think they'll stop? I'd think people want to get their religion at home with their families on Sundays," Elizabeth said. She was concerned about his idea.

"People will stop whenever they need forgiveness," Dennis said. He bent down to see how the shelving was fastened to the floor. "Gotta get a good drill motor in here."

"The boys Callie hired, Pete and Robert. They're good workers. They could help you with this," Elizabeth said. She worried about them not having work.

"I've already hired them," Dennis said. "That daughter of yours had the same concern. Practically made hiring them part of the conditions for sale."

"That's good of you," she said. They walked to the back of the store.

"Dennis here is a regular philanthropist," said the Realtor. "He's been spreading the money around. Even paid me commission on the deal I brokered for the billboard."

"I think you mean entrepreneur," Elizabeth said. "What's this about a commission?" asked Elizabeth.

"He's sold the rights to the sign to that business just up the street, across from the motel."

"You mean Eddie's convenience store?" Elizabeth asked.

"No. The other store, just next to Eddie's," said the Realtor, looking away from Elizabeth.

She thought about the street and could picture only the pornography shop with its XXX above the door and metal shed "Annexxx," which could be rented by the hour. "Surely not!"

The Realtor looked at the floor, but Dennis smiled wide and Elizabeth saw that he had tobacco-yellow teeth. "The way I figure it, the best way to get men to church is let them sin a little and then feel bad enough to repent. I got Sean over at the emporium to put a little billboard up at the end of his property—one that the truckers will see on their way out. It says, 'God Loves You Too' with directions to our church."

"It's not God they ought to be thinking about, but their wives back home. You can't be with a hooker and do a little praying to make up for that," Elizabeth said. She went to the front of the store and ripped down the wanted posters of Deb. "Forgiveness is a much harder process."

"God knows that," Dennis said, following her. "He just wants me to get them to the door. And the best way I know how to do that is let them get an illicit poke in first."

The Realtor laughed. It was a high, thin sound that reminded Elizabeth of squealing pigs. She pushed the keys into Dennis's hand and fled to her car.

Anna sat on the back porch. She'd pulled her rocker into the one bit of sun that the branches of the maples were not able to obscure, and although her eyes were closed, Elizabeth knew she was resting, but not asleep. This was part of her secret; since turning one hundred, she'd started remaining as still as possible unless another person was around. She said that this conservation of energy, this hibernation, gave her extra time, that a minute spent in this suspended state was another minute on the earth.

"Daughter," Anna said as Elizabeth approached.

Elizabeth said, "One of my grandsons was telling me that we need to stay out of the sun. That it somehow pokes tiny invisible holes in your skin and that's what causes all of our wrinkles and our age spots."

"Those grandchildren of yours are know-it-alls," Anna said. "Besides I've had wrinkles since I was thirty—what's a few more going to hurt?"

"Don't tell him that. He's one of those cancer doctors that will yell at you about your skin and cell mutations."

"No one, especially doctors, tells me what to do anymore," Anna said. Elizabeth smiled at her mother.

It was true. What could they say to a woman who'd lived to be a hundred and thirteen? Anna was confident that her body was perfect. It was old, but it worked well. Elizabeth wondered when the doctors would stop chiding her.

"How's Frank?" asked Anna.

Her mother always had been able to do this. Sense the purpose of a visit, drill down to the reason for a person's arrival on her doorstep. Elizabeth was surprised by the honesty of her answer. "I just couldn't go see him today. After giving the keys to that Realtor, you know Lucy's grandson. Well, I just couldn't face Frank. He's forgotten so much. He thinks he's twenty-five."

"We all think we're twenty-five. You know it's only when I glance in the mirror or look at you and see how old you've gotten that I remember how much time has passed."

"It's different," Elizabeth said.

"I know." Her mother gestured for her to join her on the rocker on the porch.

The sun warmed Elizabeth's skin. The smell and the talk of Frank reminded her of the summer he proposed. It was 1927 and the valley was just coming out of a winter of heavy snows. Shasta, in the distance, seemed smaller, for all the snow that covered the mountain, and by June, when the rush of melting snow usually slowed, there was a second summer melting. The river was wide and it became a place where folks liked to go and watch. The farmers whose land touched its banks began backing up in May. Jerry Sims had even hired a team of horses to move his barn, and Barry James had emptied his grain silo—paid his neighbors to store it for him.

In early June, after most of the work in the groves had been done, Frank showed up at the house and asked to take her down to watch the river. Elizabeth was not a pretty girl. She'd come to terms with this early. At nineteen, some generous people, who might have been farsighted, described her as handsome. She was taller than most of the men she met and had a hard angular face. She and Frank had grown up together. His family's orchard, although not one of the original seven that made up Kidron, was purchased and planted shortly after Kidron's historic move. His family had been Mormon—his mother married to a man with seventeen other wives until it had become illegal.

Frank was courting another young woman at the time. A petite girl named Frances, who was friendly with his younger sisters. He took her to the movie theater that the Rodgerses had built in town and out for sodas at her family's drugstore. Still, Frank would show up at Elizabeth's house once a week, and they'd go for walks or ride the horses. His family had never had a stable, but he rode like a man born into the saddle.

That summer that the riverbanks flooded, they rode out in the early afternoons and sat on the trunk of a sequoia that overlooked the river. Elizabeth's mind didn't hold all that they talked about, only words that suggested Frank's thoughts on God or the best way to increase olive production. In August, when the river finally started to recede, revealing logs and boulders pulled down from Shasta itself, he proposed. Those words she remembered clearly. He grabbed her by the shoulders and said, "You've got to marry me. I couldn't stand it being anyone else. Their perfume, their silliness, their petticoats."

"Do you love me?" Elizabeth asked him.

"You are more than I deserve," he said.

In that moment, Elizabeth understood. There were no other suitors in her life, and the whole town talked to her like she'd be a spinster, the kind ones giving her Jane Austen to read or Emily Dickinson, and the less kind telling her that they were sure Anna was glad to have a child who would never leave home.

"Will there be children?" she asked.

"I'll give you what I can," Frank said. He'd picked up a water-soaked tree branch and poked at the carcass of a possum. It was bloated and much of its hair had floated away.

"I'll take what I can get," Elizabeth said.

He confided his secret to her on their wedding night. What he'd said exactly was, "My plumbing doesn't work right. I might be able to get it turned on when you need it."

Elizabeth tracked her cycles methodically and let Frank know when she needed it. Still it took them four years to conceive, and watching his grim, determined face as he focused on getting his plumbing to work long enough, soured Elizabeth on sex.

A cloud passed in front of the sun, and a chill swept across Elizabeth's body. She turned toward her mother. "You should come see Frank with me today."

"I go on Sundays. Those nurses of his will yell at us for upsetting his routine. Why risk it?" Anna scooted her chair closer to the railing to be more fully in the sun.

"I want you to tell me if I'm understanding something right. It's about Frank and our boys and how he really is." Elizabeth left her chair in the shade. She let her mind drift to the signs she'd been seeing between Frank and Guy at the retirement facility.

The nurses at Golden Sunsets loved Frank. He'd been there longer than any other patient. They were mostly young and as such were progressive about Frank's crush. "It's nothing to be embarrassed about," they tittered when she'd asked them. "Nothing works anymore for either of them and to see them holding hands and kissing, well it is just a sweet thing." They told her of real problems between some of the younger patients. Confided that some of those in their seventies got their hands on Viagra a while back and then they'd had a real problem. "You wouldn't believe the outbreak of the clap that went around."

Elizabeth would believe anything. She told the nurses this. "One advantage of living so long, no surprises left." Her children would be surprised at Dr. Hashmi's DNA evidence. And surprise wasn't good for people; it led to hurt. Elizabeth had let go of expectations earlier than most. She didn't expect much from the world around her, and it kept her from being disappointed.

Anna pulled her from her thoughts. "You going to tell me?"

Elizabeth opened her eyes and turned toward her mother. "They're not Frank's boys."

"Of course they're not," Anna said. "But you can't tell them until he's passed. It'll be too hard on them, too much guilt."

"How could you know?" Elizabeth had been wrong. She'd not expected this, not from Anna. "Do you think they know?"

"They know and they don't know." Anna was fully alert now, sitting up with her back straight and looking out over the orchards.

"That's what you said about your own secret." Elizabeth searched her mother's face. Anna's eyes remained focused on the gnarled limbs of the trees just below the hill.

"I always wondered if you knew about my mother. Wealthy was a wise man. People don't give him enough credit, think he threw his life away chasing easy money."

"So I shouldn't tell them?" Elizabeth still felt she needed someone to tell her what to do. Someone to tell her not to take Dr. Hashmi's advice.

"Are they happy?"

Elizabeth wondered why Anna didn't already know the answer to this question. The boys were happy. Their lives were ordinary and right—the only bits of heartache coming as a few of the grandchildren and now even great-grandchildren found the trouble they went looking for. She didn't know about Callie. Happiness had eluded her for so long, but her voice was bright when she called from Pittsburgh, and Dr. Hashmi had told Elizabeth privately that he'd taken her to a counselor to talk about overusing her pain medication.

"I could never tell Callie," Elizabeth said.

"Then let her and the boys have their joy for a bit. You tell them that Frank isn't their daddy, it is going to bring a bit of unhappiness, like a rainstorm, but it will pass."

Anna settled back in her chair and began the rhythmic rocking. Elizabeth stood and kissed her mother on the top of her head. She thought that her mother's joy had come from learning her true paternity. She'd expected Anna, who must have had some previous doubts about her own ancestry, to tell her to unburden herself, to give her boys that same gift. The world was full of unexpected answers.

CHAPTER THIRTY-FIVE

Sin

*E*lizabeth knew little about the fathers of her boys. She wished she'd had other choices. One of her grandsons had told her a few years ago at Christmas how he and his wife had ordered sperm through the mail. All they had to do was pick the attributes they were looking for and send two hundred dollars to a sperm bank. He'd pointed to his children, who were playing in the yard with their cousins—they were all as blond as he and his wife. Elizabeth picked the fathers of her boys from the men who were in the Red Horseshoe, a bar in Redding. It was a popular spot for cowboys and women of loose morals, which was what the newspaper had said a few years after she'd stopped visiting the bar. It had been closed in 1942, when the whole country got a little bit more uptight.

She walked to the back of the house, where her bedroom had been as a girl, and where it was now. In the back of her closet, in a hatbox, was a yellowed piece of paper folded into quarters. There were four names on it, along with birth dates. These were the men who'd fathered her boys. She'd opened their wallets and copied the information from their drivers' licenses and then crept out the doors of the motels or flophouses. Why had she done this? There were dozens of names she'd had to throw away—months when despite her careful timing she didn't get pregnant. There'd been six men before her last son was conceived on one rainy Christmas eve. It had been too many; she'd started to enjoy herself, looking forward to putting on a dress and driving the hour north. Johnny's father had been young, and although it made Elizabeth blush to think of it, she may have been the boy's first. He took her three times and then talked to her about his father's restaurant in Modesto before he fell asleep and she could sneak back home.

Frank said nothing when she went out. Although he was as anxious as she when two weeks after her trips to Redding, she waited to see whether she'd bleed. He loved Elizabeth so deeply when she was pregnant—held the door open for her when she got out of the car and shooed her out of the orchard when the weather was anything but seventy degrees and sunny. He was wonderful with the babies when they came, cradling them in the crook of his elbow, and singing in Gaelic to them, as his grandmother had.

Callie was suspicious about Elizabeth's pregnancies. As a girl, she would poke her mother's belly as it extended and pout. "No baby," she'd say. "I'm enough." Frank thought this was as funny as could be and taught her to say "I'm spectacular." He also promised her that she'd be the only girl—Elizabeth prayed that this was true. She thinks now that a sister would have crushed Callie's spirit.

The names on the folded paper seemed unspectacular to Elizabeth. After so many years of reading them and wondering what they'd done with their lives, she was surprised to see how plain the names were: *Joseph Appleton, Gary Chandler, Michael Adams, Elton Petrik*. She wouldn't be surprised if they were all dead now. And why did she have their names? So that someday her boys or their children or their grandchildren could find Elton's great-grandson and tell them they were related? She crumpled the paper in her hand and then let it drop to the floor.

"Grams?" Erin's voice echoed down the hallway.

Elizabeth quickly stepped back and shut the closet door. She tripped over the hatbox, which she'd left by the bed, and fell backward, banging her elbow on her maple dressing table. There was a loud crack, and then Erin rushed through the door, the baby attached to her in that primeval sling. The rapid movement woke Keller, and he started crying.

"I'm fine. I'm fine," Elizabeth said. She sat up, holding her left elbow with her right hand. She'd forgotten how small an infant's cry was—more like mewing than wailing. The pain was sharp, like getting poked with a stick. To make it ebb, to take her mind from it, Elizabeth started to count backward from a hundred. She could hear Erin talking but couldn't concentrate on what she was saying. By the time she finished counting, Erin had taken the baby out of its contraption and started nursing him. She was reading one of the pamphlets that had fallen out of the hatbox when she tripped. It was a brochure for the flight program with United. The one Callie had attended.

"They sure had a different vision of women back then," Erin said. She read a bit of the text aloud, which described the ideal candidate as being in good physical shape with a waist of no more than twenty inches and a bust of at least thirty-six inches. "It's like they wanted Barbie."

Elizabeth held her arm out and straightened it. The pain was less intense. "Callie just wanted to fly. She'd been convinced since she was five that the world was bigger than Kidron."

"Was she satisfied? Is that why she came back?"

Elizabeth smiled. Her daughter had never been satisfied. "No. She came back to heal, and by the time she was fixed up, she had all those children and a restaurant to run."

"It's not the same now. I feel her absence and I feel my mom's absence." Erin looked quickly at Elizabeth and then away again.

"You've heard from her?"

"She's in Florida," Erin said quietly.

"Never would have put her there. I sent her to the Cascades," Elizabeth said. She wanted to say more, but a lifetime of keeping and holding secrets had taught her patience. The story would come.

Erin sank down onto the edge of the bed. Keller raised his head up and she moved him to the other breast. "I feel like we're coming unhinged here."

"We've stayed in Kidron a long time," Elizabeth said. "It's natural we should start leaving."

"That's what Mom said. She wants me to go back to Europe, to try to work some sort of arrangement out with Keller's dad. She says it isn't right to be away from one of your parents."

"Depends on the parent." Elizabeth lay down on the bed.

"She's got a job. Cleans up for a bed-and-breakfast on the coast." Erin lay down too and then rolled over on her side, so she was looking Elizabeth in the eyes. "Think they'll catch her?"

"Not in a million years," Elizabeth said. "Not in a million years."

"I think all of Kidron feels her absence," Erin said.

They didn't resume talking until Keller had finished. Erin held the boy out to Elizabeth and asked her to burp him. "You'll just have to do a better job of avoiding the spit-up. I imagine you've got a few tricks, having raised all those boys."

Elizabeth laid the child facedown on her lap, with his head extended just slightly past the end of her knees, and began to rub his back. She didn't want to risk getting spit-up all over her again. The boy let out a huge burp, and they laughed. "He's so new."

Erin nodded. "I don't think I understood how worn-out our bodies are until I had him."

"You've spent too many years with us," Elizabeth said. "We were tired when we got you."

"That might be true of other grandmothers, but all of you have Anna's blood. I'm practically convinced you'll live forever."

Erin's tone was light, and as Elizabeth watched her, she realized how much the girl thought she could control. "No one wants to live forever," she said and then lifted the baby off her knees and folded him against her chest. When she was younger, holding a child, anyone's child, made her chest tighten, and she'd feel the old pressure of milk against her nipples. A phantom pressure, as if her body remembered. Now she felt nothing. Her breasts were flat and hardened, like the rest of her skin, dull to sensation.

"Don't say that." Erin looked away from Elizabeth. "You've got years and years left. I expect you'll be at Keller's graduation, and there will be other children."

Elizabeth shouldn't have been honest. She took it all back. Put her hand on her great-granddaughter's knee and murmured assurances that she'd be there for all of it. "Maybe by the time you're my age, they'll have found a cure for death. For all of us. Figured out a way to bottle immortality."

With Keller asleep, the two of them stood and walked out to the porch to join Anna in her rocking. They talked about their upcoming trip to Australia, with Erin and Anna giddy at the prospect of such a journey and the potential of finding someone else who shared their genes, their mutation. Elizabeth looked out at the setting sun and wondered how she could keep her secrets for an eternity.

CHAPTER THIRTY-SIX

Grafting

The next morning, Elizabeth walked the orchard. She left her room before the sun rose, impatient with the day. Sleep was different in her old age. When she was younger and her muscles were fresh, she slept like the dead, waking in the same position she'd fallen asleep in. But sometime in her seventies, after Frank had been sent to Golden Sunsets, her sleep became restless. She often rose when the morning star was still visible and walked through the orchard, checking on the trees. In August, the trees were already getting ready for fall. She ran her fingers over some of the branches in the older section, twigs that she'd helped her father to graft. After more than half a century, the limbs looked like nothing more than part of the tree.

At the joint, where her father had made a small notch, the bark was thicker, like scar tissue over an old burn. The branches had become limbs and sprouted their own branches and network of switches that gave the tree its shape. She walked to the newer part of the grove and saw the work that the foreman had been doing. It was a different world, now that they leased their orchards and were responsible for nothing but paying the taxes on their acreage. She had no ownership over these newer trees; she didn't feel the need to speak to them, to cajole them into producing fine olives. She'd not climbed them when she was a girl.

The sun's pink and orange lights began to filter through the grove and Elizabeth made her way toward the Hill House. Now that the sun had come up, she could go and see her husband. She'd been wrong to skip her visit to Frank the day before. She wanted to be there as soon as the nurses would allow her to enter. As she left the shelter of the trees, the wind blew up the legs of her pants and she hurried into the house.

Even with the early morning orchard walk, she'd still arrived too early. The day nurses started their shifts at 7:00 A.M. and she knew them well enough that they'd let her in, even though visiting hours didn't begin until nine. She watched the night shift stagger out through the electric glass doors and blink wearily at the dawn. It surprised her to see that most of those who worked at night were Hispanic, and as they made their way to their waiting cars in the far reaches of the parking lot, she imagined she understood the snatches of Spanish they exchanged.

Frank was wearing a hat, a derby she thought, and his iron gray hair, which was too long, lay like a fringe on the collar of his shirt. The front desk nurse said he was having a good day.

"He's chipper. Keeps walking around singing *we're in the money* and telling everyone it's a good day to play the lotto." The girl squinted up at Elizabeth and smiled. "I think I will get one of those mega tickets at lunch."

Elizabeth watched Frank for a bit from the door to the rec room. Her husband was in excellent spirits, and she thought if she'd asked him, he'd tell her that the war in Europe was nothing to worry about and that if it came to it, he fancied himself a navy man. He turned away from the man in the wheelchair he'd been talking to and saw her at the door.

"Were you looking for me?" he asked, taking off his hat and smoothing his hair. "They said you were coming today. It's been so long that I hardly know you."

Elizabeth could see that he was struggling to decide who she was. His eyes were trained on her, waiting for her to give some indication of who she was to him. "I've missed you, Frankie," she said.

The diminutive allowed him to believe that she was an older female relative. Sometimes he picked his sister and other times his mother. Frank's sisters had families of their own when he was born, and his older brothers were already squabbling over who would inherit his family's forty acres. Elizabeth knew that he adored his sisters but felt distanced from his mother, who never got over having a son when she was nearly fifty. Elizabeth never lied to him, never called him brother or son, but she let him choose who she was to him.

"Sister," he said and grinned.

"Brother," she said, opening her arms for an embrace.

They hugged long enough that Elizabeth began to hope a small part of Frank knew who she was. She was on the verge of whispering into his ear when he pulled away and motioned to the man in the wheelchair, who was wearing an improbably dark toupee.

"Do you know Guy?"

Elizabeth did in fact know Guy. She'd been introduced to him at nearly every visit since he took up residence at Golden Sunsets seven years earlier. He was Frank's boyfriend. He was a delicate man with a fine bone structure and strong Roman features. He did not have dementia, like her husband, but always played along when Frank introduced them. His family had abandoned him in the 1980s when his wife had died and he'd burned through her family money on a series of much younger lovers. He'd had a stroke about fifteen years earlier, which had left him with limited use of his left side and brought him to Golden Sunsets.

For all these reasons, Elizabeth wanted to dislike Guy, but she couldn't. He was one of the most charming men she'd ever met. Callie, when she'd met him, said it was like Clark Gable had stepped off the screen and into a retirement facility in Kidron. "What's he doing here?" she'd asked.

Before Elizabeth understood about her husband and Guy, she'd come to Golden Sunsets on the pretense of visiting Frank and then gather around Guy to hear him tell of his USO adventures. He'd been a sound man and traveled with all the big name stars to the concerts they gave servicemen. It was where he'd met his wife, who'd been part of a sister act that only managed to put out two records. "They could have done more," Guy lamented. "The thing about dames is they like to go and get themselves knocked up." This way of talking, as braggarts had done when Elizabeth was younger, made her laugh. He didn't always speak this way though; when he wasn't entertaining, as he called it, he spoke languorously with a bit of a midwestern accent.

Those first few months, she'd arrive at Golden Sunsets and find Guy and Frank in the corner playing checkers. Their conversation would be about their childhoods—dogs they'd had, swimming holes, movies Elizabeth never remembered seeing.

Guy had tried to tell her what was happening between them. One fall afternoon when Frank had fallen asleep, he confessed preference for men to Elizabeth. *St. Elizabeth* he called her. He told her that the last straw for his son had been when a lover, a prostitute really, had taken his wallet and left him stranded in Reno. "The boy I was with was no older than my grandson at the time. Kids both of them, and my son looked at me like he did the year I told him the truth about the tooth fairy and said he was done bailing me out. That was in 1989 and I haven't seen him since. It was his wife that paid for all this." Guy's hand swept across the air, and the gesture, although small, made the entire place feel larger.

The daughter-in-law, as it turned out, was a second cousin to one of Elizabeth's uncles, and she'd put her own grandmother in Golden Sunsets. "It's pretty easy to be related to us," she'd said to him. They both looked at Frank at that moment, and then Guy turned to Elizabeth and put his hand on her knee.

"There's not many of us, you know. Maybe one in a couple of hundred, and for a person my age . . ." He trailed off, and Elizabeth for the first time found she wasn't charmed by Guy. His voice had flattened and slowed and she saw that his eyes were on Frank.

She wished now he'd been explicit about his relationship with her husband.

"Now which sister are you? Winifred?" Guy asked, and shook her hand.

"Please call me Winnie," Elizabeth said.

Guy winked at her and told Frank to sit down. "Did I ever tell you about the time Bob Hope fell out the back of a jeep and broke his arm?"

Elizabeth hadn't heard this story, but she couldn't focus on Guy's voice. She felt the pressure of the last few days building up on her, and she began to pray that Frank would have just a glimmer or two of lucidity. She needed him to be himself long enough to ask him if she should confess her own sins to their children—tell the boys that Frank wasn't their father. The nurses said that such lucidity was rare. It had been more than two years since his last clear moment. There were some nurses who believed that it only came when a patient was on the verge of death. Elizabeth talked to enough other spouses to know there was no pattern. One man she'd met brought violets every visit because the smell of them sometimes would bring his wife into the present.

Frank interrupted her thoughts. "You're no fun today, Winnie."

"She's just tired," Guy said, and Elizabeth saw that they were holding hands. His thumb stroked her husband's softly.

"Let's get out of here," Frank said.

"Can't," Guy said, indicating his chair and then the room they were in.

Elizabeth had, on occasion, taken Frank out of Golden Sunsets, especially in those early years. When she spoke to him in the rec center, he asked too many questions. He wanted to know who Callie was and Deb and how he was related to them. Being outside the reach of the smell of antiseptic and the sea of aged faces quieted Frank's mind. He didn't feel like he needed to make sense of his world, he just let Elizabeth talk. There were times right after Deb had been sent to prison, that she would put him in the car and they would drive for hours, Frank's head resting against the window and Elizabeth unspooling all her pent-up feelings about their daughter and their granddaughter.

Frank looked at Elizabeth. "She can take us. She drives."

"It's too much," Guy said.

"No, she wants to. Do you see how beautiful it is out there?" Frank walked to the window, which looked out over the small courtyard where residents were allowed to wander. "She doesn't want to be here any more than you do, than I do."

Elizabeth protested; she mentioned that her car was small and that there wouldn't be a place for the wheelchair. Privately, she had concerns about how she'd get Guy in and out of the car. She wasn't strong enough to lift him.

Guy assured her that he'd be fine getting in and out of the car and that the chair could be left behind. "It's just a drive, and it may do us some good."

She felt herself waver—wanting to believe that a change of location would change their reality, erase the heaviness that had settled into her bones since talking with Dr. Hashmi, and most of all change Frank into someone she knew.

There was a flurry of activity around the three of them as they left Golden Sunsets. The desk nurse gave strict instructions about how long they were to be gone and where they were to go. The other residents, overhearing the commotion, looked toward the three of them and frowned. Elizabeth didn't know if their looks were out of disappointment at having to stay or disapproval for disrupting the routine.

CHAPTER THIRTY-SEVEN

The River

W here to, boys?" Elizabeth asked. Beside her, Frank had rolled down the window and let his head lean ever so slightly into the wind. Guy was spread across the rear seat with his back against the door. They were both smiling.

"Las Vegas," Guy said.

"Mexico," Frank said.

Elizabeth made a left onto Sixth Avenue and headed toward the river. She thought about taking them to the casino in Red Bluff, but worried that Guy wouldn't be able to get out of the car. It had taken him a good five minutes to get himself into the backseat, and that had been with the front desk nurse watching closely, ready to call the trip off if he stumbled. This time of year, the park down by the river was typically beautiful, and it would be a good place to sit and talk.

Frank and Guy talked across the seat and occasionally broke into giggles. They made jokes about the nursing staff and traded gossip about the other residents. Guy did impressions of a woman they called Gladys, although Elizabeth couldn't place the name. He sucked in his cheeks and batted his eyelashes and dropped his voice two or three octaves to deliver her come-ons.

She drove past Frank's old family farm, which had been sold and turned into tract homes. They were identical structures with large, imposing garages that faced the streets and tile roofs that somehow managed to look like plastic instead of clay. She started to point it out to Frank, but then changed her mind. Instead she tried to explain to Guy what the land had looked like when she was young, how she could look down from Hill House and see row after row of olive trees.

"Driving past the rows of ordered trees could give a person vertigo," she said, thinking of the optical illusion the rows of trees created.

"I don't like olives," Guy said. "Too salty."

Elizabeth felt a chill and rolled up the windows in the car. Frank turned to Guy and asked if he'd ever tried olives that weren't cured in brine. She glanced quickly at her husband. This was something Frank would have asked before his dementia. He rarely talked about olives anymore. She slowed down to make the turn into the river park.

"Tried 'em all," Guy said, listing off all the olives he knew. "Don't like the oil either, it puts too much of itself into whatever you're making. Canola oil is better, just gives food a little bit of slipperiness."

Elizabeth pulled into a parking spot, surprised to find few other cars in the lot. It was summer and the children were out of school. When she'd come down before with Erin, a few weeks earlier, there had been scads of young people tossing disks and kicking around balls to one another. Even the playground was quiet, no squeaking swings or squeal of children as they slid down the aluminum slide that heated up to an almost unbearable temperature on hot, sunny days.

Frank said, "Have you ever tried my daughter's oil? I guess it is still made from olives, but she uses the fruit from a special grove of trees that Anna's father planted when he arrived here from Australia."

Elizabeth's breath caught.

"Honey," Frank said turning to her. "Tell him what I mean. Callie's oil has special properties, right?"

Guy sat up and leaned toward Frank. "What do you know?"

Elizabeth put her hand on her husband's arm. "Frank? Do you know who I am?"

He laughed and then kissed her on the forehead before getting out of the car.

She hurried after him, and then remembered Guy. She turned the key and rolled all the windows down in the car, speaking quickly to him, trying to explain about Dr. Hashmi and her children and that lucidity was so rare.

Guy shushed her. "Go after him," he said. "I'll be fine. I can see the river from here, and the air smells sweet. Not a trace of disinfectant."

When she reached Frank, he was standing on the sidewalk that ran parallel to the river. She slid her hand into his and realized then why the park was empty. The thunderstorms of the past month had overloaded the river. It had crept past its banks and covered the strip of grass where the teenagers usually spread their blankets and played their games. The water lapped at the edge of the playground, soaking the wood curls that were spread six inches deep around the structures to keep the children from cracking their heads. The few other cars in the parking lot belonged to people who needed a place to ponder. She looked over her shoulder to check on Guy and saw the people in their cars, eyes closed, heads resting on steering wheels or eyes focused on a point in the horizon. She'd parked on the far side of the lot so that the view of the river was through the back window of her Skylark. She saw Guy's face, round as the moon, squinting at them.

"I need to talk to you about the boys," she said.

"How's Callie doing? I worry about her and Deb. When is she up for parole?"

Elizabeth squeezed his hand tightly. She wanted to tell him about that summer, about Deb's escape, Erin's baby, their planned trip to Australia, and the incredible news about Anna, but she couldn't waste time with it. He needed to know about Callie, that she was finally happy.

"Your daughter is in love," she said. "She's like a teenager, but he's a good man, a scientist, widowed."

"Is he from someplace else? Pakistan? India? Did I meet him?" Frank's blue eyes searched her face. "I did, didn't I?"

Elizabeth rushed to assure him. "He's part of this. What I need to talk with you about. He did some tests on us—"

"Are you all right? Do you have cancer? Are you dying?" Frank's voice was high, and he sounded like a child.

"No. Quite the opposite. The doctor gave Anna another thirty years and me fifty if I want them," Elizabeth said.

"That's another lifetime," he said.

"He knows about the boys. Knows what I did to get them."

Frank's eyes narrowed, and he straightened up, pulling his shoulder blades close together. This was the posture they'd taught boys in high school, when they were readying everyone for war. "Why would he have checked them? Everyone knows it isn't the men who live so long, not at least when compared to you Keller women."

"They have daughters, you know. Your sons have become grandfathers." She didn't think Frank was slipping back into dementia. It was difficult for her to remember that her rough and tumble boys had grown into men and then lost their hair and had hips replaced.

"If they're so old as that, I guess they're old enough to know that I'm not their father."

Elizabeth had wanted a more definitive answer from him. "You're their dad, though."

"I'm not anything," Frank said.

They stared at the water for a time. Elizabeth fiddled with her necklace and wondered how aware Frank was about his memory loss. He bent down and picked up a few stones and bits of concrete that were strewn around the ground and then began throwing them into the river. Elizabeth felt her opportunity slipping away with each plunk of stone hitting water. She put her hand on his arm, stopping him from throwing his last few rocks into the river.

In one breath, Elizabeth asked him, "Should I tell the boys you're not their father?"

He hurled his handful of rocks at the water, and they hit like a spray of buckshot. She felt the impact of those stones in her heart, and she wished that he'd been born fifty years later so that he never would have had to choose between a family and love. No, that wasn't right. Frank loved her; it just wasn't the same sort of love that other married people had; there was no desperation, no attraction, just resignation.

"Can Callie handle it?" he asked. "If they know, she needs to know. I worry that she's not strong enough to live with it, to understand. But maybe she's learning to be stronger at that flight school."

Elizabeth smiled. She'd forgotten how protective Frank had been before Callie left for school. How he didn't see that his influence, his parenting, had given his daughter the wings she needed to leave Kidron. If Callie hadn't been in that plane crash, then Elizabeth would have told them all years ago about their fathers. Frank would have told them himself and explained their actions.

"It's hot out here," Frank said.

She was lost in her thoughts about Callie and the boys, so she didn't react quickly enough when Frank reached down and rolled his pant legs up. He kicked off his shoes, slippers really. How had she not noticed his footwear when they left Golden Sunsets? He waded into the water.

"Don't," Elizabeth said, reaching for him, but he stepped away from her farther into the water. He turned, waving her off, and then a branch fallen from a large spruce tree hit the back of his knees causing them to buckle. He fell backward into the water and his head submerged for just long enough for him to swallow water. She saw his throat constricting at the sudden influx of water.

"Frank!" she screamed.

He made an effort to stand. What had seemed like placid water had a brisk current and somehow in his flailing, Frank was pulled from the backwater into the current and struggled to stay afloat.

From behind her, she heard Guy scream. "Go after him. Go after him. Oh God. You've got to reach him."

"Stand up!" she shouted to her husband. She trotted along the sidewalk, watching his stumbling, desperate attempts to gain footing on the river bottom. She saw a tree ahead of him, one that at one point had been a shady spot for the Frisbee players to lounge under. "Grab the tree!"

Elizabeth was not a strong swimmer. She hesitated, looking around her for something to extend to Frank. She heard him call her name, and looking up she realized that he'd managed to use the tree to stop himself. He had his back against the trunk and was half sitting, half standing in the water. It was too deep for him to sit, but shallow enough that he was able to keep his upper torso above the water.

She heard Guy yelling again. He sounded closer, and when she looked back at the car, she saw that he'd opened the door and managed to crawl out onto the pavement. A woman who'd been sitting in a blue sedan was walking toward them with a phone in her hand.

"Mama. Please. Mama!" Frank was crying. He'd fully returned to his dementia. Elizabeth could only wonder what he thought as he looked around him. She did look like his mother, it was one of the reasons he'd married her, and now that she was old and wrinkled, she looked like everyone's mother or grandmother.

She stepped into the water and felt it course across her ankles and into her sneakers. She felt safer with them on, thought that stepping onto the soggy grass beneath the water would be less slippery. He wasn't far from the sidewalk, but she could see that he'd exhausted himself. He'd lost his hat, and she saw the age spots on the crown of his head, along with the jagged scar he'd gotten when his brother had hit him with a stick they had used to play ball. The scar ran from just over his left ear down his neck and looked like a crack in glass just before it broke.

"Help," he called again.

Elizabeth was within an arm's reach of him and the water was above her knees. She felt the current pulling at her slacks, and as she stepped, the water splashed up into her face. It was not clean, and now that she was in it, she began to worry about sewage and dead animals and snakes. "You've got to stand up, Frank," she said.

He grabbed onto her shoulder and pulled hard enough that she stumbled into the tree. He clawed at her, and she felt herself begin to lose her balance. The water flowed much more quickly around the tree; it pushed against her. Frank fell backward and his head again slipped under the water. She leaned over, grabbing desperately at his shirt, trying to pull him up toward her. She stepped backward to give herself more leverage and the current took her legs out from under her. The last image she had was of Frank's brown eyes opened wide in terror under the water. His mouth gaped, and she knew that he wasn't going to make it.

The water was cold. Elizabeth thought she should panic, flail her arms and yell for help, but she couldn't find the energy. She realized that she wanted to sink, to join Frank on the bottom of the river. She was tired of her secrets, tired of living. Hadn't she done enough? Wasn't ninety years more than enough? The water slammed her arm into a boulder, and for a moment a blinding pain ripped through her body. She screamed and a bit of water, which tasted like day-old fish, rushed into her mouth. She felt her shirt catch on a limb that was trapped between rocks on the bottom of the bank, and it held her in place.

The air was smoky in this section of the river. She realized she'd floated miles downriver of Woodson Bridge to where the rice farmers were ending their season by burning the stubble of their harvested crops. The smoke hung low in places around the edges of the bank, making it impossible to see if anyone had come after Elizabeth. She wondered if Guy had seen her be carried away, or whether the woman on the phone had reached help. The water was loud, like standing next to a waterfall, and she thought she heard voices drifting from the bank or a pleasure boat. There were murmurs of the constantly changing river channel. A man talking about snags and shoal, and maybe a woman crying, and the memory of Mims talking about how land never belonged to a family until they had laid their dead in it.

She looked up at the sky as the branch held her in place and water rushed around her. The river was running faster than its normal four miles per hour, and she could tell by the trees and the gravel that she was just a few hundred yards from Foster Island. Above her an osprey flew with a stick in his talons. His brown-and-white-striped feathers outstretched as he rode the air currents, the white cross of his belly and the edges of his wings spread like fingertips. She closed her eyes against the sun and relaxed her body. The water, which had been pushing against her rigidity, rolled her body over. With her face pressed against the river water, she tried to raise up her neck to get a breath of air, but the water was moving too quickly and the angle at which she was twisted made it too awkward for her to move. She stopped fighting and opened her eyes, but the water was too murky, too filled with sediment for her to see the bottom of the river.

KELLER, AUGUST 1, 2017

I am too old for bedtime stories, but each night when my mother sits on the edge of my sister's bed and calls to me to come across the hall, I go. When it is cold I come wrapped in blankets and when the dry winds from the desert heat the valley, I lie on the wood floor, pressing my face into its coolness. We live in an old house on a hill, and from the windows of my bedroom, I can see the olive orchard planted by my great-great-great-great-grandfather.

The beginning of the stories is always the same. "There is a curious girl who lives in a curious place. She has as many friends as a girl her age can keep track of, but her closest companion is a tortoise who tells people he is as old as dirt, but really has only lived for a hundred and seventy-two years. The tortoise has no name and is simply called Tortoise by the girl, who has a name, but prefers to be called Girl."

Often my little sister, who is four, demands that the Girl be given a proper name, usually Athena, which is also my sister's name. My mother never indulges her and insists on calling the girl "Girl" and the tortoise "Tortoise." All the women in our family are more stubborn than they need to be. "This is how the stories go," she'll tell my sister and lightly pat her leg through the covers. Tonight my sister refrains from trying to put her own stamp on the story. I think it is because Anna is in the room with us.

We all know that Anna, who is improbably my still living great-great-great-grandmother, is the little girl in the story. Tonight she is one hundred and twenty-two years and one hundred sixty-five days old. Normally nobody cares about how many days old a person is, but today is a record breaker for Anna. She has lived the longest of any other human being on Earth. At least that one can document. My friend Jim, who is faster than me in the forty-yard dash, says that Methuselah lived to be almost 969, but I told him it didn't count because nobody can prove that he did. I could tell he wanted to hit me for saying that what he learned at Sunday school wasn't true, but instead he challenged me to a race and took great satisfaction when he beat me by at least two full seconds.

Some of the stories are about adventure, others full of silliness, but the one tonight Mom tells is the sad story. I've only heard it once when I was younger than Athena, and all that I remember is that the Tortoise dies. I guess I've given away the ending now. But it doesn't matter because, to me, all the other stories became better because I knew that eventually the magical world where there was just the Tortoise and the Girl ends. All the best animal companions die. Billy lost Old Dan and Little Ann, Travis had to shoot Yeller, and even though Wilbur managed not to become bacon, we still had to say good-bye to Charlotte.

My mother's voice is like the sound of the ocean trapped inside a shell. People pay good money to listen to her sing in all those foreign languages, but her voice is best in English, and when she tells stories, the words seem to travel up to your ears from the inside of your body. The shells know that trick, too. My fourth grade teacher told us last year that the sound inside of a shell is nothing more than an amplification of all the noises our bodies make that we can't hear—like the blood moving through our veins and our own heart beating. Anyway, that's what my mother sounds like when she tells us the stories.

"The Tortoise is the only family the girl has ever known. He tells her that she'd been born in one of the great copper cauldrons that the women of the village use for washing. She crawled out one evening during twilight as the Tortoise moved from the tall grass to a wallow formed by the runoff from the washing cauldrons. It has become the habit of the great Tortoise to sleep in this mud pit during particularly cool nights."

Grandma Anna reaches over and pats my mother's arm. "That Tortoise doesn't hear so well," she says, interrupting. "That's why he doesn't notice the Girl until she is right in front of him and don't forget to tell them about the hibiscus flowers."

Earlier today, there were dozens of reporters at the house—all here to talk to Grandma Anna and to ask her what she thought of the world now. They kept calling her the grandmother of humanity. She told them that though the stuff around us had changed, we humans were the same as we've ever been, and then she told them that time was an illusion we'd dreamed up to keep our lives from happening all at once. "I'm just better at stretching my illusion out," she'd said, and a smattering of applause rippled through the crowd.

Mom leans over and kisses Anna on the cheek. Because our parents travel so much, Grandma Anna helps look after us. Right now my dad is in Germany directing a production of *Alcina* for the Semper. They take turns leaving us, but lately Dad has been gone more often than Mom. I think it is because she is worried about how much longer she has with Grandma Anna. The other grandmothers worry, too. Grandma Callie and her husband, Grandpa Amrit, who isn't really my grandfather, were here to celebrate Anna's milestone. They had to get back to Pittsburgh though because of his research.

Mom starts up where she was interrupted and tells my sister about one particular day when, "the Girl feeds the Tortoise hibiscus flowers and talks about a man she's seen in town. Because the Girl has no father or mother, while the Tortoise sleeps in the afternoons, she's gotten into the habit of sitting near the fish market on the town's eastern edge near the quay and looking up into the faces of the adults as they pass by.

"'He had gold eyes,' the Girl says.

"'I only know one other person with gold eyes,' the Tortoise says.

"The girl looks at him and blinks slowly."

Athena stands up in bed and shouts, "The Girl. It's the Girl. She has gold eyes."

"I'm glad to see you remember," Grandma Anna says, settling Athena back under the covers.

My mother looks at me, and it seems that she is asking if Athena is ready to hear the next part of the story. I get up off the cool floor and hug my knees to my chest. She takes this as a yes and continues the story.

"For many days, the Girl and the Tortoise watch the man. He seems to be making preparations to leave their town. He has men come to his house, which is nearly hidden inside the lush greenery in the bush outside of town, and carry all that he owns onto a ship. There is a woman bustling about inside the house who the Girl can never see clearly and a boy somewhat older than the Girl who looks down sadly at his father from the windows of the house. The more the Girl watches the man with the gold eyes, the more she comes to believe he is her father.

"'He peels his bananas from the bottom up,' she says to the Tortoise.

"'He chews on bunya sticks,' the Tortoise says to the Girl. He's long disapproved of this habit, thinking that her teeth were falling out because of it. Because he is a Tortoise, he doesn't know that humans have baby teeth.

"On the third day they watch him, the woman and the boy emerge from the house with him and together they walk down to the docks and onto the ship where all their possessions have been loaded."

"Don't forget about the twin girls," Anna says as my mother takes a breath.

"Ah, yes. There are two little girls who look exactly the same except that one has red hair and one has blond hair. They were about the same age as the Girl, and seeing them in their matching blue dresses makes her sad. The Tortoise sees the tears in the Girl's eyes and tells her that nothing is as beautiful as a dress made from eucalyptus leaves.

"'If he leaves, I won't know if he's my father,' the Girl says to the Tortoise.

"They continue to watch the boat and just as the Tortoise is getting very hungry and feeling like the Girl should at least offer to get him some hibiscus flowers, the large white sails of the ship go up, turning what had looked like spindly dead trees into majestic spires anchoring what appears to the Girl to be clouds.

"The Tortoise, who knows more than the Girl, realizes that the man and his family are never coming back. He doesn't want to tell the Girl this because he is afraid of what she will do. He knows in his heart that a Tortoise isn't a proper family for the girl, but he loves her and he likes the hibiscus flowers, which he'd never been able to reach on his own.

"'Do you think he knows he has a daughter?' the Girl asks.

"'The boat is moving.'

"'He can't leave now.'

"The girl looks wildly about the dock and then her gaze settles on the Tortoise. She knows he can't swim well, but she's seen him float as easily as a cork in the wallow down by the laundry cauldrons. She doesn't even have to ask. The Tortoise moves to the water's edge, and then she blinks and he is in the water, motioning with his head for her to climb atop his great carapace."

"Shell," I say, knowing my sister looked as confused as I had hearing that word for the first time.

"Does she get there?" Athena asks me, because she knows better than to ask Mom to jump ahead in the story.

"Wait and see," I say.

"Grandma Deb could never wait either," Grandma Anna says from her corner of the room. "She always wanted to know the ending before the beginning. Used to read the last page of a book first, just so she could see where she was headed."

I've only met Grandma Deb once. She lives in Florida and works in a place where you can swim with the dolphins. We went there when I was six, just after Mom and Dad finally got married. But we had to pretend we didn't know who she was and her name tag said LORNA. She was in charge of handing out and collecting the wet suits we wore in the water.

"Shhhh," my mom says. It is late, and although Athena's eyes are wide open, the rest of her looks to be on the verge of sleep.

"What happens?" Athena asks.

"Using her hands, the Girl paddles the Tortoise near the boat. It takes them hours to catch up to it, but finally, they are near enough that the Girl stretches out and grabs on to a ladder that hangs down the side of the ship. She reaches into the water and tries to pull the Tortoise up with her, but she is too small to carry him and his legs are too short to climb the ladder.

"'I'll let the current carry me back to shore,' the Tortoise says. His eyes are closed and his head is barely lifted out of the water.

"'I can't leave you,' the Girl says. She does not think she's ever seen her old friend look so tired.

"'Kiss me on the nose. It'll bring you luck and a life long enough so that we may meet again.'

"The Girl keeps one hand tight on the ladder and leans over to kiss the Tortoise on the nose. She's never done it before and is surprised at how soft his skin feels. They bump noses and then he kisses her. She climbs the ladder and once she is safely atop the boat, she looks in all directions for some sign that the Tortoise is still in the water. In the darkening light, she thinks every wave cap is the

Tortoise's shell. She sees him everywhere and nowhere, and when the sun has finally set, she turns her back on the ocean and goes in search of her father."

"The end?" Athena asks with her eyes closed.

"The end," my mother says, rising and kissing the top of Athena's head.

I take Grandma Anna's arm, and as we walk out of the room together, she says, "You know, I'm still looking for that Tortoise."

ACKNOWLEDGMENTS

I have a tattoo of a quill, which I got when I was eighteen and believed that it would always remind me that I was a writer. It did not, but my husband did. Not only did he believe that I could write this book, he took the kids to the movies, to the park, to ride bikes on Saturday afternoons so that I could write this book.

The year I turned thirty, chance and Richard Bausch put me in a group of writers who had nothing more in common than wanting to be better writers. We spent a winter sharing our work with one another and learning as Richard gently walked us through his lessons on writing (it is show-and-tell). I am still with those wonderful writers and they have shepherded me through many more winters with grace, humor, and honest critique of my writing. Thank you Beverly, David, Elizabeth, Jerry, Lisa, Marjorie, Patti, and Ray.

The students and faculty who are a part of the University of Memphis' MFA program are incredibly talented and generous. If not for their help and guidance (and good old-fashioned competiveness) this book would still be a story about an old woman, a pregnant woman, and a turtle. Thank you to Tom Russell for helping me start this novel in his workshop and thank you to Cary Holladay for being the best thesis advisor. Cary is a brilliant writer who is generous with her time.

My agent, Alexandra Machinist, found me, fought for me, and in the process made me believe that dreams do come true. She, along with Stephanie Koven, have done more than their fair share of hand-holding to help me through all that I didn't know about what happens after someone says yes to your book.

There is no better editor than Carrie Feron. She embraced

my book and told me where it needed work. Without her valuable insights into my characters, this novel would be less than it is today. It is a dream to be working with the team at William Morrow: Tavia Kowalchuk, Shawn Nicholls, Ben Bruton, Lynn Grady, Liate Stehlik, Mike Brennan, Brian Grogan, and Andrea Molitor. A special thanks to Tessa Woodward for knowing what I needed before I could ask.

Finally, thank you to my own unbroken line of women. Especially my mother and my grandmothers. I am surrounded by strong, complicated, interesting women with more stories than I'll ever be able to write.

An interview with
Courtney Miller Santo

THE ROOTS OF THE OLIVE TREE **has its basis in your own family. How closely do the details mirror them and did you run into any problems with their reaction to the book?**

One of the reasons I grew up to be a writer is that my family believed the only reason to keep any skeletons in the closet was to be able to pull them out when a good story was needed. Because of that my family's reaction has been overwhelmingly positive to the book. I took inspiration from my own great-grandmother (who is 104) to create the character of Anna, but the two women are as different as they are alike. I think what they share, and what I drew inspiration from, is that my great grandmother has a great zest for life. She was determined to outlive her older brother, Wealthy, who died at the age of 101 and so far she's got him beat by several years. In addition, instead of waiting for life to happen to her, my great-grandmother and Anna are the type of women who go out and get the life they want.

The only criticism I've had about the book from my family came from my grandmother who told me there was a bit too much sex in it for her taste.

314 / COURTNEY MILLER SANTO

What was your route to writing your first novel?

For a great many years, I was afraid to tell people that I wanted to be a writer. It seemed quite impractical and foolish to admit that my life's goal consisted of putting words on a page for entertainment. So, instead of getting an English degree, I got a degree in journalism, which at the time was quite practical and as a bonus, I got to see my name in print nearly every day.

Once I had children and my husband had a steady job with benefits, it seemed less wasteful to focus on telling stories, and so I went back to school. However, I knew that unlike many of my fellow students I didn't have time to waste figuring out what I wanted to write. I decided I would only do the program if my final project was a novel—and of course it had to be the story that I'd been thinking of writing for years, which is the story of a very old woman and a young pregnant woman. That project turned into *The Roots of the Olive Tree*.

I wouldn't have written the book without the discipline of the MFA program at the University of Memphis. For me, seeing writers like Richard Bausch, Cary Holladay, and Tom Russell at work, changed the entire picture I had in my head of what it meant to be a writer. They taught me that writing is about two things: putting words on the page and then revising those words so that they tell a story in the most honest and direct way possible. Outside of the program, I've found that what I value most is the feedback I get from other writers—both about my writing and about all the emotional stuff that comes up when you write. I keep telling people that trying to get at the truth of a story is as good as talking to a therapist.

What are your favorite 'family saga' novels?

Is it obvious that I'm a huge fan of family sagas? For me any book that gets at the complications and complexities of intergenerational families gets a prize spot on my bookshelf. My favorite of the genre is *The Stone Diaries* by Carol Shields, but I love *The Thorn Birds* and *The Godfather* almost as much. The first family saga I ever read was *East of Eden*, by Steinbeck, and it holds a special place in my heart, although the problem with a book that good is that it becomes intimidating to try to write when you realize perfection already exists. I also have always loved the big, sprawling mess that is any Tolstoy novel, but especially *Anna Karenina*. And any list wouldn't be complete without *One Hundred Years of Solitude*.

I'm sure you've been asked about a continuation of the story. Is this something you're thinking about in the near future?

When I was a small child, our family would visit my grandmother at the beach and the first thing my siblings and I would do when we entered her house was to head straight for this yellow cookie jar shaped like a pear. I have such strong memories of that jar and the various types of cookies we'd find in there. Sometimes they'd be freshly homemade and other times they'd be store-bought and soft for having sat so long. I was shocked a few years ago to hear my cousins discuss that same cookie jar with the same bit of reverence that our family talked of it. What I realized is that family stories are that way also. I fully expect Deb and Anna and the other Keller women to show up in future stories and my guess is that readers who've read *The Roots of the Olive Tree* will find a new facet or a bit more information on how their lives turn out that is contained in this novel. I told my husband about this and he compared it to cross overs on television and I suppose in some ways he's right. I prefer to think of it as every family member having a different story about the skeleton in their grandmother's closet.

How much research did you need to do on the subject of longevity to complete the character of Amrit? Were you always intrigued by this question given your own family's longevity?

I think most people, as they age, become interested in longevity. I didn't go to my first family funeral until I was nearly an adult, which I came to understand much later in life how unusual that experience was. So, for me, there exists this assumption that people live well into their nineties. My husband had the opposite experience, losing his father early in his teenage years. So, when we started having children, I started to think about the question of mortality and whether or not it is influenced by genetics or environment.

To answer that question in the book, I needed someone like Amrit and in order to write Amrit, I had to do some research. The wonderful part about writing fiction is that it doesn't have to be true, it just has to have the appearance of truth. I'm sure I've taken some liberties and gotten some of the science wrong, but I think as far as the bigger questions about genetics and longevity, the science agrees with Amrit. If you want to be a super-ager, take a look at your grandparents to assess your chances. Oh, and eating well and exercising regularly doesn't hurt.

Although the book is about lots of different kinds of relationship, female family bonds are at its heart. Why do you think these bonds are so strong, yet often so complicated?

My husband would tell you that relationships between fathers and sons are just as complicated. However, I've spent my life surrounded by generations of mothers and daughters and so my interest naturally lies in these relationships. When I became a parent (and of course I had a daughter first) I realized I had to stop kidding around about my life. I made plans to be better—skinnier, healthier, more interesting, your basic New Year's resolution stuff—but the only part of that I was able to change was my writing. I wanted to be more for my daughter. And isn't that what drives these complicated relationships? Living up to your mother's expectations and then living up to your own expectations. And there are hormones and insecurities and this idea that you owe your life to another person.

In the book, I talk about not being able to choose your family and I think that is at the root of all complicated mother and daughter relationships. Of course, I'm talking about relationships that aren't fundamentally broken by abuse, abandonment, or addiction. In my own case, I think my relationship with my mother became less complicated and fraught when I realized motherhood is about a series of choices, or rather compromises. You do the best that you can. In *Roots*, I think the women come to understand that about each other by the end of the book.

The lifespan of your characters causes them to be witness to great changes in society, not least in the treatment of women. Was the 'sweep of history' something you had in mind or is it just impossible to avoid once you have the different generations in play?

I was fascinated by the image of a very old woman holding a newborn. That is the picture I began with when I started writing this novel—one that is from my own life when my great-grandmother held my infant daughter. I saw the two of them and what I thought about was how much less cosmic time suddenly seemed. Here was a woman who'd seen more than a century of life and she was holding my daughter, who in all likelihood, will live to see another century of life. So in one frame you have two hundred years. As I wrote the book, I realized that the women themselves were less interested in the things that changed around them and more interested in how little people change. In some ways you can see the advancement of what a woman's life can be through my characters, but you also see how an individual's choices can make even more of a difference. My own great-grandmother used to tell me the only good to come from technology was having more time to worry about all that you hadn't gotten done yet.

When you're writing, what is foremost in your mind that you want to communicate? Are you thinking of emotions, dynamics, impressions, or characters? Or is it more a case of capturing your own experience?

Gosh, for me I'm working at trying to capture the enormity of the rich, full, interesting characters that are chattering to me about their lives in words. I believe the beauty of fiction is that it is the only chance you get to read someone else's mind, and doing so can have the effect of changing how you see the world—or it can just be entertaining. My own experience colors every part of what I write, but I'm less interested in what I have to say than I am in what my characters are doing and why they're doing it. But having said that, it's such an imperfect medium. There's so much I can't translate from my brain to the page, and my only hope is that the reader forgives these trespasses and is able to let Anna and Bets and Erin live in their own heads in a way that gives them the same full life they have in my head.

What part of writing do you find most rewarding?

What is it they say? The best part of writing is having written. That's rewarding for me. I'm happier, more productive, and a better human being when I've had a good writing day. It has become therapy for me and I'm so very blessed that other people are interested in what I'm writing. It makes me feel much less alone in the world.

If you enjoyed THE ROOTS OF THE OLIVE TREE, why not
download the FREE prequel...

Under the Olive Tree

In a small town in Northern California, the olives are ripening and
the Keller women, a multigenerational family of firstborn daughters, are preparing to send their youngest, Erin, abroad. Although
she worries about forsaking her family, she is compelled to take a
chance at living her dream.

A crisis the day before she is to leave makes Erin question her choice.
Is it possible that before she can return to Hill House, she might lose
one of her beloved grandmothers? Because, although she has three
caretakers—Anna, her great-great-grandmother; Bets, her great-
grandmother; and Callie, her grandmother—Erin has no mother.
It is an absence keenly felt and never mentioned.

Under the Olive Tree offers a tantalizing glimpse into the secrets of
the Keller women...

To download free of charge, search for *Under the Olive Tree* in the Amazon Kindle store

JOIN THE HAY HOUSE FAMILY

As the leading self-help, mind, body and spirit publisher in the UK, we'd like to welcome you to our family so that you can enjoy all the benefits our website has to offer.

 EXTRACTS from a selection of your favourite author titles

 COMPETITIONS, PRIZES & SPECIAL OFFERS Win extracts, money off, downloads and so much more

 LISTEN to a range of radio interviews and our latest audio publications

 CELEBRATE YOUR BIRTHDAY An inspiring gift will be sent your way

 LATEST NEWS Keep up with the latest news from and about our authors

 ATTEND OUR AUTHOR EVENTS Be the first to hear about our author events

 iPHONE APPS Download your favourite app for your iPhone

 HAY HOUSE INFORMATION Ask us anything, all enquiries answered

join us online at **www.hayhouse.co.uk**

 292B Kensal Road, London W10 5BE
T: 020 8962 1230 E: info@hayhouse.co.uk